THE
GÜNTER
GRASS
READER

THE
GÜNTER
GRASS
READER

EDITED BY
HELMUT FRIELINGHAUS

A HARVEST ORIGINAL • HARCOURT, INC.

Orlando   Austin   New York   San Diego   Toronto   London

Requests for permission to make copies of any part of the work should be
mailed to the following address: Permissions Department, Harcourt, Inc.,
6277 Sea Harbor Drive, Orlando, Florida 32887-6777.

www.HarcourtBooks.com

Library of Congress Cataloging-in-Publication Data
Grass, Günter, 1927–
[Selections. 2004]
The Günter Grass reader/Günter Grass; edited by Helmut Frielinghaus.
p. cm.
ISBN 0-15-101176-1   ISBN 0-15-602992-8 (pbk.)
1. Grass, Günter, 1927– Translations into English.   I. Title.
PT2613.R338A6   2004
838'.91409—dc22   2004011446

Text set in Garamond MT
Designed by Cathy Riggs

Printed in the United States of America
First edition
A C E G I K J H F D B
A C E G I K J H F D B (pbk.)

Permission acknowledgments begin on page 309
and constitute a continuation of the copyright page.

CONTENTS

THE
GÜNTER
GRASS
READER

WHEN THE *LZ-126* DREW CLOSE
TO NEW YORK

from MY CENTURY (1999)

THE DATE COLUMBUS WEIGHED ANCHOR WAS THE DATE we chose. Columbus set sail from Genoa in 1492, heading for India, though in fact he landed in America; our venture, our more accurate instruments notwithstanding, was every bit as risky. The dirigible was actually ready on the morning of the eleventh: it lay in its open hangar with precisely calculated quantities of fuel for the five Maybach engines and water for ballast on board; the ground crew had ropes in hand. But the *LZ-126* refused to float: it was heavy and remained so because a layer of fog and warm air masses had suddenly rolled in and settled over the entire Lake Constance region. Since we could not spare either water or fuel, we had to postpone the takeoff until the following morning. The jeering crowd was hard to bear. We did take off on the twelfth, however.

Twenty-two men strong. For a long time it was touch and go whether I would be allowed to serve as mechanic:

I was one of the ones who by way of national protest had destroyed the last four military airships waiting in Friedrichshafen to be delivered up to the enemy, just as more than seventy ships from our fleet—including a dozen battleships and regular-service ships due to be handed over to the English—were scuttled by our own people in July 1919 at Scapa Flow. The Allies promptly demanded compensation; the Americans alone wanted us to cough up three million gold marks. But then the Zeppelin people proposed that the debt be paid off by our delivering an airship built to the latest standards. And since the American military had shown more than lively interest in our most recent model, which had a capacity of seventy thousand cubic meters of helium, the horse trading worked. *LZ-126* was to be flown to Lakehurst, New Jersey, and presented to the Americans upon landing.

Many of us looked upon that as a disgrace. I did. Hadn't we been humiliated enough at Versailles? Hadn't the enforced peace placed a heavy enough burden on the Fatherland? We—that is, several of us—toyed with the thought of undermining the sordid deal. Only after long inner turmoil was I able to discern anything positive in the undertaking, and not until I had expressly promised Dr. Eckener, whom we all respected as our captain and an honest man, that I had given up any idea of sabotage was I allowed to take part.

LZ-126 was so stunning I can picture her even today. Yet at first, while we were still above the European continent, only fifty meters above the saddles of the Côte-d'Or, I was still obsessed with the idea of destroying her. Though designed to provide luxurious accommodation for two dozen, she had no passengers aboard, only a few American military personnel who kept a sharp eye on us round the clock. But when we hit some strong downdrafts over the Spanish coast at Cape Ortegal and the ship started swaying so violently that all hands were occupied keeping her on course and the Americans had to turn to matters of navigation, a takeover would have been possible. All we would have had to do was force an early landing by pitching a few fuel containers overboard. I was tempted again when the Azores lay beneath us. Indeed, day and night I sought opportunities, suffering doubt and temptation. Even when we climbed two thousand meters over the Newfoundland fog or shortly thereafter, when a stay snapped during a storm, I harbored thoughts of averting the imminent ignominy. But thoughts they remained.

What held me back? Certainly not fear. During the war I had been exposed to mortal danger over London whenever the searchlights reached our airship. No, I knew no fear. The only thing that kept me from acting was Dr. Eckener's will. Although I could not share his conviction—namely, that in the face of the victors' despotism it was our duty to give proof of German productivity in the form of our shiny, silver, celestial cigar—in the end I bowed totally to his will, for a piddling, merely symbolic, as it were, breakdown would have made little or no impression, especially as the Americans had sent two cruisers to meet us and we were in constant radio contact with them: they would have come to our aid had we had an emergency, whether a strong headwind or the slightest hint of sabotage.

Only now can I see how right I was to renounce all attempts at an "act of liberation," but even then, when the

LZ-126 drew close to New York, when the Statue of Liberty greeted us through the mist of the morning of 15 October, when we headed up the bay and the metropolis with its mountain chain of skyscrapers lay beneath us and the boats in the harbor welcomed us with their sirens, when we flew the entire length of Broadway, back and forth, twice, at middle altitude, then rose up to three thousand meters to give all the inhabitants of New York a chance to admire German productivity sparkling in the morning sun, and when we finally headed for Lakehurst and made ourselves presentable, washing and shaving with the last of our water supply, I felt proud, unrestrainedly proud.

Later, when the sad delivery ceremony was over and our pride and joy was rechristened the *Los Angeles,* Dr. Eckener thanked me and told me that he had experienced the same turmoil as I. "But one's inner swinish tendencies are easier to resist," he said, "than the inborn commandment to maintain one's dignity and achieve results." I wonder what he felt when thirteen years later the finest expression of the Reich restored, the *Hindenburg,* powered unfortunately by flammable hydrogen rather than helium, went up in flames upon landing at Lakehurst. Was he as certain as I that it was sabotage? It was the Reds! They didn't hold back. Their dignity hinged on another commandment.

Translated by Michael Henry Heim

THE STOCKTURM. LONG-DISTANCE
SONG EFFECTS

from THE TIN DRUM (1959)

DR. HORNSTETTER, THE LADY DOCTOR WHO DROPS IN
on me almost every day just long enough to smoke a ciga-
rette, who is supposed to be taking care of me but who,
thanks to my treatment, leaves the room after every visit a
little less nervous than she was when she came, a retiring
sort who is intimate only with her cigarettes, keeps insisting
that I suffered from isolation in my childhood, that I didn't
play enough with other children.

Well, as far as other children are concerned, she may be
right. It is true that I was so busy with Gretchen Scheffler's
lessons, so torn between Goethe and Rasputin, that even
with the best of intentions I could have found no time for
ring-around-a-rosy or post office. But whenever, as schol-
ars sometimes do, I turned my back on books, declaring
them to be the graveyards of the language, and sought con-
tact with the simple folk, I encountered the little cannibals
who lived in our building, and after brief association with
them, felt very glad to get back to my reading in one piece.

Oskar had the possibility of leaving his parents' flat through the shop, then he came out on Labesweg, or else through the front door that led to the stairwell. From here he could either continue straight ahead to the street, or climb four flights of stairs to the attic where Meyn the musician was blowing his trumpet, or, lastly, go out into the court. The street was paved with cobblestones. The packed sand of the court was a place where rabbits multiplied and carpets were beaten. Aside from occasional duets with the intoxicated Mr. Meyn, the attic offered a view and that pleasant but deceptive feeling of freedom which is sought by all climbers of towers and which makes dreamers of those who live in attics.

While the court was fraught with peril for Oskar, the attic offered him security until Axel Mischke and his gang drove him out of it. The court was as wide as the building, but only seven paces deep; in the rear it was separated from other courts by a tarred board fence topped with barbed wire. The attic offered a good view of this maze which occupied the inside of the block bordered by Labesweg, by Hertastrasse and Luisenstrasse on either side, and Marienstrasse in the distance. In among the irregularly shaped courts that made up the sizable rectangle there was also a cough-drop factory and several run-down repair shops. Here and there in the yards one could discern some tree or shrub indicative of the time of year. The courts varied in size and shape, but all contained rabbits and carpet-beating installations. The rabbits were present and active every day; carpets, however, as the house regulations decreed, were beaten only on Tuesdays and Fridays. On Tuesdays and Fridays it became evident how large the block really was.

Oskar looked and listened from the attic as more than a hundred carpets, runners, and bedside rugs were rubbed with sauerkraut, brushed, beaten, and bullied into showing the patterns that had been woven into them. With a great display of bare arms a hundred housewives, their hair tied up in kerchiefs, emerged from the houses carrying mounds of carpets, threw the victims over the rack supplied for that very purpose, seized their plaited carpet beaters, and filled the air with thunder.

Oskar abhorred this hymn to cleanliness. He battled the noise with his drum and yet, even in the attic, far away from the source of the thunder, he had to admit defeat. A hundred carpet-beating females can storm the heavens and blunt the wings of young swallows; with half a dozen strokes they tumbled down the little temple that Oskar's drumming had erected in the April air.

On days when no carpets were being beaten, the children of our building did gymnastics on the wooden carpet rack. I was seldom in the court. The only part of it where I felt relatively secure was Mr. Heilandt's shed. The old man kept the other children out but admitted me to his collection of vises, pulleys, and broken-down sewing machines, incomplete bicycles, and cigar boxes full of bent or straightened nails. This was one of his principal occupations: when he was not pulling nails out of old crates, he was straightening those recovered the day before on an anvil. Apart from his salvaging of nails, he was the man who helped on moving day, who slaughtered rabbits for holidays, and who spat tobacco juice all over the court, stairs, and attic.

One day when the children, as children do, were cooking soup not far from his shed, Nuchi Eyke asked old man

Heilandt to spit in it three times. The old man obliged, each
time with a cavernous clearing of the throat, and then dis-
appeared into his shanty, where he went on hammering the
crimps out of nails. Axel Mischke added some pulverized
brick to the soup. Oskar stood to one side, but looked on
with curiosity. Axel Mischke and Harry Schlager had built
a kind of tent out of blankets and old rags to prevent
grownups from looking into their soup. When the brick
gruel had come to a boil, Hänschen Kollin emptied his
pockets and contributed two live frogs he had caught in
Aktien Pond. Susi Kater, the only girl in the tent, puckered
up her mouth with disappointment and bitterness when
the frogs vanished ingloriously into the soup without the
slightest attempt at a swan song or a last jump. Undeterred
by Susi's presence, Nuchi Eyke unbuttoned his fly and peed
into the one-dish meal. Axel, Harry, and Hänschen Kollin
followed suit. Shorty tried to show the ten-year-olds what
he could do, but nothing came. All eyes turned toward Susi,
and Axel Mischke handed her a sky-blue enamel cook pot.
Oskar was already on the point of leaving. But he waited
until Susi, who apparently had no panties on under her
dress, had squatted down on the pot, clasping her knees,
looking off expressionlessly into space, and finally crinkling
her nose as the pot emitted a tinny tinkle, showing that Susi
had done her bit for the soup.

At this point I ran away. I should not have run; I should
have walked with quiet dignity. Their eyes were all fishing in
the cook pot, but because I ran, they looked after me. I
heard Susi Kater's voice: "What's he running for, he's going
to snitch on us." It struck me in the back, and I could still
feel it piercing me as I was catching my breath in the loft
after hobbling up the four flights of steps.

I was seven and a half. Susi may have been nine. Shorty was just eight. Axel, Nuchi, Hänschen, and Harry were ten or eleven. There was still Maria Truczinski. She was a little older than I, but she never played in the court; she played with dolls in Mother Truczinski's kitchen or with her grown-up sister Guste who helped at the Lutheran kindergarten.

Is it any wonder if to this day I can't abide the sound of women urinating in chamberpots? Up in the attic Oskar appeased his ears with drumming. Just as he was beginning to feel that the bubbling soup was far behind him, the whole lot of them, all those who had contributed to the soup, turned up in their bare feet or sneakers. Nuchi was carrying the pot. They formed a ring around Oskar, Shorty arrived a moment later. They poked each other, hissing: "Go on, I dare you." Finally, Axel seized Oskar from behind and pinned his arms. Susi laughed, showing moist, regular teeth with her tongue between them, and said why not, why shouldn't they. She took the tin spoon from Nuchi, wiped it silvery on her behind, and plunged it into the steaming brew. Like a good housewife, she stirred slowly, testing the resistance of the mash, blew on the full spoon to cool it, and at length forced it into Oskar's mouth, yes, she forced it into my mouth. Never in all these years have I eaten anything like it, the taste will stay with me.

Only when my friends who had been so concerned over my diet had left me, because Nuchi had been sick in the soup, did I crawl into a corner of the drying loft where only a few sheets were hanging at the time, and throw up the few spoonfuls of reddish brew, in which I was surprised to find no vestiges of frogs. I climbed up on a chest placed beneath the open attic window. Crunching powdered brick, I looked out at distant courts and felt an urge for action. Looking toward the distant windows of the houses in Marienstrasse, I screamed and sang in that direction. I could see no results and yet I was so convinced of the possibilities of long-distance action by singing that from then on the court and all the many courts became too small for me. Thirsting for distance, space, panorama, I resolved to take advantage of every opportunity to leave our suburban Labesweg, whether alone or with Mama, to escape from the pursuits of the soup-makers in the court that had grown too small.

Every Thursday Mama went into the city to shop. Usually she took me with her. She always took me along when it became necessary to buy a new drum at Sigismund Markus' in Arsenal Passage off the Kohlenmarkt. In that period, roughly between the ages of seven and ten, I went through a drum in two weeks flat. From ten to fourteen I demolished an instrument in less than a week. Later, I became more unpredictable in my ways; I could turn a new drum into scrap in a single day, but then a period of mental balance might set in, and for as much as three or four months I would drum forcefully but with a moderation and control that left my instrument intact except for an occasional crack in the enamel.

But let us get back to the days when I escaped periodically from our court with its carpet beating and its soup chefs, thanks to my mama, who took me every two weeks to Sigismund Markus' store, where I was permitted to select a new drum. Sometimes Mama let me come even when my old drum was in relatively good condition. How I relished those afternoons in the multicolored old city; there was always something of the museum about it and there was always a pealing of bells from one church or another. Usually our excursions were pleasantly monotonous. There were always a few purchases to be made at Leiser's, Sternfeld's, or Machwitz'; then we went to Markus'. It had got to be a habit with Markus to pay Mama an assortment of the most flattering compliments. He was obviously in love with her, but as far as I know, he never went any further than to clutch my mother's hand, ardently described as worth its weight in gold, and to impress a silent kiss upon it—except for the time I shall speak of in a moment, when he fell on his knees.

Mama, who had inherited Grandma Koljaiczek's sturdy, imposing figure and her lovable vanity tempered with good nature, put up with Markus' attentions. To some extent, no doubt, she was influenced by the silk stockings—he bought them up in job lots but they were of excellent quality—which he sold her so cheap that they were practically gifts. Not to mention the drums he passed over the counter every two weeks, also at bargain prices.

Regularly at half past four Mama would ask Sigismund if she might leave me, Oskar, in his care, for it was getting late and she still had a few important errands. Strangely smiling, Markus would bow and promise with an ornate turn of phrase to guard me, Oskar, like the apple of his eye, while she attended to her important affairs. The mockery in his tone was too faint to give offense, but sometimes it brought a blush to Mama's cheeks and led her to suspect that Markus knew what was what.

As for me, I knew all about the errands that Mama characterized as important and attended to so zealously. For a

time she had let me accompany her to a cheap hotel in Tis-
chlergasse, where she left me with the landlady and van-
ished up the stairs for exactly three-quarters of an hour.
Without a word the landlady, who as a rule was sipping
half-and-half, set a glass of some foul-tasting soda pop be-
fore me, and there I waited until Mama, in whom no par-
ticular change was discernible, returned. With a word of
good-bye to the landlady, who didn't bother to look up
from her half-and-half, she would take me by the hand. It
never occurred to her that the temperature of her hand
might give me ideas. Hand in overheated hand, we went
next to the Café Weitzke in Wollwebergasse. Mama would
order mocha, Oskar lemon ice, and they would wait, but
not for long, until Jan Bronski should happen by, and a sec-
ond cup of mocha should be set down on the soothingly
cool marble table top.

They spoke in my presence almost as though I were not
there, and their conversation corroborated what I had long
known: that Mama and Uncle Jan met nearly every Thurs-
day to spend three-quarters of an hour in a hotel room in
Tischlergasse, which Jan paid for. It must have been Jan
who objected to these visits of mine to Tischlergasse and
the Café Weitzke. Sometimes he was very modest, more so
than Mama, who saw no reason why I should not witness
the epilogue to their hour of love, of whose legitimacy she
always, even afterward, seemed to be convinced.

At Jan's request, then, I spent almost every Thursday af-
ternoon, from half past four to shortly before six o'clock,
with Sigismund Markus. I was allowed to look through his
assortment of drums, and even to use them—where else
could Oskar have played several drums at once? Mean-

while, I would contemplate Markus' hangdog features. I didn't know where his thoughts came from, but I had a pretty fair idea where they went; they were in Tischlergasse, scratching on numbered room doors, or huddling like poor Lazarus under the marble-topped table at the Café Weitzke. Waiting for what? For crumbs?

Mama and Jan Bronski left no crumbs. Not a one. They ate everything themselves. They had the ravenous appetite that never dies down, that bites its own tail. They were so busy that at most they might have interpreted Markus' thoughts beneath the table as the importunate attentions of a draft.

On one of those afternoons—it must have been in September, for Mama left Markus' shop in her rust-colored autumn suit—I saw that Markus was lost in thought behind his counter. I don't know what got into me. Taking my newly acquired drum, I drifted out into Arsenal Passage. The sides of the cool dark tunnel were lined with sumptuous window displays: jewelry, books, fancy delicatessen. But desirable as these articles may have been, they were clearly beyond my reach. They did not hold me; I kept on going, through the passage and out to the Kohlenmarkt. Emerging in the dusty light, I stood facing the Arsenal. The basalt gray façade was larded with cannonballs dating back to various sieges, which recorded the history of the city of Danzig for the benefit of all who should pass by. The cannonballs were of no interest to me, particularly as I knew that they had not stuck in the wall of their own accord, that there lived in the city of Danzig a mason employed and paid conjointly by the Public Building Office and the Office for the Conservation of Monuments, whose function it was to immure the ammunition of past centuries in the façades of various churches and town halls, and specifically in the front and rear walls of the Arsenal.

I decided to head for the Stadt-Theater, whose portico I could see on the right, separated from the Arsenal only by a short unlighted alley. Just as I had expected, the theater was closed—the box office for the evening performance opened only at seven. Envisaging a retreat, I drummed my way irresolutely leftward. But then Oskar found himself between the Stockturm and the Langgasser Gate. I didn't dare to pass through the gate into Langgasse and turn left into Grosse Wollwebergasse, for Mama and Jan Bronski would be sitting there; and if they were not there yet, it seemed likely that they had just completed their errand in Tischlergasse and were on their way to take their refreshing mochas on the little marble table.

I have no idea how I managed to cross the Kohlenmarkt, to thread my way between the streetcars hastening to squeeze through the arch or popping out of it with a great clanging of bells and screeching round the curve as they headed for the Holzmarkt and the Central Station. Probably a grown-up, perhaps a policeman, took me by the hand and guided me through the perils of the traffic.

I stood facing the Stockturm, steep brick wall pinned against the sky, and it was only by chance, in response to a faint stirring of boredom, that I wedged my drumsticks in between the masonry and the iron mounting of the door. I looked upward along the brickwork, but it was hard to follow the line of the façade, for pigeons kept flying out of niches and windows, to rest on the oriels and waterspouts for the brief time it takes a pigeon to rest before darting downward and forcing my gaze to follow.

Those pigeons really got on my nerves with their activity. There was no point in looking up if I couldn't follow the wall to its end in the sky, so I called back my gaze and, to dispel my irritation, began in earnest to use my drumsticks as levers. The door gave way. It had no need to open very far, already Oskar was inside the tower, climbing the spiral staircase, advancing his right foot and pulling the left one after it. He came to the first dungeons and still he climbed, on past the torture chamber with its carefully preserved and instructively labeled instruments. At this point he began to advance his left foot and draw the right one after it. A little higher he glanced through a barred window, estimated the height, studied the thickness of the masonry, and shooed the pigeons away. At the next turn of the staircase he met the same pigeons. Now he shifted back to his right foot and after one more change reached the top. He felt a heaviness in his legs, but it seemed to him that he could have kept on climbing for ages. The staircase had given up first. In a flash Oskar understood the absurdity, the futility of building towers.

I do not know how high the Stockturm was (and still is; for it survived the war). Nor have I any desire to ask Bruno my keeper for a reference work on East German brick Gothic. My guess is that it must measure a good 150 feet from top to toe.

I was obliged—because of the staircase that lacked the courage of its convictions—to stop on the gallery that ran around the spire. I sat down, thrust my legs between the supports of the balustrade, and leaned forward. I clasped one of the supports in my right arm and looked past it, down toward the Kohlenmarkt, while with my left hand I made sure that my drum, which had participated in the whole climb, was all right.

I have no intention of boring you with a bird's-eye view of Danzig—venerable city of many towers, city of belfries and bells, allegedly still pervaded by the breath of the Middle Ages—in any case you can see the whole panorama in dozens of excellent prints. Nor shall I waste my time on pigeons, or doves as they are sometimes called, though some people seem to regard them as a fit subject for literature. To me pigeons mean just about nothing, even gulls are a little higher in the scale. Your "dove of peace" makes sense only as a paradox. I would sooner entrust a message of peace to a hawk or a vulture than to a dove, which is just about the most quarrelsome animal under God's heaven. To make a long story short: there were pigeons on the Stockturm. But after all, there are pigeons on every self-respecting tower.

At all events it was not pigeons that held my eyes but something different: the Stadt-Theater, which I had found closed on my way from the Arsenal. This box with a dome on it looked very much like a monstrously blown-up neo-classical coffee mill. All the Temple of the Muses lacked was a crank with which to grind up its contents, actors and public, sets and props, Goethe and Schiller, slowly but exceedingly small. The building annoyed me, especially the column-flanked windows of the lobby, sparkling in the rays of a sagging afternoon sun which kept mixing more and more red in its palette.

Up there on the tower, a good hundred feet above the Kohlenmarkt with its streetcars and throngs of homeward-bound office workers, high above Markus' sweet-smelling shop and the Café Weitzke with its cool marble table tops, two cups of mocha, far above Mama and Jan Bronski, above all courtyards, all bent and straightened nails, all juvenile soupmakers—up there on the tower, I who had hitherto screamed only for good and sufficient reason, became a gratuitous screamer. Until the day when I took it into my head to climb the Stockturm I had projected my cutting notes upon glasses, light bulbs, beer bottles, but only when someone wanted to take away my drum; now on the tower I screamed though my drum was not even remotely threatened.

No one was trying to take Oskar's drum away, and still he screamed. No pigeon had sullied his drum with its droppings. Near me there was verdigris on copper plates, but no glass. And nevertheless Oskar screamed. The eyes of the pigeons had a reddish glitter, but no one was eying him out of a glass eye; yet he screamed. What did he scream at? What distant object? Did he wish to apply scientific method to the experiment he had attempted for the hell of it in the loft after his meal of brick soup? What glass had Oskar in mind? What glass — and it had to be glass — did Oskar wish to experiment with?

It was the Stadt Theater, the dramatic coffee mill, whose windowpanes gleaming in the evening sun attracted the modernistic tones, bordering on mannerism, that I had first tried out in our loft. After a few minutes of variously pitched screams which accomplished nothing, I succeeded in producing an almost soundless tone, and a moment later Oskar noted with joy and a blush of telltale pride that two of the middle panes in the end window of the lobby had been obliged to relinquish their share of the sunset, leaving two black rectangles that would soon require attention from the glazier.

Still, the effect had to be verified. Like a modern painter who, having at last found the style he has been seeking for years, perfects it and discloses his full maturity by turning out one after another dozens of examples of his new manner, all equally daring and magnificent, I too embarked on a productive period.

In barely a quarter of an hour I succeeded in unglassing all the lobby windows and some of the doors. A crowd, from where I was standing one would have said an excited crowd, gathered outside the theater. But the stupidest incident draws a crowd. The admirers of my art made no particular impression on me. At most they led Oskar to discipline his art, to strive for greater formal purity. I was just getting ready to lay bare the very heart of things with a still more daring experiment, to send a very special cry through the open lobby, through the keyhole of one of the loge doors into the still darkened theater, a cry that should strike the pride of all subscribers, the chandelier with all its polished, facetted, light-reflecting and refracting hardware, when my eye lit on a bit of rust-brown material in the crowd outside of the theater: Mama was on her way back from the Café Weitzke, she had had her mocha and left Jan Bronski.

Even so, it must be admitted that Oskar aimed a cry at the chandelier. But apparently it had no effect, for the newspapers the next day spoke only of the windows and doors that had burst asunder for unknown, mysterious reasons. For several weeks purveyors of scientific and semiscientific theories were to fill the back pages of the daily press with columns of fantastic nonsense. The *Neueste Nachrichten* spoke of cosmic rays. The unquestionably well-informed staff of the local observatory spoke of sunspots.

I for my part descended the spiral staircase as quickly as my short legs would carry me and, rather out of breath, joined the crowd outside the theater. Mama's rust-brown autumn suit was nowhere to be seen, no doubt she was in Markus' shop, telling about the destruction wrought by my voice. And Markus, who took my so-called backwardness and my diamond-like voice perfectly for granted, would be wagging the tip of his tongue and rubbing his yellowed white hands.

As I entered the shop the sight that met my eyes made me forget all about my success as a singer. Sigismund Markus was kneeling at Mama's feet, and all the plush animals, bears, monkeys, dogs, the dolls with eyes that opened and shut, the fire engines, rocking horses, and even the jumping jacks that guarded the shop, seemed on the point of kneeling with him. He held Mama's two hands in his, there were brownish fuzzy blotches on the backs of his hands, and he wept.

Mama also looked very solemn, as though she were giving the situation the attention it deserved. "No, Markus," she said, "please, Markus. Not here in the store."

But Markus went on interminably. He seemed to be overdoing it a little, but still I shall never forget the note of supplication in his voice. "Don't do it no more with Bronski, seeing he's in the Polish Post Office. He's with the Poles, that's no good. Don't bet on the Poles; if you gotta bet on somebody, bet on the Germans, they're coming up, maybe sooner maybe later. And suppose they're on top and Mrs. Matzerath is still betting on Bronski. All right if you want to bet on Matzerath, what you got him already. Or do me a favor, bet on Markus seeing he's just fresh baptized. We'll go to London, I got friends there and plenty stocks and bonds if you just decide to come, or all right if you won't come with Markus because you despise me, so despise me. But I beg you down on my knees, don't bet no more on Bronski that's meshugge enough to stick by the Polish Post Office when the Poles are pretty soon all washed up when the Germans come."

Just as Mama, confused by so many possibilities and impossibilities, was about to burst into tears, Markus saw me in the doorway and pointing five eloquent fingers in my direction: "Please, Mrs. Matzerath. We'll take him with us to London. Like a little prince he'll live."

Mama turned toward me and managed a bit of a smile. Maybe she was thinking of the paneless windows in the theater lobby or maybe it was the thought of London Town that cheered her. But to my surprise she shook her head and said lightly, as though declining a dance: "Thank you, Markus, but it's not possible. Really it's impossible — on account of Bronski."

Taking my uncle's name as a cue, Markus rose to his feet and bowed like a jackknife. "I beg your pardon," he said. "That's what I was thinking all along. On account of him you couldn't do it."

It was not yet closing time when we left the shop, but Markus locked up from outside and escorted us to the streetcar stop. Passersby and a few policemen were still standing outside the theater. But I wasn't the least bit scared, I had almost forgotten my triumph. Markus bent down close to me and whispered, more to himself than to us: "That little Oskar! He knocks on the drum and hell is breaking loose by the theater."

The broken glass had Mama worried and he made gestures that were intended to set her mind at rest. Then the car came and he uttered a last plea as we were climbing into the trailer, in an undertone for fear of being overheard: "Well, if that's the case, do me a favor and stay by Matzerath what you got him already, don't bet no more on that Polisher."

When today Oskar, lying or sitting in his hospital bed but in either case drumming, revisits Arsenal Passage and the Stockturm with the scribbles on its dungeon walls and its well-soiled instruments of torture, when once again he looks down on those three windows outside the lobby of the Stadt-Theater and thereafter returns to Arsenal Passage and Sigismund Markus' store, searching for the particulars of a day in September, he cannot help looking for Poland at the same time. How does he look for it? With his drumsticks. Does he also look for Poland with his soul? He looks for it with every organ of his being, but the soul is not an organ.

I look for the land of the Poles that is lost to the Germans, for the moment at least. Nowadays the Germans have started searching for Poland with credits, Leicas, and compasses, with radar, divining rods, delegations, and moth-eaten provincial students' associations in costume. Some carry Chopin in their hearts, others thoughts of revenge. Condemning the first four partitions of Poland, they are busily planning a fifth; in the meantime flying to Warsaw via Air France in order to deposit, with appropriate remorse, a wreath on the spot that was once the ghetto. One of these days they will go searching for Poland with rockets. I, meanwhile, conjure up Poland on my drum. And this is what I drum: Poland's lost, but not forever, all's lost, but not forever, Poland's not lost forever.

Translated by Ralph Manheim

In the Tunnel

(1960)

A young woman—dressed with a sporty elegance—was sitting in the compartment across from Breitscheidt, reading a book. He thought he could make out some of the words. This meant she wasn't a foreigner—or else that she was one of those well-educated globe-trotters whose knowledge of German would permit her to follow his own torrent of speech, if only he opened his mouth.

It's hard to talk to someone who is reading a book. The train was rushing through Switzerland, winding through Switzerland. The countryside was colorful and inviting, just as it is on those ingenious official tourist posters. The mountains towered overhead, slicing open the fair-weather clouds; the valleys tapered to points; spotted cows and homesick expatriates alike feasted on the green grass.

That was no light book she was reading; Breitscheidt could see it was an India-paper edition. India paper—the words somehow fit the lady, who seemed to meditate over each thin page. Her blouse was cream colored, with open-work trim. Her brassiere looked as if it had been designed to lightly accentuate her nipples. The train was ascending; they were ascending. Breitscheidt was looking forward to St. Gotthard and that hole in the middle of the mountains. He realized the tunnel had a special aura that brought those who were sitting on opposite sides of the compartment a little closer, that acted as a springboard for conversation. In Göschenen he bought a ham sandwich and some café au lait from a vendor who handed everything to him through the open window of the compartment. Afterward he had a hard time getting the window to close again. He had to take off his jacket and put it back on: that was embarrassing. The speakers announced the departing train in two languages, and seconds later the tunnel swallowed whatever was bound for Airolo and beyond. Everything went cramped and gray inside his ears; he leaned back in his seat. The words and phrases and sentences towered up in his head and came crashing back down, then sprang back up even more rampant and random and inexpressible than before. A tunnel like that is as long and monotonous as a Sunday afternoon. Maybe it was the fault of the mountain, that corpse full of holes, but all the pointed compliments, the tender words and propositions he had thought up, which traveled as far as Rimini, where they conjured up a hotel room overlooking the blue Adriatic, where, together with her, both together, then, together—everything inside Breitscheidt settled into a laconic rage: "What's she reading anyway, in that India-paper book of hers? Doesn't she want to be with me? Doesn't she like me? Just because I had a hard time getting the window up? As if it's my fault the thing got stuck!"

The lady closed her book and refocused her eyes from the text to the window, where she meant to see Nature, and said: "Are we already in the tunnel?"

"Yes," Breitscheidt answered, too loudly.

"Will it go on long?" Her gray-checked legs were crossed.

"Not much longer," Breitscheidt was able to affirm, adding: "No, Fräulein, it won't be much longer." Then he laughed, expansively and excessively, before slowly letting up, until finally only the train or the mountain was laughing—or the train, the mountain, and the tracks—and the tunnel took a turn.

After that Breitscheidt, too, crossed his legs—first attending to the crease in his trousers—and both passengers had no choice but to submit to the general tunnel cheer. It was all he could do to come out with the line: "You know, I'll bet the sun will be shining as soon as we come out the other side." And as he uttered this prophecy he suddenly uncrossed his legs and leaned alarmingly forward, full of genuine praise for the openwork blouse, the India-paper edition, the Adriatic, etc., just to give the last bit of tunnel some meaning, and then suddenly everything went bright, too bright: no more cheery humor, just the milky, white window—and rain.

Now they were sitting very far apart. She took a cigarette in her secretarial fingers but he was too late on the draw. She lit it herself and opened the India-paper book. Breitscheidt wondered wearily if he ought to open the light metal ashtray for her. He didn't. He reached into his jacket pocket, found his trusty tin, sprinkled some of the contents into his open hand and then into his mouth, until the peppermint flavor drowned out his sadness.

Translated by Philip Boehm

KINDERLIED   (1960)

Wer lacht hier, hat gelacht?
Hier hat sich's ausgelacht.
Wer hier lacht, macht Verdacht,
daß er aus Gründen lacht.

Wer weint hier, hat geweint?
Hier wird nicht mehr geweint.
Wer hier weint, der auch meint,
daß er aus Gründen weint.

Wer spricht hier, spricht und schweigt?
Wer schweigt, wird angezeigt.
Wer hier spricht, hat verschwiegen,
wo seine Gründe liegen.

Wer spielt hier, spielt im Sand?
Wer spielt, muß an die Wand,
hat sich beim Spiel die Hand
gründlich verspielt, verbrannt.

Wer stirbt hier, ist gestorben?
Wer stirbt, ist abgeworben.
Wer hier stirbt, unverdorben,
ist ohne Grund verstorben.

NURSERY RHYME

Who laughs here, who has laughed?
Here we have ceased to laugh.
To laugh here now is treason.
The laugher has a reason.

Who weeps here, who has wept?
Here weeping is inept.
To weep here now means too
a reason so to do.

Who speaks here or keeps mum?
Here we denounce the dumb.
To speak here is to hide
deep reasons kept inside.

Who plays here, in the sand?
Against the wall we stand
players whose games are banned.
They've lost, thrown in their hand.

Who dies here, dares to die?
"Defector!" here we cry.
To die here, without stain,
is to have died in vain.

Translated by Michael Hamburger

By the Time the War Broke Out

from Cat and Mouse (1961)

. . . AND ONE DAY, AFTER MAHLKE HAD LEARNED TO swim, we were lying in the grass, in the Schlagball field. I ought to have gone to the dentist, but they wouldn't let me because I was hard to replace on the team. My tooth was howling. A cat sauntered diagonally across the field and no one threw anything at it. A few of the boys were chewing or plucking at blades of grass. The cat belonged to the caretaker and was black. Hotten Sonntag rubbed his bat with a woolen stocking. My tooth marked time. The tournament had been going on for two hours. We had lost hands down and were waiting for the return game. It was a young cat, but no kitten. In the stadium, handball goals were being made thick and fast on both sides. My tooth kept saying one word, over and over again. On the cinder track the sprinters were practicing starts or limbering up. The cat meandered about. A trimotored plane crept across the sky, slow and loud, but couldn't drown out my tooth. Through the stalks of grass the caretaker's black cat showed a white bib. Mahlke was asleep. The wind was from the east, and the crematorium between the United Cemeteries and the Engineering School was operating. Mr. Mallenbrandt, the gym teacher, blew his whistle: Change sides. The cat practiced. Mahlke was asleep or seemed to be. I was next to him with my toothache. Still practicing, the cat came closer. Mahlke's Adam's apple attracted attention because it was large, always in motion, and threw a shadow. Between me and Mahlke the caretaker's black cat tensed for a leap. We formed a triangle. My tooth was silent and stopped marking time: for Mahlke's Adam's apple had become the cat's mouse. It was so young a cat, and Mahlke's whatsis was so active—in any case the cat leaped at Mahlke's throat; or one of us caught the cat and held it up to Mahlke's neck; or I, with or without my toothache, seized the cat and showed it Mahlke's mouse: and Joachim Mahlke let out a yell, but suffered only slight scratches. . . .

BY THE TIME the war broke out, the ports of Gdynia, Putzig, Heisternest, and Hela were bereft of naval vessels except for an obsolete former French cruiser that served as a training ship and dormitory, the minelayer *Gryf,* built in the Norman dockyards of Le Havre, a heavily armed vessel of two thousand tons, carrying three hundred mines. Otherwise there were a lone destroyer, the *Wicher,* a few former German torpedo boats, and the six minesweepers of the *Czaika* class, which also laid mines. These last had a speed of eighteen knots; their armament consisted of a 75-millimeter forward gun and four machine guns on revolving mounts; they carried, so the official handbooks say, a complement of twenty mines.

And one of these one-hundred-and-eighty-five-ton vessels had been built specially for Mahlke.

The naval battle in the Gulf of Danzig lasted from the first of September to the second of October. The score, after the capitulation on Hela Peninsula, was as follows: The Polish units *Gryf, Wicher, Baltyk,* as well as the three minesweepers of the *Czaika* class, the *Mewa,* the *Jaskolka,* and the *Czapla,* had been destroyed by fire and sunk in their ports; the German destroyer *Leberecht* had been damaged by artillery fire, the minesweeper *M 85* ran into a Polish antisubmarine mine north of Heisternest and lost a third of its crew.

Only the remaining, slightly damaged vessels of the *Czaika* class were captured. The *Zuraw* and the *Czaika* were soon commissioned under the names of *Oxthöft* and *Westerplatte*; as the third, the *Rybitwa,* was being towed from Hela to Neufahrwasser, it began to leak, settle, and wait for Joachim Mahlke; for it was he who in the following summer raised brass plaques on which the name *Rybitwa* had been engraved. Later, it was said that a Polish officer and a bosun's mate, obliged to man the rudder under German guard, had flooded the barge in accordance with the well-known Scapa Flow recipe.

For some reason or other it sank to one side of the channel, not far from the Neufahrwasser harbor buoy and, though it lay conveniently on one of the many sandbanks, was not salvaged, but spent the rest of the war right there, with only its bridge, the remains of its rail, its battered ventilators, and the forward gun mount (the gun itself had been removed) emerging from the water—a strange sight at first, but soon a familiar one. It provided you, Joachim

Mahlke, with a goal in life; just as the battleship *Gneisenau,*
which was sunk in February '45 just outside of Gdynia har-
bor, became a goal for Polish schoolboys; though I can
only wonder whether, among the Polish boys who dove
and looted the *Gneisenau,* there was any who took to the
water with the same fanaticism as Mahlke.

HE WAS NOT a thing of beauty. He could have had his
Adam's apple repaired. Possibly that piece of cartilage was
the whole trouble.

But it went with the rest of him. Besides, you can't prove
everything by proportions. And as for his soul, it was never
introduced to me. I never heard what he thought. In the
end, all I really had to go by was his neck and its numerous
counterweights. It is true that he took enormous bundles of
margarine sandwiches to school and to the beach with him
and would devour quantities of them just before going into
the water. But this can only be taken as one more reminder
of his mouse, for the mouse chewed insatiably.

There were also his devotions at the altar of the Virgin.
He took no particular interest in the Crucified One. It
struck me that though the bobbing on his neck did not
cease when he joined his fingertips in prayer, he swallowed
in slow motion on these occasions and contrived, by ar-
ranging his hands in an exaggeratedly stylized pose, to dis-
tract attention from that elevator above his shirt collar and
his pendants on strings, shoelaces, and chains—which
never stopped running.

Apart from the Virgin he didn't have much truck with
girls. Maybe if he had had a sister? My girl cousins weren't
much use to him either. His relations with Tulla Pokriefke

don't count, they were an anomaly and would not have been bad as a circus act—remember, he was planning to become a clown—for Tulla, a spindly little thing with legs like toothpicks, might just as well have been a boy. In any case, this scrawny girl child, who swam along with us when she felt like it during our second summer on the barge, was never the least embarrassed when we decided to give our swimming trunks a rest and sprawled naked on the rusty bridge, with very little idea what to do with ourselves.

You can draw a good likeness of Tulla's face with the most familiar punctuation marks. The way she glided through the water, she might have had webs between her toes. Always, even on the barge, despite seaweed, gulls, and the sour smell of the rust, she stank of carpenter's glue, because her father worked with glue in her uncle's carpenter's shop. She was all skin, bones, and curiosity. Calmly, her chin in the cup of her hand, Tulla would look on when Winter or Esch, unable to contain himself, produced his modest offering. Hunching over so that the bones of her spine stuck out, she would gaze at Winter, who was always slow in getting there, and mutter: "Man, that's taking a long time!"

But when, finally, the stuff came and splashed on the rust, she would begin to fidget and squirm, she would throw herself down on her belly, make little rat's eyes and look and look, trying to discover heaven-knows-what, turn over, sit up, rise to her knees and her feet, stand slightly knock-kneed over the mess, and begin to stir it with a supple big toe, until it foamed rust red: "Boy! That's the berries! Now you do it, Atze."

Tulla never wearied of this little game—yes, game, the whole thing was all perfectly innocent. "Aw, you do it," she would plead in that whining voice of hers. "Who hasn't done it yet? It's your turn."

She always found some good-natured fool who would get to work even if he wasn't at all in the mood, just to give her something to goggle at. The only one who wouldn't give until Tulla found the right words of encouragement— and that is why I am narrating these heroic deeds—was the great swimmer and diver Joachim Mahlke. While all the rest of us were engaging in this time-honored, nay Biblical, pursuit, either one at a time or—as the manual puts it—with others, Mahlke kept his trunks on and gazed fixedly in the direction of Hela. We felt certain that at home, in his room between snowy owl and Sistine Madonna, he indulged in the same sport.

He had just come up, shivering as usual, and he had nothing to show. Schilling had just been working for Tulla. A coaster was entering the harbor under its own power. "Do it again," Tulla begged, for Schilling was the most prolific of all. Not a single ship in the roadstead. "Not after swimming. I'll do it again tomorrow," Schilling consoled her. Tulla turned on her heel and stood with outspread toes facing Mahlke, who as usual was shivering in the shadow of the pilothouse and hadn't sat down yet. A high-seas tug with a forward gun was putting out to sea.

"Won't you? Aw, do it just once. Or can't you? Don't you want to? Or aren't you allowed to?"

Mahlke stepped half out of the shadow and slapped Tulla's compressed little face left right with his palm and the back of his hand. His mouse went wild. So did the screwdriver. Tulla, of course, didn't shed one single tear, but gave a bleating laugh with her mouth closed; shaking

with laughter, she arched her india-rubber frame effort-
lessly into a bridge, and peered through her spindly legs at
Mahlke until he—he was back in the shade again and the
tug was veering off to northwestward—said: "OK. Just so
you'll shut your yap."

Tulla came out of her contortion and squatted down
normally with her legs folded under her, as Mahlke stripped
his trunks down to his knees. The children at the Punch-
and-Judy show gaped in amazement: a few deft movements
emanating from his right wrist, and his pecker loomed so
large that the tip emerged from the shadow of the pilot-
house and the sun fell on it. Only when we had all formed
a semicircle did Mahlke's jumping Jim return to the shadow.

"Won't you let me just for a second?" Tulla's mouth hung
open. Mahlke nodded and dropped his right hand, though
without uncurving his fingers. Tulla's hands, scratched and
bruised as they always were, approached the monster,
which expanded under her questioning fingertips; the veins
stood out and the glans protruded.

"Measure it!" cried Jürgen Kupka. Tulla spread the fingers
of her left hand. One full span and another almost. Some-
body and then somebody else whispered: "At least twelve
inches!" That was an exaggeration of course. Schilling, who
otherwise had the longest, had to take his out, make it stand
up, and hold it beside Mahlke's: Mahlke's was first of all a size
thicker, second a matchbox longer, and third looked much
more grownup, dangerous, and worthy to be worshiped.

He had shown us again, and then a second time he
showed us by producing not one but two mighty streams in
quick succession. With his knees not quite together,
Mahlke stood by the twisted rail beside the pilothouse, star-

ing out in the direction of the harbor buoy, a little to the rear of the low-lying smoke of the vanishing high-seas tug; a torpedo boat of the *Gull* class was just emerging from the harbor, but he didn't let it distract him. Thus he stood, showing his profile, from the toes extending just over the edge to the watershed in the middle of his hair: strangely enough, the length of his sexual part made up for the otherwise shocking protuberance of his Adam's apple, lending his body an odd, but in its way perfect, harmony.

No sooner had Mahlke finished squirting the first load over the rail than he started in all over again. Winter timed him with his waterproof wristwatch; Mahlke's performance continued for approximately as many seconds as it took the torpedo boat to pass from the tip of the breakwater to the buoy; then, while the torpedo boat was rounding the buoy, he unloaded the same amount again; the foaming bubbles lurched in the smooth, only occasionally rippling swell, and we laughed for joy as the gulls swooped down, screaming for more.

Joachim Mahlke was never obliged to repeat or better this performance, for none of us ever touched his record, certainly not when exhausted from swimming and diving; sportsmen in everything we did, we respected the rules.

For a while Tulla Pokriefke, for whom his prowess must have had the most direct appeal, courted him in her way; she would always be sitting by the pilothouse, staring at Mahlke's swimming trunks. A few times she pleaded with him, but he always refused, though good-naturedly.

"Do you have to confess these things?"

Mahlke nodded, and played with his dangling screwdriver to divert her gaze.

"Will you take me down sometime? By myself I'm scared. I bet there's still a stiff down there."

For educational purposes, no doubt, Mahlke took Tulla down into the fo'c'sle. He kept her under much too long. When they came up, she had turned a grayish yellow and sagged in his arms. We had to stand her light, curveless body on its head.

After that Tulla Pokriefke didn't join us very often and, though she was more regular than other girls of her age, she got increasingly on our nerves with her drivel about the dead sailor in the barge. She was always going on about him. "The one that brings him up," she promised, "can you-know-what."

It is perfectly possible that without admitting it to ourselves we all searched, Mahlke in the engine room, the rest of us in the fo'c'sle, for a half-decomposed Polish sailor; not because we really wanted to lay this unfinished little number, but just so.

Yet even Mahlke found nothing except for a few half-rotted pieces of clothing, from which fishes darted until the gulls saw that something was stirring and began to say grace.

No, HE DIDN'T set much store by Tulla, though they say there was something between them later. He didn't go for girls, not even for Schilling's sister. And all my cousins from Berlin got out of him was a fishy stare. If he had any tender feelings at all, it was for boys; by which I don't mean to suggest that Mahlke was queer; in those years spent between the beach and the sunken barge, we none of us knew exactly whether we were male or female. Though later there may have been rumors and tangible evidence to the contrary, the fact is that the only woman Mahlke cared about was the Catholic Virgin Mary. It was for her sake alone that he dragged everything that can be worn and displayed on the human neck to St. Mary's Chapel. Whatever he did, from diving to his subsequent military accomplishments, was done for her or else—yes, I know, I'm contradicting myself again—to distract attention from his Adam's apple. And perhaps, in addition to Virgin and mouse, there was yet a third motive: Our school, that musty edifice that defied ventilation, and particularly the auditorium, meant a great deal to Joachim Mahlke; it was the school that drove you, later on, to your supreme effort.

Translated by Ralph Manheim

Execution on the Playground

from My Century (1999)

Our schoolyard games didn't end with the bell; they ran from recreation period to recreation period under the chestnut trees and around the single-story lavatory building we called the piss hut. We fought. The piss hut, which was next to the gym, was the Toledo Alcázar. True, the event had taken place the year before, but in our schoolboy dreams the Falangists were still heroically defending the walls, the Reds storming them in vain. Part of the reason for the latter's failure lay in our lack of enthusiasm: nobody wanted to be a Red, myself included. All of us considered ourselves stalwart supporters of General Franco. In the end, a few of the older boys had us draw lots, and I, never suspecting the future significance of the draw, was one of several first-year boys who drew Red. Clearly the future starts making itself felt in the schoolyard.

And so we laid siege to the piss hut. We had to accept one compromise, however: during regular truces imposed by the teachers on schoolyard duty both neutral and combatant groups were to be allowed to obey calls of nature. One of the high points in the battle scenario was the telephone conversation between the commander of the Alcázar, Colonel Moscardó, and his son Luis, whom the Reds had captured and threatened with execution should the fortress refuse to surrender. Helmut Kurella, a third-year boy with an angelic face and the voice to match, played the role of Luis. My job was to hand the phone over to Luis in the person of Caballo, the Commissar of the Red Militia. "Hello, Papa," said Luis in a voice that rang out clear as day over the schoolyard. "What's wrong, my lad?" "Oh, nothing. They say they're going to shoot me if the Alcázar doesn't surrender." "If that is so, my son, then commend your soul to God, cry 'Viva España!' and die a hero's death." "Farewell, Father. I embrace you warmly."

That was the angelic Helmut as Luis. Whereupon I as the Red Commissar, coached by an older boy, cried out "Viva la muerte!" and shot the brave boy to death under a blossoming chestnut tree.

Actually, I'm not sure I'm the one who was charged with the execution, though I may have been. In any case, the battle went on from there. During the next recreation period the tower was blown up. We did it acoustically. But the Falangists refused to surrender. What was later called the Spanish Civil War played itself out in the schoolyard of the Conradinum in Danzig-Langfuhr as a single event repeatable ad infinitum. The Falange was eventually victorious, of course, the encirclement being pierced from without by a horde of overly zealous fourth- and fifth-year boys. Embraces all around. Colonel Moscardó greeted the liberators with his by then famous "Sin novedad," which means something like "Nothing to report," and we Reds were liquidated forthwith.

By the end of recreation the piss hut could be used as usual again, but on the next day of school we were back at our game. And so it went until the summer holidays. It was 1937. We could have acted out the bombing of the Basque town of Guernica. The German newsreel had shown it to us, this strike by our volunteers, before the feature film. On 26 April the town was turned into a rubble heap. I can still hear the engines and the background music. But all I got to see were our Heinkels and Junkers approaching, diving, departing. They might as well have been on maneuvers. There was no heroic feat for us to reproduce in the schoolyard.

Translated by Michael Henry Heim

Roll Your Own

(1974)

I'M A SMOKER. AND, WHAT'S MORE, I'M LEFT-HANDED. All you need are papers and tobacco. The edge of the cigarette paper is the edge of the world; that little strip lined with adhesive separates the person rolling his own from the outside world, sets him apart from the smokers of packaged brands, who are forever fretting about whether the next vending machine might be broken, or broken into.

God the Father also rolled his own,
after making us out of next to nothing.

Wedge the paper along the fold against middle and index fingers of one hand; then, with the thumb, index finger, and middle finger of your other hand knead a quantity of tobacco—measured according to whim—into a little sausage, calmly, without rushing (as if the world weren't forever coming to an end).

It's the same hold you use for breadcrumbs, loam, and
    assorted odd junk.
In the womb, as an alternative, I rolled myself.
Don't reach for the ready-made: shape and distort.

Now the index and middle fingers of your left hand hold
the shaped tobacco that's been patted into the center
crease of the paper, while the other hand returns both to-
bacco pouch and cigarette papers to your pocket—still
without rushing: that way we gain a little time, without a
smoke, but possibly long enough for a thought to find its
needle's eye.

And because everyone likes a slogan, I will say (with
    reservations),
Self-rolled is half-smoked.
Because I often interrupt the slow process to scribble
    something down, type a line or two,
flee into another century that's far enough away.

Finally—because meanwhile some time has slipped by—
your thumbs middle and index fingers of both hands hold
the paper with the tobacco in the crease horizontally, at
about navel height, in perfect symmetry.

Of course people talk: about Ivan and his cheap loose-leaf
    tobacco, his *machorka*
(crumbled up in old editions of *Pravda*),
or else they think of Grandpa,
who also rolled his own (in the bad times), from his own
    crop.

When you roll your own, you have to radically renounce all
the fluffy pieces that refuse to fit in. Only then, when the
tobacco is firmly ensconced along the bottom third of the
paper, firm to the touch—only then do you take your
tongue and moisten the strip of adhesive along the far edge
of the paper, using your index finger behind it as a backing.

What we all miss, apart from a new religion,
is a type of cigarette paper you can get in Holland,
which doesn't have any adhesive but still sticks and which
    turns brown
while you smoke it because it's been moistened with the
    tongue:
no less than the bland filters.

Beginners have a hard time wrapping the moistened edge
of the paper around the tobacco without sacrificing the
uniform pressure that a tautly rolled cigarette ought to
have. Now remoisten the seam. And meanwhile another
child has come into the world.

In order to keep the tobacco from burning my tongue,
    I give a little twist
to the left end, to make a mouth-sized point, because
when you draw it through a moist little cone like that,
the smoke becomes cool and spiritual.

Maria started rolling her own, too, after she took a picture of
me rolling mine while I was telling her the story of the
bearded man who wanted to revert to infancy so he could
once again suck and all that that entails: now we both smoke.

It's cheap. Lots of fun. Passes the time. And there are
    other advantages;
for instance, self-rolled stubs are all unique, each
is artistically curved, and every day
my ashtray lets me know
how my crisis is progressing.

Translated by Philip Boehm

There Was Once a City

from Dog Years (1963)

There was once a city —

in addition to the suburbs of Ohra, Schidlitz, Oliva, Emmaus, Praust, Sankt Albrecht, Schellmühl, and the seaport suburb of Neufahrwasser, it had a suburb named Langfuhr. Langfuhr was so big and so little that whatever happens or could happen in this world, also happened or could have happened in Langfuhr.

In this suburb, with its kitchen gardens, drill grounds, drainage fields, slightly sloping cemeteries, shipyards, athletic fields, and military compounds, in Langfuhr, which harbored roughly 72,000 registered inhabitants, which possessed three churches and a chapel, four high schools, a vocational and home-economics school, at all times too few elementary schools, but a brewery, with Aktien Pond and icehouse, in Langfuhr, which derived prestige from the Baltic Chocolate Factory, the municipal airfield, the railroad station, the celebrated Engineering School, two movie houses of unequal size, a car barn, the always overcrowded Stadium, and a burned-out synagogue; in the well-known suburb of Langfuhr, whose authorities operated a municipal poorhouse-and-orphanage and a home for the blind, picturesquely situated near Heiligenbrunn, in Langfuhr, incorporated in 1854, a pleasant residential section on the fringe of Jäschkental Forest where the Gutenberg monument was located, in Langfuhr, whose streetcar lines went to Brösen, the seaside resort, Oliva, the episcopal seat, and the city of Danzig—in Danzig-Langfuhr, then, a suburb made famous by the Mackensen Hussars and the last Crown Prince, a suburb traversed from end to end by the Striessbach, there lived a girl by the name of Tulla Pokriefke, who was pregnant but didn't know by whom.

In the same suburb, actually in the same apartment house on Elsenstrasse, which like Hertastrasse and Luisenstrasse connects Labesweg with Marienstrasse, lived Tulla's cousin; his name was Harry Liebenau, he was serving as an Air Force auxiliary in the Kaiserhafen AA battery and was not one of those who might have impregnated Tulla. For Harry merely cogitated in his little head what others actually did. A sixteen-year-old who suffered from cold feet and always stood slightly to one side. A knowledgeable young man who read a hodgepodge of books on history and philosophy and took care of his handsomely wavy medium-brown hair. A bundle of curiosity who mirrored everything with his gray, but not cold gray, eyes and had a fragile, porous feeling about his smooth but not sickly body. An always cautious Harry, who believed not in God but in the Nothing, yet did not want to have his sensitive tonsils removed. A melancholic, who liked honey cake, poppy-seed

cake, and shredded coconut, and though not a good swim-
mer had volunteered for the Navy. A young man of in-
action, who tried to murder his father by means of long
poems in school copybooks and referred to his mother as
the cook. A hypersensitive boy, who, standing and lying,
broke out in sweat over his cousin and unswervingly though
secretly thought of a black shepherd dog. A fetishist, who
for reasons carried a pearl-white incisor tooth in his purse.
A visionary, who lied a good deal, spoke softly, turned red
when, believed this and that, and regarded the never-ending
war as an extension of his schooling. A boy, a young man, a
uniformed high school student, who venerated the Führer,
Ulrich von Hutten, General Rommel, the historian Hein-
rich von Treitschke, for brief moments Napoleon, the
panting movie actor Emil Jannings, for a while Savonarola,
then again Luther, and of late the philosopher Martin Hei-
degger. With the help of these models he succeeded in
burying a real mound made of human bones under medi-
eval allegories. The pile of bones, which in reality cried out
to high heaven between Troyl and Kaiserhafen, was men-
tioned in his diary as a place of sacrifice, erected in order
that purity might come-to-be in the luminous, which trans-
luminates purity and so fosters light.

In addition to the diary, Harry Liebenau kept up an
often languishing and then for a time lively correspondence
with a girl friend, who under the stage name of Jenny An-
gustri danced in the German Ballet in Berlin and who in the
capital and on tours of the occupied regions appeared first
as a member of the *corps de ballet,* later as a soloist.

When Air Force auxiliary Harry Liebenau had a pass, he
went to the movies and took the pregnant Tulla Pokriefke.

Before Tulla was pregnant, Harry had tried several times in vain to persuade her to attend the movies by his side. Now that she was telling all Langfuhr: "Somebody's knocked me up"—though there were still no visible signs—she was more indulgent and said to Harry: "It's OK with me if you'll pay."

They let several films flicker past them in Langfuhr's two movie houses. The Art Cinema ran first the newsreel, then the educational film, then the feature. Harry was in uniform; Tulla was sitting there in a much too spacious coat of navy serge, which she had had tailored especially for her condition. While grapes were being harvested on rainy screen and peasant girls, festooned with grapes, wreathed with vine-leaves, and forced into corsets, were smiling, Harry tried to clinch with his cousin. But Tulla disengaged herself with the mild reproach: "Cut that out, Harry. There's no sense in it now. You should have come around sooner."

In the movies Harry always had a supply of raspberry drops on him, which were paid out in his battery every time you had laid low a specific number of water rats. Accordingly, they were known as rat drops. In the darkness, while up front the newsreel started up with a din, Harry peeled paper and tin foil from a roll of raspberry drops, thrust his thumbnail between the first and the second drop, and offered Tulla the roll. Tulla lifted off the raspberry drop with two fingers, clung to the newsreel with both pupils, sucked audibly, and whispered while up front the muddy season was setting in in Center Sector: "Everything stinks in that battery of yours, even the raspberry drops, of that whatchacallit behind the fence. You ought to ask for a transfer."

But Harry had other desires, which were fulfilled in the

movies: Gone: the muddy season. No more Christmas
preparations on the Arctic front. Counted: the gutted T-34
tanks. Docked: the U-boat after a successful expedition.
Taken off: our fighter planes to attack the terror bombers.
Different music. Different cameraman: a quiet pebble-
strewn afternoon, sunlight sprinkling through autumn
leaves: the Führer's headquarters. "Hey, look. There he
runs stands wags his tail. Between him and the aviator. Sure
thing, that's him: our dog. Our dog's dog, I mean; it's him
all over. Prinz, that's Prinz, that our Harras . . ."

For a good minute, while the Führer and Chancellor
under low-pulled visor cap, behind anchored hands, chats
with an Air Force officer—was it Rudel?—and walks back
and forth among the trees at the Führer's headquarters, an
obviously black shepherd is privileged to stand beside his
boots, rub against the Führer's boots, let the side of his
neck be patted—for once the Führer unlocks his anchored
hands, only to recouple them as soon as the newsreel has
captured the cordiality prevailing between master and dog.

Before Harry took the last streetcar to Troyl—he had to
change at the Main Station for the Heubude train—he took
Tulla home. They talked by turns: neither listened: she about
the feature; he about the newsreel. In Tulla's picture a girl
was raped while picking mushrooms and consequently—
something Tulla refused to understand—jumped in the
river; Harry tried, in Störtebeker's philosophical language,
to keep the newsreel alive and at the same time define it:
"The way I see it, dog-being—the very fact of it—implies
that an essent dog is thrown into his there. His being-in-the-
world is the dog-there, regardless of whether his there is a
carpenter's yard or the Führer's headquarters or some realm

removed from vulgar time. For future dog-being is not later than the dog-there of having-beenness, which in turn is not anterior to being-held-out-into the dog-now."

Nevertheless, Tulla said outside the Pokriefkes' door: "Beginning next week I'll be in my second month, and by Christmas you're sure to see something."

Harry dropped in at his parents' apartment for fifteen minutes, meaning to take some fresh underwear and edibles. His father, the carpenter, had swollen feet because he had been on them all day: from one building site to another. Consequently he was soaking his feet in the kitchen. Large and gnarled, they moved sadly in the basin. You couldn't tell from the carpenter's sighs whether it was the well-being bestowed by his footbath or tangled memories that made him sigh. Harry's mother was already holding the towel. She was kneeling and had taken off her reading glasses. Harry pulled a chair over from the table and sat down between father and mother: "Want me to tell you a terrific story?"

As his father took one foot out of the basin and his mother expertly received the foot in the Turkish towel, Harry began: "There was once a dog, his name was Perkun. Perkun sired the bitch Senta. And Senta whelped Harras. And the stud dog Harras sired Prinz. And do you know where I just saw our Prinz? In the newsreel. At the Führer's headquarters. Between the Führer and Rudel. Plain as day, out of doors. Might have been our Harras. You've got to go see it, Papa. You can leave before the feature if you've had enough. I'm definitely going again, maybe twice."

With one dry but still steaming foot, the carpenter nodded absently. He said of course he was glad to hear it and would go see the newsreel if he could find time. He was too tired to be pleased aloud though he tried hard, and later, with two dry feet, actually did put his pleasure into words: "You don't say, our Harras' Prinz. And the Führer patted him in the newsreel. And Rudel was there too. You don't say."

THERE WAS once a newsreel;

it showed the muddy season in Center Sector, Christmas preparations on the Arctic front, the aftermath of a tank battle, laughing workers in a munitions plant, wild geese in Norway, Hitler Cubs collecting junk, sentries on the Atlantic Wall, and a visit to the Führer's headquarters. All this and more could be seen not only in the two movie houses of the suburb of Langfuhr, but in Salonika as well. For from there came a letter written to Harry Liebenau by Jenny Brunies, who under the stage name of Jenny Angustri was performing for German and Italian soldiers.

"Just imagine," Jenny wrote, "what a small world it is: last night—for once we weren't playing—I went to the movies with Herr Haseloff. And whom did I see in the newsreel? I couldn't have been mistaken. And Herr Haseloff also thought the black shepherd, who was there for at least a minute in the headquarters scene, could only be Prinz, your Harras' Prinz.

"The funny part of it is that Herr Haseloff can't possibly have seen your Harras except in the photographs I've shown him. But he has tremendous imagination, and not only in artistic matters. And he always wants to know about things down to the slightest details. That's probably why he has sent in a request to the propaganda unit here. He wants a copy of the newsreel for purposes of documentation. He'll probably get it, for Herr Haseloff has connections all over, and it's unusual for anyone to refuse him anything. Oh, Harry, then we'll be able to look at the newsreel together, any time we please, later, when the war is over. And someday when we have children, we'll be able to show them on the screen how things used to be.

"It's stupid here. I haven't seen a bit of Greece, just rain. Unfortunately we had to leave our good Felsner-Imbs in Berlin. The school goes on even when we're on tour.

"But just imagine—but of course you know all about it—Tulla is expecting a baby. She told me about it on an open postcard. I'm glad for her, though I sometimes think she's going to have a hard time of it, all alone without a husband to take care of her or any real profession . . ."

Jenny did not conclude her letter without pointing out how very much the unaccustomed climate fatigued her and how very much—even in far-off Salonika—she loved her Harry. In a postscript she asked Harry to look out for his cousin as much as possible. "In her condition, you know, she needs a prop, especially as her home isn't exactly what you would call well regulated. I'm going to send her a package with Greek honey in it. Besides, I've unraveled two practically new sweaters I was recently able to buy in Amsterdam. One light blue, the other pale pink. I'll be able to knit her at least four pairs of rompers and two little jackets. We have so much time between rehearsals and even during performances."

THERE WAS once a baby,
    which, although rompers were already being knitted for him, was not to be born. Not that Tulla didn't want the

baby. She still showed no sign, but she represented herself, with a sweetness verging on the maudlin, as an expectant mother. Nor was there any father growling with averted face: I don't want a child! for all the fathers that might have come into consideration were absorbed from morning till night in their own affairs. To mention only the tech sergeant from the Kaiserhafen battery and Air Force auxiliary Störtebeker: the tech sergeant shot crows with his carbine and ground his teeth whenever he made a bull's-eye: Störtebeker soundlessly drew in the sand what his tongue whispered: errancy, the ontological difference, the world-project in all its variations. How, with such existential occupations, could the two of them find time to think of a baby that suffused Tulla Pokriefke with sweetness though it did not yet round out her expressly tailored coat?

Only Harry, the receiver of letters, the writer of letters, said: "How are you feeling? Are you sick to your stomach before breakfast? What does Dr. Hollatz say? Don't strain yourself. You really ought to stop smoking. Should I get you some malt beer? Matzerath will give me dill pickles for food tickets. Don't worry. I'll take care of the child later on."

And sometimes, as though to replace the two plausible but persistently absent fathers in the expectant mother's eyes, he stared gloomily at two imaginary points, ground inexperienced teeth in the tech sergeant's manner, drew Störtebeker's symbols in the sand with a stick, and prattled with Störtebeker's philosophical tongue, which, with slight variations, might also have been the tech sergeant's tongue: "Listen to me, Tulla, I'll explain. The fact is that the average everydayness of child-being can be defined as thrown, projected being-in-the-child-world, which in its child-being-in-the-world and its child-being-with-others involves the very core of child-being capacity. —Understand? No? Let's try again . . ."

But it was not only his innate imitativeness that inspired Harry with such sayings; in the becoming uniform of an Air Force auxiliary he occasionally took up his stance in the middle of the Pokriefkes' kitchen and delivered self-assured lectures to Tulla's grumbling father, a dyspeptic Koshnavian from the region between Konitz and Tuchel. He made no profession of fatherhood, but took everything on himself. He even offered—"I know what I'm doing"—to become his pregnant cousin's future husband, yet was relieved when, instead of taking him up, August Pokriefke found troubles of his own to chew on: August Pokriefke had been drafted. Near Oxhöft —he had been declared fit only for home-front duty—he had to guard military installations, an occupation which enabled him, in the course of long weekend furloughs, to tell the whole family—the master carpenter and his wife were also obliged to lend their ears—interminable stories about partisans; for in the winter of '43 the Poles began to extend their field of operations: whereas previously they had made only Tuchler Heath insecure, now partisan activity was also reported in Koshnavia. Even in the wooded country inland from the Gulf of Danzig and extending to the foot of Hela Peninsula, they were making raids and imperiling August Pokriefke.

But Tulla, with flat hands on still-flat tummy, had other things to think about besides guerrillas stealthy and insidious, and guerrilla-fighter groups. Often she stood up in the middle of a night attack west of Heisternest and left the kitchen so noticeably that August Pokriefke was unable to bring in his two prisoners and save his motor pool from plunder.

When Tulla left the kitchen, she went to the lumber shed. What could her cousin do but follow her as in the years when he had been permitted to carry the school satchel on his back. Tulla's hiding place was still there among the timber. The logs were still piled in such a way as to leave an empty space just big enough for Tulla and Harry.

There sit an expectant sixteen-year-old mother and an Air Force auxiliary who has enlisted in the Army and is looking forward to his induction, in a children's hiding place: Harry had to lay a hand on Tulla and say: "I can feel something. Plain as day. There it is again." Tulla potters with tiny wood-shaving wigs, weaves wood-shaving dolls from soft linden shavings, and as ever disseminates her aroma of bone glue. Unquestionably the baby, as soon as emerged, will distill his mother's unbanishable smell; but only months later, when sufficient milk teeth are present, and still later at the sand-box age, will it become apparent whether the child often and significantly grinds his teeth or whether he prefers to draw little men and world-projects in the sand.

Neither bone-glue aroma nor grinding tech sergeant nor sign-setting Störtebeker. The baby didn't feel like it; and on the occasion of an outing—Tulla obeyed Harry, who, putting on the airs of a father, said an expectant mother needed plenty of fresh air—under the open sky, the infant gave it to be understood that it had no desire to disseminate the aroma of bone glue after the manner of its mother, or to perpetuate the paternal habits of teeth-grinding or world-projecting.

Harry had a weekend pass: an existential pause. Because the air was so Decemberly, cousin and cousin decided to go out to Oliva Forest and, if it wasn't too much for Tulla, to walk as far as the Schwedenschanze. The streetcar, Line

Number 2, was crowded, and Tulla was furious because nobody stood up for her. Several times she poked Harry, but the sometimes bashful Air Force auxiliary was disinclined to speak up and demand a seat for Tulla. In front of her, with rounded knees, sat a dozing infantry p.f.c. Tulla fumed at him: Couldn't he see she was expecting? Instantly the p.f.c. transformed his rounded sitting knees into neatly pressed standing knees. Tulla sat down, and on all sides total strangers exchanged glances of complicity. Harry was ashamed not to have demanded a seat and ashamed a second time that Tulla had asked for a seat so loudly.

The car had already passed the big bend on Hohenfriedberger Weg and was jogging from stop to stop on a stretch that was straight as a die. They had agreed to get out at "White Lamb." Right after "Friedensschluss," Tulla stood up and directly behind Harry pushed her way through winter coats to the rear platform. Even before the trailer reached the traffic island at "White Lamb"—so called after an inn favored by excursionists—Tulla was standing on the bottommost running board, screwing up her eyes in the head wind.

"Don't be a fool," said Harry above her.

Tulla had always liked to jump off streetcars.

"Wait till it stops," Harry had to say from above.

From way back, jumping on and off had been Tulla's favorite sport.

"Don't do it, Tulla, watch out, be careful!" But Harry didn't hold her back.

Beginning roughly in her eighth year, Tulla had jumped from moving streetcars. She had never fallen. Never, as stupid, foolhardy people do, had she risked jumping against the motion of the car; and now, on the trailer of the Number 2, which had been running between Main Station and the suburb of Oliva since the turn of the century, she did not jump from the front platform, but from the rear platform. Nimbly and light as a cat, she jumped with the motion of the car and landed with an easy flexing of the knees and gravel-scraping soles.

Tulla said to Harry, who had jumped off right behind her: "Watcha always nagging for? You think I'm dumb?"

They took a dirt road to one side of the White Lamb Inn. Turning off through the fields at right angles to the rectilinear streetcar line, it led toward the dark forest, huddled on hills. The sun was shining with spinsterish caution. Rifle practice somewhere near Saspe punctuated the afternoon with irregular dots. The White Lamb, haven of excursionists, was closed, shuttered, boarded. The owner, it seemed, had been jailed for economic subversion—buying canned fish on the black market. The furrows of the field and the frozen ruts of the road were filled with windblown snow. Ahead of them hooded crows were shifting from stone to stone. Small, under a sky too high and too blue, Tulla clutched her belly first over, then under, the material of her coat. For all the fresh December air, her face couldn't produce a healthy color: two nostrils dilated with fright in a shrinking, chalky phiz. Luckily Tulla was wearing ski pants.

"Something's gone wrong."

"What's wrong? I don't get it. You feel sick? You want to sit down? Or can you make it to the woods? What is it, anyway?"

Harry was frightfully excited, knew nothing, understood nothing, half suspected, and didn't want to know. Tulla's nose crinkled, the bridge sprouted beads of sweat that didn't want to fall off. He dragged her to the nearest stone—the crows abandoned it—then to a farm roller, its shaft spitting the December air. Then at the edge of the woods, after crows had had to move another few times, Harry leaned his cousin against the trunk of a beech tree. Her breath flew white. Harry's breath too came in puffs of white steam. Distant rifle practice was still putting sharp pencil points on nearby paper. From crumbly furrows ending just before the woods, crows peered out with cocked heads. "It's good I got pants on, or I wouldn't have made it this far. It's all running off!"

Their breath at the edge of the woods rose up and blew away. Undecided. "Should I?" First Tulla let her navy serge coat slip off. Harry folded it neatly. She herself undid her waistband, Harry did the rest with horrified curiosity: the finger-size two-months-old fetus lay there in her panties. Made manifest: there. Sponge in gelatin: there. In bloody and in colorless fluids: there. Through world onset: there. A small handful: unkept, beforelike, partly there. Dismal in sharp December air. Grounding as fostering steamed and cooled off quickly. Grounding as taking root, and Tulla's handkerchief as well. Unconcealed into what? By whom attuned? Space-taking never without world-disclosure. Therefore: panties off. Ski pants up, no child, but. What a vision of essence! Lay there warm, then cold: Withdrawal provides the commitment of the enduring project with a hole at the edge of Oliva Forest: "Don't stand there! Do something. Dig a hole. Not there, that's a better place." Ah, are we ourselves ever, is mine ever, now under the leaves, in the ground, not deeply frozen; for higher than reality is potentiality: here manifested: what primarily and ordinarily does not show itself, what is hidden but at the same time is an essential part of what does primarily and ordinarily show itself, namely, its meaning and ground, which is not frozen but loosened with heels of shoes from the Air Force supply room, in order that the baby may come into its there. There into its there. But only project there. Shorn of its essence: there. A mere neuter, a mere impersonal pronoun—and the impersonal pronoun not there in the same sense as the there in general. And happening-to-be-present confronts being-there with the facticity of its there and without disgust sets it down with bare fingers, unprotected by gloves: Ah, the ecstatic-horizontal structure! There only toward death, which means: tossed in layers, with a few leaves and hollow beechnuts on top, lest the crows, or if foxes should come, the forester, diviners, vultures, treasure seekers, witches, if there are any, gather fetuses, make tallow candles out of them or powder to strew across thresholds, ointments for everything and nothing. And so: fieldstone on it. Grounding in the ground. Placedness and abortion. Matter and work. Mother and child. Being and time. Tulla and Harry. Jumps off the streetcar into her there, without stumbling. Jumps shortly before Christmas, nimbly but too overarchingly: pushed in two moons ago, out through the same hole. Bankrupt! The nihilating Nothing. Lousy luck. Come-to-be in errancy. Spitting cunt. Not even transcendental but vulgar ontic unconcealed ungrinded unstörtebekert. Washed up. Error fostered. Empty egg. Wasn't a pre-Socratic. A bit of care. Bullshit. Was a latecomer. Vaporized, evaporated, cleared out. "You shut your trap. Stinking luck. Why did it have to happen to me? Beans. I was going to call him Konrad or after *him*. After who? After him. Come on, Tulla. Let's go. Yes, come on, let's go."

And cousin and cousin left after securing the site with one large and several small stones against crows, foresters, foxes, treasure seekers, and witches.

A little lighter, they left; and at first Harry was allowed to support Tulla's arm. Distant practice shots continued irregularly to punctuate the written-off afternoon. Their mouths were fuzzy. But Harry had a roll of raspberry drops in his breast pocket.

When they were standing at the "White Lamb" car stop and the car coming from Oliva grew yellow and larger, Tulla said out of gray face into his rosy face: "We'll wait till it starts to move. Then you jump in front and me on the rear platform."

THERE WAS once an abortion

named Konrad, and no one heard about him, not even Jenny Brunies, who, under the name of Jenny Angustri, was dancing in Salonika, Athens, Belgrade, and Budapest in pointed slippers for sound and convalescent soldiers and knitting little things from unraveled wool, pink and blue, intended for a girl friend's baby who was supposed to be named Konrad, the name by which they had called the girl friend's little brother before he drowned while swimming.

In every letter that came fluttering Harry Liebenau's way—four in January, in February only three—Jenny wrote something about slowly growing woolies: "In between I've been working hard. Rehearsals drag out dreadfully, because there's always something wrong with the lighting and the stage hands here act as if they didn't understand a word. Sometimes, when they take forever to shift scenes, one's tempted to think of sabotage. At any rate the routine here leaves me lots of time for knitting. One pair of rompers is done and I've finished the first jacket except for crocheting the scallops on the collar. You can't imagine how I enjoy doing it. Once when Herr Haseloff caught me in the dressing room with an almost finished pair of rompers, he had a terrible scare, and I've kept him on the hook by not telling him whom I was knitting for.

"He certainly thinks I'm expecting. In ballet practice, for instance, he sometime stares at me for minutes on end, in the weirdest way. But otherwise he's nice and ever so considerate. For my birthday he gave me a pair of fur-lined gloves, though I never wear anything on my fingers, no matter how cold it is. And about other things, too, he's as kind as he could be: for instance, he often talks about Papa Brunies, in the most natural way, as if we were expecting him back any minute. When we both know perfectly well that it will never be."

Every week Jenny filled a letter with her babbling. And in the middle of February she announced, apart from the completion of the third pair of rompers and the second jacket, the death of Papa Brunies. Matter-of-factly and without making a new paragraph, Jenny wrote: "The official notice has finally come. He died in Stutthof Camp on November 12, 1943. Stated cause of death: heart failure."

The signature, the unvarying "As ever, your faithful and somewhat tired Jenny," was followed by a postscript with a bit of special news for Harry: "Incidentally, the newsreel came, the one with the Führer's headquarters and your Harras' pup in it. Herr Haseloff ran the scene off at least

ten times, even in slow motion, so as to sketch the dog.
Twice was as much as I could bear. Don't be cross with me,
but the news of Papa's death—the announcement was so
awfully official—has affected me quite a lot. Sometimes I
feel like crying the whole time, but I can't."

THERE WAS once a dog,
   his name was Perkun, and he belonged to a Lithuanian
miller's man who had found work on the Vistula delta.
Perkun survived the miller's man and sired Senta. The bitch
Senta, who belonged to a miller in Nickelswalde, whelped
Harras. The stud dog, who belonged to a carpenter in
Danzig-Langfuhr, covered the bitch Thekla, who belonged
to a Herr Leeb, who died early in 1942, shortly after the
bitch Thekla. But the dog Prinz, sired by the shepherd male
Harras and whelped by the shepherd bitch Thekla, made
history: he was given to the Führer and Chancellor for his
birthday and, because he was the Führer's favorite dog,
shown in the newsreels.
   When dog breeder Leeb was buried, the carpenter at-
tended his funeral. When Perkun died, a normal canine ail-
ment was entered on the studbook. Senta had to be shot
because she grew hysterical and did damage. According to
an entry in the studbook, the bitch Thekla died of old age.
But Harras, who had sired the Führer's favorite dog Prinz,
was poisoned on political grounds with poisoned meat, and
buried in the dog cemetery. An empty kennel was left
behind.

Translated by Ralph Manheim

DIXIELAND!

from MY CENTURY (1999)

BECAUSE WE'D FIRST FOUND EACH OTHER, ANNA AND me—it was 1953 in January-cold Berlin—on the Egg Shell dance floor, we decided to go dancing (and because our only salvation was to leave the Book Fair premises, with its umpteen thousand new publications and umpteen thousand blithering insiders) at the publisher's expense (Luchterhand's—or was it S. Fischer's?—brand-new beehive building, in any case it certainly wasn't Suhrkamp's polished parquet; no, it must have been a place rented by Luchterhand), hot to trot, seeking and finding each other, Anna and me, as always, by dancing, this time to a tune with the rhythm of our youth—Dixieland!—as if only dancing could save us from the brouhaha, the flood of books, the self-important people, remove us, tripping the light fantastic, from their twaddle—"It's Böll, Grass, and Johnson comin' round the bend!"—and at the same time riding out our inkling of something coming to an end, something getting off the ground, now we have a name, getting over it in a quick spin and on rubber legs, up close or touching fingertips, because the only way we could deal with the Book Fair babble—*"Billiards, Speculations, Tin Drum"*—and party buzz—"German postwar prose has made it at last!"—and military intelligence—"Forget Sieburg and the *Frankfurter Allgemeine,* this is the breakthrough!"—was to turn a deaf ear, let ourselves go, step to a combination of Dixieland and heartbeat, which drowned them out, made us light and airy, gave us wings, so that the weight of the tome—seven hundred and thirty pages fat—was offset by the dancing and we went from printing to printing, fifteen, no, twenty thousand, till all at once, just as somebody cried out, "Thirty thousand!" and started listing possible contracts with France, Japan, and Scandinavia, up we went, outbidding the new success by dancing aboveground, and Anna lost her petticoat with its embroidered mouse-tooth hem and three levels of frills when the elastic gave up or, like us, lost its inhibitions, whereupon Anna, released, floating up over the fallen linen, tossed it with the tip of one foot in the direction of a group of onlookers, Fair people, with even a reader or two among them, who were celebrating at the publisher's (Luchterhand's) expense what was by now a best-seller and shouting "Oskar!" and "Oskar's dancing!" but it wasn't Oskar Matzerath on the floor doing "Jimmy the Tiger" with a telephone operator, it was Anna and me going at it with great gusto, having left Franz and Raoul, our baby boys, with friends and taken the train all the way from Paris, where I had shoveled coal into the stove to heat our cold-water flat and written chapter after chapter staring at the oozing walls, while Anna, whose fallen petticoat was an heirloom from her grandmother, sweated it out daily at Madame Nora's barre, Place Clichy, until I typed up the last pages, sent the proofs off to Neuwied, and finished painting the dust jacket with a blue-eyed Oskar, whereupon the editor (Reifferscheid, his name was) invited us to Frankfurt and the Book Fair so we could experience, no, savor the acclaim together, from foretaste to aftertaste, but mostly what we did was dance, later too, after making a name for ourselves, though having less and less from dance to dance to say to each other.

Translated by Michael Henry Heim

A LOOK BACK AT *THE TIN DRUM*, OR:
THE AUTHOR AS DUBIOUS WITNESS

First published in the *Süddeutsche Zeitung* (Munich), January 12, 1974.

I HAD HARDLY FINISHED CORRECTING THE LAST GAL-
leys when my book abandoned me. That was fourteen
years ago; since then, I've lost track of *The Tin Drum*. Now
translated into Croatian, Japanese, Finnish, it ambitiously
set off to disconcert the middle-class readers of the world.
Danzig-Langfuhr, my lost territory, has made itself scarce
the world over.

Yet my own access to it seems to have been blocked by
so many layers of interlocking critiques and preconceptions,
for I've never actually read my *Tin Drum* as a coherent,
printed whole. Something that for a good five years—in
outline or blueprint, in first, second, or third draft—de-
fined every moment of my waking life and dream life, up
and disappeared. The books that came after— *Dog Years,*
the volumes of poetry—remain available to me.

It might be a kind of writerly loathing that has spoiled
me for reading the printed and bound *Tin Drum* to this day.

For even now, when I've been asked to talk about how I wrote my first novel, I haven't been able to manage much more than aimlessly leafing through it, reading a chapter opening here and there. I'm still not sufficiently prepared to examine my conditions and impulses from that time; I'm almost afraid of finding myself out. Where his own book is concerned, the author is a dubious witness.

Pleading incompetence, I can always heap up the re-maindered copies and attempt to avoid those constructive lies that, like cuttings, make the greenhouse of German Studies thrive.

There was no creative certainty (when or how), no long-pending decision (I'll do it now!), no higher purpose or pointing of the finger (the sacred calling), that got me to sit down at the typewriter. It was my petit bourgeois background that served, inasmuch as I had some distance to cover, as my most dependable engine; it was those thoroughly fusty delusions of grandeur, augmented by an interrupted secondary school education (I never made it beyond ninth grade), that I could present to the world something it could not ignore. A dangerous impetus, often the pilot of hubris. But I knew my background and its propulsive power, and so I spared no effort in making use of it, playfully and calmly: writing is a process that requires detachment, and is therefore ironic, and begins privately no matter how publicly its products end up flaunting themselves or falling flat.

My mother died in 1954 at the age of fifty-six. Helene Grass had possessed not only a petit bourgeois sensibility but also the love of theater that goes with it, and so she mockingly dubbed her twelve- to-thirteen-year-old son—who enjoyed confecting tall tales and promises of trips to Naples and Hong Kong, of treasure and Persian coats—Peer Gynt. *The Tin Drum* was published five years after her death and may well have been what Peer Gynt had imagined as success. I had always wanted to prove myself to my mother, but it was her death that finally freed my initiative.

Because I felt myself to be at a disadvantage, I gauged myself by those authors whose typewriters were anointed with a sense of social responsibility, that is, not by the incurable egotists but by those who practiced their profession with a view to the whole of society. I had no lofty ambition to enrich German postwar literature with a robust showpiece. Nor was I able to fulfill the then crass demands for "coming to terms with the German past"—for my attempts at surveying my own (lost) homeland and at clearing away, layer by layer, deposits of its so-called middle class (a half proletarian, half petit bourgeois loam of debris) had brought me no consolation or catharsis. Perhaps I managed to loosen a few new-seeming ideas, to unearth behavior that had already put on new disguises, to undermine with a cold laugh the insincere horror with which National Socialism was demonized, and to give free rein to a language until then only anxiously called to heel; but coming to terms with the past was something I neither could nor wanted to do.

Aesthetic delight—the fun of switching forms and the attendant pleasure of creating alternate realities on paper; in short, the instrument of every kind of artistic venture—was there, waiting to wrestle with an all-consuming subject matter. But the subject matter was there, too, waiting for transmutation. Fear of its enormity and my proneness to distraction initially prevented me from making the effort.

As ever, private circumstances were what freed me. For when, following my mother's death in the spring of 1954, I married Anna Margaretha Schwarz, there began for me a period of concentration, ruled by a bourgeois ethic of work and achievement, and I staunchly resolved to prove myself to all those who by marriage had come snowing into my nonexistent house: solid Swiss burghers of a frugal, puritan disposition, who observed my fidgety gymnastics on over-sized equipment with a mixture of forbearance and liberal appreciation of the arts.

The situation was a funny one in that Anna, who had only just escaped the custody of the bourgeoisie, was more inter-ested in uncertainty and wanted to explore (if cautiously) the bohemian life of postwar Berlin. She certainly had not planned on becoming the wife of a so-called great writer.

However interesting that collision between the interests of a petit bourgeois social climber and the emancipatory desires of the daughter of a patrician family may have been, it was my marriage to Anna that made me determined to write my novel, although what first triggered the composi-tion of *The Tin Drum* dated from a time before we met.

In the spring and summer of 1952, I hitchhiked the length and breadth of France. I lived on nothing, drew sketches on packing paper, and wrote uninterruptedly: I succumbed to language as a kind of diarrhea. In addition to (what I remember as) numerous knock-off ballads about the slum-bering helmsman Palinurus, I wrote a long and proliferat-ing poem in which Oskar Matzerath, before he was called that, appeared as a stylite.

He was a young man, an existentialist, as was the fashion then. A stonemason. He was a man of our time. Uncultivated and rather haphazardly educated, he was generous with quotations. Even before the era of prosperity arrived, he was sick of prosperity: infatuated with his own nausea. And so, in the center of his small town (which remained nameless), he erected a pillar, mounted it, and chained himself to the top. His mother cursed and passed him his meals in a lunch box attached to the end of a long pole. Her attempts to tempt him down off the pillar were backed by a chorus of mythologically coiffed girls. Small-town traffic circled around his pillar, and friends and enemies alike congregated under it, a community of uplifted eyes. Calmly shifting his weight from one leg to the other, he, the stylite, looked down; he had found his place and point of view and responded to the onlookers with a flurry of metaphors.

This long poem, which was not very good, ended up getting lost somewhere. I only have fragments of it left, which show at most just how strongly influenced I was at the same time by Trakl and Apollinaire, Ringelnatz and Rilke, and a badly translated Lorca. The only interesting thing about it was my search for a displaced perspective: the stylite's high altitude was too static. Only with Oskar Matzerath's three-year-old stature did I find both mobility and distance. Oskar Matzerath is, if you like, an inverted stylite.

Later that same summer, as I was passing from the south of France through Switzerland toward Düsseldorf, not only did I meet Anna for the first time, but I was also put off my stylite, by something I just happened to see. On a perfectly banal afternoon, I watched a three-year-old boy, with a tin drum hanging from his neck, standing amidst a group of adults who were drinking coffee. What I noticed then and retained in my memory was how completely lost in his instrument the three-year-old was, and how he ignored the world of the adults, their afternoon conversation and coffee.

For a good three years this "find" remained buried. I moved from Düsseldorf to Berlin, found a new sculpture instructor, met Anna again, married her the following year, brought my sister back from the convent she had run away to, sketched and modeled birdlike structures, grasshoppers, and filigree chickens, attempted my first long story, "The Barrier," which borrowed its form from Kafka and its extravagant metaphors from the early Expressionists and ended tragically. Only then, being under less pressure, did I write my first more informal poems, figures tested by being illustrated, which kept their distance from their author and acquired the kind of independence that grants publication: *The Advantages of Windfowl,* my first book, poems and drawings, case-bound.

Later—though I still had my day job as a sculptor—I wrote short plays, one-acts like *Uncle, Uncle* and *Flood,* which I presented with some success at meetings of Gruppe 47, to which I'd meanwhile been invited. Also, because Anna danced, I wrote ballet libretti.

I even made several attempts to create ballets out of plot structures that would later work their way into *The Tin Drum* as chapters, such as the opening chapter, "The Wide Skirt"; the story of the figurehead "Niobe"; and "The Last Streetcar," which Oskar Matzerath and his friend Vittlar rode through nighttime Düsseldorf; even scenes of the Polish cavalry attacking German tanks. But nothing came of these libretti. I gave them up. They all wandered into the authorial shredder.

With this kind of baggage—built-up material, vague plans, and precise ambitions: I wanted to write my novel; Anna was looking for more vigorous ballet training— we left Berlin at the beginning of 1956, penniless but carefree, and moved to Paris. Near Place Pigalle, Anna found Madame Nora, a demanding Russian ballet mistress, and while I was still polishing my play *The Wicked Cooks,* I began the first draft of a novel that bore alternating provisional titles: *Oskar the Drummer, The Drummer, The Tin Drum.*

And precisely here is where my memory gets stuck. While I know that I drew numerous sketches for scenes, sketches in which the entire narrative material was condensed, and covered them with notes, they canceled each other out and were voided one by one as the work progressed.

But even the manuscripts of the first and second drafts and, eventually, the third ended up feeding the coal furnace in my workroom, which I will come back to later. No matter how high-flying I may have been back then, it has never been my intention to satisfy the lust of Germanists for secondary texts with variants of my own.

From the first sentence, "Granted: I am an inmate of a mental hospital . . . ," the door shut and locked; language turned the screws; my memory and my fantasy, my playful enjoyment and obsession with detail seized the reins and ran ahead; chapter followed upon chapter; and where holes blocked the flow of narration I hopped over them; history accommodated me with local offerings; vials jumped up and released odors; I acquired a wildly proliferating family and struggled with Oskar Matzerath and his penchant for streetcars and their routes, with concurrent plotlines and the absurd constraint of chronology, with Oskar's entitlement to give account in the first or third person, with his pretense of wanting to father a child, with his real indebtedness and imaginary guilt.

This was how my attempt to provide him, the maverick, with a malicious little sister came to grief over Oskar's objections; it may be that the prohibited sister later on came to demand her right to literary existence as Tulla Pokriefke.

To answer a common question: I did not write *The Tin Drum* for an audience, because I did not know any audiences. I wrote first of all and second of all and third of all for myself, for Anna, and for friends and acquaintances who happened to drop in and were forced to listen to this or that chapter, and I suppose I also wrote for an audience summoned by my imagination. The living and the dead crouched around my typewriter: my meticulous friend Geldmacher; my literary mentor Alfred Döblin with his thick glasses on; my stepmother Rabelais, whose literary expertise never interfered with his belief in the good, the true, and the beautiful; my old German teacher, whose eccentric notions I still find more useful than the dried pedagogical fruit we're given today; and my deceased mother, whose objections and corrections I always tried countering with documents and who never believed me without reservations.

If I listen closely, I can hear again the lengthy discussions I held with this not uncritical audience, which had they been written down and added to the book as an appendix would have enriched the final product by a good two hundred pages.

Or the appendix would have been swallowed up by the coal furnace at 111 Avenue d'Italie. Or else even those discussions would have become an extra source for my fiction.

I remember my workroom far better than any writing process: a damp cave at ground level that first served as a studio for nascent sculptures, but after the onset of *The Tin Drum* increasingly housed crumbling ones. My writing schedule dovetailed with my household job as stoker. Whenever I hit a snag in my work on the manuscript, I would walk out of the covered cellar door behind the front house, a bucket in each hand, to fetch coal. My workroom was filled with the smell of dry rot and the cosy scent of gas. Dripping walls kept my imagination flowing. Oskar Matzerath's wit may well have been a reaction to the room's dampness.

Once a year, during the summer months, I had the opportunity, since Anna is Swiss, to spend a few weeks writing in the open air of Tessin. There I would sit at a stone table under a grapevine-covered arbor, gazing out at the glimmering backdrop of that southern landscape, all the while sweating to recall the icy Baltic.

Sometimes, for a change of scene, I would scribble chapter drafts sitting in Paris bistros like the ones we see in movies. There, ensconced between tragically embracing lovers, old women concealed in overcoats, wall-length mirrors, and art nouveau décor, I would write something about elective affinities: Goethe and Rasputin.

All the while, during those four years, Anna was dealing with my work process. I don't mean only her readiness— mostly voluntary, sometimes not—to listen to my long interim reports, which often varied only in the details. In retrospect, I think a greater difficulty for Anna may have been trying to recognize in her aloof husband, who generally appeared in a thick cloud of cigarette smoke, the man she had married. I was largely indigestible as a real person because I was almost entirely dependent on the characters in my fiction: I was a coordinating instrument that had to feed a multitude of circuits connecting a myriad of layers, each interrupting another at all times. They call it *obsessed*.

And yet at the same time I must have been living heartily, cooking attentively, and seizing every opportunity to dance with Anna out of sheer delight in her dancing legs, for in September 1957—I was in the middle of the second draft—our twin sons Franz and Raoul were born. Here was a financial problem, not a writing one. Taking everything into account, we lived on a carefully budgeted DM 300 per month, which I earned under the table, as it were. I sold drawings and lithographs at the yearly meeting of Gruppe 47; Walter Höllerer came to Paris now and then and funded me, as was his way, by commissioning and accepting manuscripts; and in distant Stuttgart, Helmut Heissenbüttel had my unstaged theater pieces broadcast as radio plays. But then the following year, while I was already toiling over the final draft, I was awarded the Gruppe 47 Prize, and for the first time came into a fat sum of money, DM 5,000. With it we bought a record player that still emits noises and now belongs to our daughter, Laura.

Sometimes I think I was protected by the simple fact (and a disgrace to my parents) that I never took the *Abitur*. With this examination I would have had job offers, would have ended up the night-program editor of some radio station, would have tended an unfinished manuscript in my desk drawer, and as a would-be writer would have harbored growing spite toward all those who willy-nilly write whatever they want while the Heavenly Father somehow sustains them.

Now and then, I had conversations with Paul Celan; or rather, I was an audience for his monologues. Now and then, I engaged in a little politics on the side—Mendès-France and the milk; raids on the Algerian quarter—or packaged in newspaper: the Polish October, Budapest, Adenauer's landslide. Now and then, there were gaps.

Work on the final draft of the chapters about the defense of the Polish post office in Danzig made it necessary for me to travel to Poland in the spring of 1958. Höllerer pulled some strings, Andrzej Wirth wrote the invitation, and I journeyed to Gdansk via Warsaw. I suspected that some of the post office defenders had survived and were living still, so I went to find out at the Polish Ministry of the Interior, which maintained an office where documents about German war crimes in Poland were stacked in heaps. I was given addresses for three former postal workers (the most recent was from 1949), along with the warning that the supposed survivors had never been recognized by the Polish postal workers' union (or by any other official body) because according to both German and Polish accounts from the autumn of 1939, all of the defenders had been killed. That was why all their names had been engraved into the stone memorial tablet: when your name is engraved in stone, it means you must be dead.

In Gdansk I went looking for Danzig and also tracked down two of the former post office workers, who had since found work in the shipyards, where they made more money than they would have with the postal service, and who were actually undisturbed by their lack of recognition. But their sons wanted heroes for fathers and had maneuvered (in vain) for official acknowledgment of their fathers as resistance fighters. Each of the postal workers (one had delivered money wires) gave me a detailed description of what had happened inside the post office during the siege. I could not have invented their escape routes.

In Gdansk I paced out the paths I had taken to school in Danzig, had conversations in cemeteries with familiar gravestones, sat (just as I once sat as a schoolchild) in the reading room of the public library, where I leafed through volumes of back issues of the *Danziger Vorposten* and smoked packs of Mottlaus and Radaunes. In Gdansk I was a stranger, yet discovered everything again as fragments: public baths, forest trails, brick Gothic houses, and the tenements on Labesweg between Max Halbe Platz and Neuer Markt; I also revisited (at Oskar's suggestion) the Church of the Sacred Heart: the unchanged Catholic fug.

And then I was standing in my Kashubian great-aunt Anna's kitchen. Not until I showed her my passport would she believe me: "Well, little Günter, you growed up, you did." I spent some time there, listening. As it turned out, her son Franz, who had worked for the Polish postal service back then, had been shot after the workers surrendered. I found his name cut in the stone of the memorial, recognized.

In Warsaw, on my return trip, I made the acquaintance of Marcel Reich-Ranicki, the now-famous West German critic. Ranicki amiably inquired of the young man who claimed to be a German writer what sort of manuscript he had written and what its social function was. After I gave him a short summary of my *Tin Drum* ("Boy stops growing at age three . . ."), he walked away from me and in distress phoned Andrzej Wirth, who had introduced us: "Watch out! This fellow is no German writer, he's a Bulgarian spy." In Poland, I, too, found it hard to prove my identity.

After I finished the manuscript, in the spring of 1959, and corrected the galleys and sent off the page proofs, I was awarded a four-month fellowship. Again, Höllerer had pulled strings. I was supposed to travel to the United States and answer some questions from students now and then. But I was not allowed to go. Back then, in order to get a visa, you had to undergo a thorough medical examination. This I did and learned that in a number of spots on my lungs, tuberculomas had begun to show, and when tuberculomas burst, they leave holes.

Because of that, and because de Gaulle had meanwhile come to power in France—and after a night in French police custody, I suddenly felt homesick for the West German police—we left Paris shortly after *The Tin Drum* appeared as a book (abandoning me), and settled in Berlin again. I had to sleep during the day, avoid alcohol, go for regular checkups, drink cream, and gulp down little white tablets, which I think were called Neoteben, three times a day, all of which made me healthy and fat.

But even before we left Paris, I had begun preparations for the novel *Dog Years,* which initially was titled *Potato Peels* and got off to a false start. It was the novella *Cat and Mouse* that set me right again. But at that time I was already famous and no longer had to feed coal to the furnace. Writing has gotten harder since then.

Have I said everything? More than I intended. Have I concealed something important? Definitely. Will I add anything else? No.

Translated by W. Martin

Two Left-handers

(1958)

Erich is watching me closely, and I'm keeping my eyes on him as well. We're both armed, and it's already been decided: we are going to use these weapons, we are going to hurt each other. Our pistols are loaded. They've been thoroughly tested over long training sessions and carefully cleaned right after practice. We hold them in front of us, our fingers slowly warming the cool metal. From a distance, firearms like these look harmless enough. After all, can't you hold a pen or a hefty key the same way, splaying a black leather glove just enough to startle a shriek out of some frightened old lady? Not for a moment do I allow myself to imagine that Erich's weapon might be fake, harmless, a toy. And I know that, for his part, Erich doesn't question the seriousness of my own piece. Besides, we stripped them down and cleaned them about half an hour ago, put them back together, loaded up, and removed the safeties. We aren't dreamers.

We picked Erich's weekend cottage as the site for our

unavoidable shoot-out. The one-story building is very iso-
lated, more than an hour's hike from the nearest train sta-
tion, so we can assume we'll be far enough away from any
prying ears. We've cleaned out the living room and taken
down the pictures—mostly hunting scenes and still lifes
with game. After all, the shots aren't meant for the chairs,
the wooden chests with their warm luster, and the richly
framed paintings. Nor do we have any desire to wound the
mirror or a piece of porcelain. We're only after each other.

We're both left-handed. We know each other from the
club. Because—like everyone else with comparable afflic-
tions—the city's southpaws have founded a club. We hold
regular meetings and attempt to train our other hand, so re-
grettably clumsy. For some time we were instructed by an
obliging right-hander, but unfortunately he doesn't come
any more. The board of directors criticized his teaching
method and decided that club members should take care of
their own retraining. So now, very casually, we meet for
events that combine group social games, designed just for
us, with special tests of skill, such as using our right hand to
thread a needle, pour drinks, loosen and fasten buttons.
Part of our mission statement reads: We shall not rest until
right feels as right as left.

However nice and powerful a declaration like that might
sound, it's utter nonsense, a goal we shall never attain. And
the extremists in our group have long been demanding that
this sentence be removed, and replaced with: We shall take
pride in our left hand and refuse to be ashamed of our nat-
ural handedness.

But this slogan, too, is untenable; we only chose that par-
ticular formulation because of its pathos, and out of a cer-

tain generosity of feeling. Both Erich and I, who belong to our club's extreme faction, know all too well how deeply rooted our shame really is. Neither at home, nor at school, nor later in the military did anyone ever teach us how to bear with dignity this slight deviation—slight in comparison with other, widespread abnormalities. It began early on, as children, when we were taught to shake hands. All those aunts and uncles, mother's girlfriends, father's colleagues, the whole horrible family photo, impossible to overlook, always looming on the horizon and casting its pall on an entire childhood. You had to hold out your hand to everyone: "Not that naughty little hand, the good one. I'm sure you'll hold out the proper hand, the good little hand, the smart one, the skillful one, the only true hand, the right one!"

I was sixteen years old when I first touched a girl. I reached my hand into her blouse and she blurted out, clearly disappointed, "You mean you're left-handed!" and pulled my hand away. Memories like that don't go away, and even if we turn to composing manifestos—Erich and I were the authors of this particular one—that is nothing more than the attempt to give a name to some unattainable ideal.

Erich has pressed his lips together and narrowed his eyes. I do the same. Our cheek muscles flex, our brows tense up, the ridges of our noses contract. Now Erich looks like a movie actor I know from any number of adventure scenes. Should I assume that I show the same embarrassing resemblance to one of these unseemly movie stars? Do we both look full of grim fury? Anyway, I'm happy that no one is watching us. As it is, any unwanted eyewitness would

probably assume that two young men of an overly roman-
tic nature were staging a duel. That they're rivals for the same
robber bride or that one said a bad word about the other.
A long-standing family feud, a bloody game for the high-
est stakes. Only mortal enemies eye each other like that.
Look how thin and colorless their lips are, how irreconcil-
able the ridges of their noses. Chewing their hate, addicted
to death.

In fact, we're friends. And as different as our professions
are—Erich works as a department manager in a ware-
house; I chose the well-paid field of precision engineer-
ing—we can count enough common interests to make a
friendship last. Erich has been in the club longer than I
have. I well remember the day I stepped into the favorite
pub of the One-siders. I was shy and overdressed; Erich
came up to me and pointed out the coat check. He looked
me over keenly but without annoying curiosity before he
said: "No doubt you're looking for us. Don't be shy; we're
here to help ourselves."

I just mentioned the One-siders. That's what we call our-
selves officially. But this name, like most of our bylaws,
seems to miss the point. It doesn't state clearly enough
what is supposed to bind us together and give us strength.
I'm convinced we'd be better off with a name like the Left-
ies or, perhaps more melodiously, the Left-handed Brother-
hood. You can guess why we had to give up on registering
those kinds of names. Nothing would be less fitting and
more offensive than allowing ourselves to be compared
with those sad souls from whom nature has withheld the
sole human possibility of satisfying love. On the contrary,
we are a colorful crew, and I can say for certain that our

ladies hold their own in beauty, charm, and good behavior with their right-handed sisters. In fact, a closer comparison of their mores might lead many a preacher to call out from his pulpit: "Oh would that you were all left-handers!"

This awful club name. Even our first president, a high official in the municipal land registry, who is unfortunately a little too patriarchal both in his thinking and his governing—even he is forced to admit now and then that we're not exactly well served by our name, that too much left has been left out, and that we are by no means one-sided—not in our thoughts or feelings or deeds.

Of course we had certain political concerns when we tossed out the better suggestions and chose a name we really shouldn't have. Ever since the members of parliament started veering from the middle to this side or that, arranging the chairs of their house to reveal our country's political situation, it has become customary to read a dangerous radicalism into every memo or speech in which the word *left* appears more than once. Well, on that matter you can rest assured. If there's any group in our city that is truly unburdened with political ambitions and completely committed to mutual aid and sociability, it is ours. And just to nip any suspicion of erotic peculiarity in the bud, I should briefly mention at this point that I met my fiancée among the girls in our youth group. As soon as an apartment opens up for us we plan to get married. And if the shadow from my first encounter with the female sex ever passes from my soul, I will have Monika to thank for that happy outcome.

Not only did our love have to cope with the usual problems, known to all and described in many books—our manual suffering, too, had to be overcome and practically transfigured for us to find our own spot of happiness. After our initial bewilderment (perfectly understandable) and our attempts to care for each other in a right-handed way, we were bound to realize how unfeeling our insensitive side actually is. Since that time we have only caressed each other with our skillful side; that is to say, skillful in the way the good Lord made us. I trust I'm not giving away too much or being indiscreet if I mention that it is Monika's dear hand that time and again gives me the strength to endure, and to keep my pledge. On our first movie date, after the film, she made me promise that I would spare her maidenhood until we had placed our rings—and here we gave in, sad to say, merely reinforcing the clumsy trend—until we had placed our rings on our right fingers. Whereas in southern, Catholic countries, in those sunny climes where the heart tends to rule, and not relentless reason, the golden emblem of marriage is worn on the left. Be that as it may, the younger ladies of our club banded together in a flurry of night work and—perhaps as a girlish form of rebellion and to demonstrate how forcefully women can advocate their cause when their interests seem in jeopardy— embroidered our green flag with a motto: The heart beats on the left.

No matter how often Monika and I have discussed this moment of exchanging rings, we always come to the same conclusion: that we will never be able to stand before an ignorant and often malicious world as two people betrothed, even after we have long been a married couple sharing good things and bad, great things and small. The whole ring business often brings Monika to tears. No matter how much we look forward to our day, a light shimmer of sadness will likely cover all the gifts and richly spread tables, and taint the general festivities.

Now Erich is again showing his good face, his normal face. I, too, relax, though for a while I still feel my jaw muscles cramping. Nor do my temples stop twitching. Obviously such grimaces and scowls aren't meant for us. Our gazes meet more calmly, and therefore more daringly; we take aim. Each has in mind the sure hand of the other. I'm absolutely certain I won't miss, and I know I can count on Erich. We've trained for too long, using nearly every spare minute we could, in an abandoned gravel pit on the edge of town—all so that we won't fail today, when so much is at stake.

You'll probably shout out that the whole thing is sadistic; worse, that it's practically self-mutilation. Believe me, we've already gone through all these arguments. It's not the first time we've stood here in this cleaned-out room. Four times we have seen each other armed like this, and four times we have let our pistols drop, shocked by our own intentions. Only today do we have clarity. The most recent incidents, both personal matters as well as issues from the club, show us how right we are: we must go on. After many misgivings—we have cast doubt on the club and the objectives of the extreme wing—we are finally reaching for our weapons. Regrettable as it is, we can no longer take part. Our consciences demand that we distance ourselves from the customs of our comrades. After all, the club has become rife with sectarianism; the reasonable in our ranks have been replaced by passionate enthusiasts, even fanatics. One group swears by the left, the other worships the right. It's hard for me to grasp: political slogans are shouted from table to table, and the hideous cult of the left-handed nailing — to signify an oath — has become so widespread that some executive sessions sound like orgies in which participants pound their way to ecstasy through violent, frenzied hammering. Moreover, despite the fact that many who had clearly succumbed to the vice have since been ousted, it cannot be denied — although no one says it aloud — that the sinful and, for me, completely incomprehensible practice of homosexual love has also found followers. And to mention the worst, even my relationship with Monika has suffered. She spends too much time with her friend, a frail, erratic woman. And she accuses me too often of giving in, of lacking courage in the matter of the rings, for me to believe that we still enjoy the same degree of trust as before, even if it is the same Monika I still hold, though now more rarely, in my arms.

Now Erich and I are trying to synchronize our breathing. The more we are together in that, the more certain we are that good feelings will guide our actions. Don't think it is the word of the Bible advising us to tear out what offends. Rather it is the burning, eternal desire to achieve clarity, and greater clarity; to know how things are with us and whether this fate is unalterable or in our own hands, whether it is possible to intervene and point our lives in a normal direction. No more silly prohibitions, bandages, or other tricks. We want to start over, honest and upright, free to choose, no longer cut off from the rest; we want to have a lucky hand.

Now our breathing is simultaneous. Without signaling, we fire together. Erich hits his mark, and I, too, do not disappoint him. As foreseen, each of us has cut through the major tendon, making it impossible to hold on to the pistols, which promptly fall to the floor, making any further shot unnecessary. We laugh and begin our great experiment by dressing our wounds—clumsily, with the right hand.

Translated by Philip Boehm

WHEN THE WALL WENT UP

First published under the title "And What Can the Writers Do?" in *Die Zeit* (Hamburg), August 18, 1961. Anna Seghers was a novelist who spent the Hitler years in France and Mexico, then returned to East Berlin in 1947 and served until 1978 as president of the Writers' Union.

Berlin, August 14, 1961

To the President
of the German Writers' Union
in the GDR

Dear Frau Anna Seghers:

Yesterday I was startled awake by one of those sudden operations so familiar to us Germans, with tank noises in the background, radio commentary, and the usual Beethoven symphony. When I did not want to believe what the radio was serving up for breakfast, I went to the Friedrichstrasse station, went to the Brandenburg Gate, and found myself face to face with naked power, which nevertheless stank of pigskin. The minute I find myself in danger, I become overanxious, like all once-burned children, and have the tendency to cry for help. I groped around in my head and heart for names, names promising help; and your name, revered Frau Anna Seghers, became the straw I do not want to let go of.

It was you who after that never-to-be-forgotten war taught my generation, or anyone who had ears to hear, to distinguish justice from injustice. Your book *The Seventh Cross* formed me, sharpened my eye, so that I can still recognize a Globke or a Schröder in any disguise, even when they call themselves humanists, Christians, or activists. The anxiety felt by your protagonist, Georg Heisler, communicated itself to me once and for all; except that the commandant of the concentration camp is no longer called Fahrenberg but Walter Ulbricht, and he presides over your state. I am not Klaus Mann, and your spirit is diametrically opposed to the spirit of the fascist Gottfried Benn, and yet, with the presumptuousness of my generation, I refer you to the letter Klaus Mann wrote to Gottfried Benn on May 9, 1933.* For you and for myself let me transform those two dead men's ninth of May into our living August 14, 1961. Up to now you have been the epitome of resistance to violence; it is impossible that you should fall prey to the irrationalism of a Gottfried Benn and fail to recognize the violent nature of a dictatorship that has scantily yet cleverly wrapped itself in your dream of socialism and communism, a dream I do not dream but which I respect, as I do any dream. . . .

Please do not tell me to wait for the future, which, as you know, being a writer, is resurrected hourly in the past. Let

---

*Klaus Mann, eldest son of the writer Thomas Mann and a prolific writer himself, sharply rebuked the Expressionist poet Gottfried Benn for supporting Hitler and National Socialism.

us stick to today, August 14, 1961. Today nightmares in the form of tanks are parked at Leipziger Strasse, disturbing all sleep and threatening citizens while claiming to protect them. Today it is dangerous to live in your state, and it is impossible to leave your state. . . .

I want to make this day our day. I want you, as a woman at once weak and strong, to arm your voice and speak out against the tanks, against this barbed wire that seems to be perpetually manufactured in Germany, the same barbed wire that once provided the concentration camps with security. . . .

This letter, revered Frau Anna Seghers, must be an "open letter." I am sending you the original by way of the Writers' Union in East Berlin. I am sending a copy to the daily *Neues Deutschland,* asking them to publish it, and a second copy to the weekly *Die Zeit* in Hamburg.*

Seeking help, I send you best regards from

Günter Grass

Translated by Krishna Winston

---

*The *Neues Deutschland* is the official party organ in East Berlin. *Die Zeit* is a highly respected intellectual weekly newspaper, left of center in its editorial policies.

Operation Travel Bureau

from My Century (1999)

Even if no one particularly cares anymore, I always say to myself looking back, Those were the best days of your life. You were given a job to do. You risked your life daily for more than a year. You were so scared you practically bit your fingernails off, but you met the danger head on, trying not to think about whether you were in for another disastrous semester. The thing was, I was a student at the Technical University—and even then interested in district heating—when from one day to the next the wall went up.

People made an enormous fuss, rushed to rallies, staged protest marches in front of the Reichstag and elsewhere. Not me. First thing, in early August, I got Elke out. She was at a teacher-training college over there. All you needed was a West German passport, which was no problem because we had the personal data on her and a picture. But by the end of the month we had to start fiddling with the entry

permits and working in groups. I was the contact. My pass-
port, which was issued in Hildesheim, where I actually
come from, worked for the next few weeks, but starting
some time in September you had to hand in your entry per-
mit as you left the eastern sector. We might have been able
to make our own if somebody had smuggled out the kind
of paper they used.

Not that people are interested nowadays. My kids cer-
tainly aren't. They either turn a deaf ear or say, "We know,
Dad. You were real noble, your generation." Well, maybe
my grandchildren will listen when I tell them how I got
their grandma out and how she took an active part in "Op-
eration Travel Bureau," which was our cover name. We
were experts at getting the official stamps right. Some used
hard-boiled eggs; others swore by finely sharpened matches.
We were mostly students and mostly leftist, but we had our
dueling society types and a few like me who couldn't get
excited about politics. It was election time in the West, and
our Berlin mayor was a candidate for the Social Democrats,
but I didn't vote for Brandt and the comrades or for old
man Adenauer either, because fancy words and ideologies
didn't mean a thing to me; what counted was what you did.
And our job was to "transfer," as we called it, passport pic-
tures into West German or foreign passports—Swedish,
Dutch. Or find contacts to bring us passports with pictures
and personal data—hair color, eye color, height, age—of
the kind we needed. We also needed the right kind of news-
papers, small change, used bus tickets—the odds and ends
that, say, a Danish girl would be likely to have in her bag. It
was tough work. And all of it free or at cost.

Nowadays, when nothing is free, nobody can believe we
didn't make a penny from it. Oh, a few held out their hands

when we started digging our tunnel. It had a crazy history, the Bernauer Strasse project. What happened was that without our knowing it an American TV company put up over thirty thousand marks for the right to make a documentary about the tunnel. We'd dug for four long months and through that Mark Brandenburg sand—it was a hundred meters long, the tunnel—and when they filmed us smuggling thirty or so people, including grandmas and grandkids, into the West, it never occurred to me they'd put it on the air there and then. But that's what they did, and the tunnel would have been discovered in no time if it hadn't flooded—despite our expensive pumping equipment—shortly before the film was shown. No matter. We carried on elsewhere.

No, we had no casualties. I know. The papers were full of reports of people jumping from the third story of border buildings and landing on the pavement a hair's breadth from the safety net. A year after the wall went up, a man by the name of Peter Fechter was shot barging his way through Checkpoint Charlie; he bled to death because nobody would come to his aid. We didn't need to worry, though, since we stuck to sure things. Still, I could tell you stories people didn't want to believe back then even. About all the folks we took through the sewers, for instance. It stank to high heaven down there. One of the routes leading from the center of East Berlin across to Kreuzberg we called "Glockengasse 4711" after the cologne, because all of us, the refugees and our people, had to wade knee-deep in raw sewage. I served later as a cover, but not in the sense you might think. It was my job to wait until everybody had disappeared down the manhole and then pull the cover back in place: the refugees themselves were so panic-stricken they'd forget to do it. We had a similar problem at the Esplanadenstrasse runoff canal in the north of the city, when a few refugees let out a mighty cheer the moment they crossed over to the West: the East German police standing guard caught on and threw tear-gas canisters down the hatch. Then there was the cemetery that had one wall in common with *the* wall, so we dug a subterranean passageway up to the graves for our clientele, harmless-looking mourners with flowers and suchlike paraphernalia, to vanish into. It worked just fine until a young woman, who was taking her baby with her, left the pram at the camouflaged entrance to the passageway, which gave things away immediately. . . .

Slips like that had to be factored in. But now let me tell you about a time when everything worked. Had enough, you say? I understand. I'm used to it. Things were different a few years back when the Wall was still up. I'd be having a Sunday beer with my co-workers from the district heating plant, and one or another of them would ask me, "What was it like, Ulli, when the Wall went up and you had to smuggle Elke into the West?" But nowadays nobody's interested, not here in Stuttgart at least. Because the Swabians never really grasped what it meant back in '61. So when the Wall came down all of a sudden . . . Actually, they liked having it there better. Because now that it's gone, they've got the solidarity tax to pay. So I'll shut up about it, even though it was the best time of my life, wading knee-deep through the sewage, crawling through the subterranean passageway. . . . My wife is right when she says, "You were another man back then. We had a real life. . . ."

Translated by Michael Henry Heim

I Like Riding the Escalator

(1974)

I just accompanied Maria to the train station, where she was catching the express to Bremerhaven. I wasn't allowed to wait on the platform to see her off. Neither one of us likes to leave the other behind — a victim of the nearly constant punctuality of the rail system.

We hugged calmly and then released each other, as if we'd be back together the next day. Now I move through the hall, bumping into people, excusing myself too late. Keeping the pack in my pocket, I coax out a cigarette; I have to buy matches.

Then I have to wait. The escalator takes its time swallowing the pedestrians in their fall clothes. Now I, too, take the step; I, too, stand in line, between two raincoats breathing out moisture. I like riding the escalator. I can lose myself completely in my cigarette, and rise just like the smoke. The whole mechanism fills me with trust. No one insisting on conversation: not from above, not from below. The moving steps speak. My thoughts fall nicely into line: By now Maria will have reached the edge of town; the train will arrive on time in Bremerhaven. With luck, she won't have any problems. Schulte-Vogelsang tells us we can count on him, and that everything will go smoothly once we're over there as well. Maybe we should have tried going through Switzerland instead? People have assured me that Vogelsang is reliable. They say he's done this for a number of others, that everything has always worked out well. Why should Maria have a problem, especially since she has only been working for us for a short time?

The woman in front of me rubs her eyes. She is sobbing through her nose.

I look back. Below me is a line of hats. And more hats and headgear clustered down at the foot of the escalator. It does me good, being no longer at the mercy of human facial details. For that reason I want to avoid looking up toward the exit. But then I turn around after all. I shouldn't do that. Up above, where the escalator swallows itself with its hard rubber jaw, sweeping away neck after neck and head after head, two men are standing, gazing intently— no doubt at me. But I no more think of turning around than I do of pushing my way down the moving staircase, against the rising flow of hats. This ridiculous sense of being safe and secure; this seductive feeling that as long as you're on the escalator, then you're alive, that as long as there's breath ahead of you and breath behind you then no one can push his way between.

The number of stairs is growing smaller; I move back a little, so my toes won't land on the hard rubber edge. I'm almost happy that I manage such a smooth landing.

The men are already calling out my name; they show their IDs and laugh as they assure me that Maria's express train will arrive in Bremerhaven right on time and that she'll find some other gentlemen waiting for her, though not with flowers, of course. How fitting that I've just finished smoking my cigarette. I follow the men.

Translated by Philip Boehm

On Writers as Court Jesters and on Non-existent Courts

Address delivered in April 1966 on the occasion of a meeting of the German literary Group 47 at Princeton University. Grass's fellow panelists were Leslie Fiedler and the German literary critic Marcel Reich-Ranicki.

THEY SELDOM MEET, AND THEN AS STRANGERS: I AM referring to our overtired politicians and our uncertain writers with their quickly formulated demands which always cry out for immediate fulfillment. Where is the calendar that would permit the mighty of our day to hold court, to seek utopian advice, or to cleanse themselves from the compromises of everyday life by listening to expositions of preposterous utopias? True, there has been the already legendary Kennedy era; and to this day an overworked Willy Brandt listens with close attention when writers tot up his past errors or darkly prophesy future defeats. Both examples are meager; at the very most they prove that there are no courts and hence no advisers to princes, or court jesters. But let's assume for the fun of it that there is such a thing as a literary court jester, who would like to be an adviser at court or in some foreign ministry; and let's assume at the same time that there is no such thing, that the literary court jester is only the invention of a serious and slow-working writer who, merely because he has given his mayor a few bits of advice that were not taken, fears in social gatherings to be mistaken for a court jester. If then we assume both that he exists and that he does not, then he exists as a fiction, hence in reality. But the question is: Is the literary court jester worth talking about?

When I consider the fools of Shakespeare and Velásquez, or let us say the dwarfish power components of the Baroque age — for there is a connection between fools and power, though seldom between writers and power — I wish the literary court jester existed; and as we shall see, I know a number of writers who are well fitted for this political service. Except that they are far too touchy. Just as a "housekeeper" dislikes to be called a "cleaning woman," they object to being called fools. "Fool" is not enough. They just want to be known to the Bureau of Internal Revenue as "writers"; nor do they wish to be ennobled by the title of "poet." This self-chosen middle — or middle-class — position enables them to turn up their noses at the disreputable, asocial element, the fools and poets. Whenever society demands fools and poets — and society knows what it needs and likes — whenever, in Germany for example, a writer of verse or a storyteller is addressed by an old lady or a young man as a "poet," the writer of verse or storyteller — including the present speaker — hastens to make it clear that he wishes to be known as a writer. This modesty, this humility, is underlined by short, embarrassed sentences: "I practice my trade like any shoemaker," or "I work seven hours a day with language, just as other self-respecting citizens lay bricks for seven hours a day." Or differing only in tone of voice and

Eastern or Western ideology: "I take my place in socialist society" or "I stand foursquare behind the pluralistic society and pay my taxes as a citizen among citizens."

Probably this well-bred attitude, this gesture of self-belittlement, is in part a reaction to the genius cult of the nineteenth century which in Germany continued to produce its pungent-smelling houseplants down to the period of Expressionism. Who wants to be a Stefan George running around with fiery-eyed disciples? Who wants to disregard his doctor's advice and live the concentrated life of a Rimbaud, without life insurance? Who does not shy away from the prospect of climbing the steps of Olympus every morning, who does not shun the gymnastics to which Gerhart Hauptmann still subjected himself or the tour de force which even Thomas Mann—if only by way of irony—performed as long as he lived?

Today we have adapted ourselves to modern life. You won't find a Rilke doing handstands in front of the mirror; Narcissus has discovered sociology. There is no genius, and to be a fool is inadmissible because a fool is genius in reverse. So there he sits, the domesticated writer, deathly afraid of Muses and laurel wreaths. His fears are legion. The already mentioned fear of being called a poet. The fear of being misunderstood. The fear of not being taken seriously. The fear of entertaining, that is, of giving enjoyment: the fear, invented in Germany but since then thriving in other countries, of producing something Lucullan. For though a writer is intent to the point of fear and trembling on being a part of society, he still wants very much to mold this society according to his fiction but chronically distrusts fiction as something smacking of the poet and fool; from the *nouveau roman* to socialist realism, writers, sustained by choruses of lettered teenagers, are earnestly striving to offer more than mere fiction. The writer who does not wish to be a poet distrusts his own artifices. And clowns who disavow their circus are not very funny.

Is a horse whiter because we call it white? And is a writer who says he is "committed" a white horse? We are all familiar with the writer who, far removed from the poet and the fool, but not satisfied with the naked designation of his trade, appends an adjective, calling himself and encouraging others to call him a "committed" writer, which always — forgive me — reminds me of titles such as "court pastry cook" or "Catholic bicycle rider." From the start, before even inserting his paper into the typewriter, the committed writer writes, not novels, poems, or comedies, but "committed literature." When a body of literature is thus plainly stamped, the obvious implication is that all other literature is "uncommitted." Everything else, which takes in a good deal, is disparaged as art for art's sake. Insincere applause from the Right calls forth insincere applause from the Left, and fear of applause from the wrong camp calls forth anemic hopes of applause from the right camp. Such complex and anguished working conditions engender manifestoes, and the sweat of anguish is replaced by professions of faith. When, for instance, Peter Weiss, who after all did write *The Shadow of the Coachman's Body,* suddenly discovers that he is a "humanist writer," when a writer and poet versed in all the secrets of language fails to recognize that even in Stalin's day this adjective had already become an empty expletive, the farce of the committed humanist writer becomes truly theatrical. It would be better if he were the fool he is.

You will observe that I confine myself, in utter provincialism, to German affairs, to the smog in which I myself am at home. However, I trust that the United States of America has committed and humanist writers and poets as well as those others who are so readily defamed, and possibly also literary fools; because it is here in this country that this topic was proposed to me: Special adviser or court jester.

The "or" means no doubt that a court jester can never be a special adviser and that a special adviser must under no circumstances regard himself as a court jester, but rather perhaps as a committed writer. He is the great sage; to him financial reform is no Chinese puzzle; and it is he, hovering high above the strife of parties and factions, who in every instance pronounces the final word of counsel. After centuries of hostility the fictitious antitheses are reconciled. Mind and power walk hand in hand. Something like this: After many sleepless nights the Chancellor summons the writer Heinrich Böll to his bungalow. At first the committed writer listens in silence to the Chancellor's troubles. Then, when the Chancellor sinks back into his chair, the writer delivers himself of succinct, irresistible counsel. Relieved of his cares, the Chancellor springs from his chair eager to embrace the committed writer; but the writer takes an attitude of aloofness, he does not wish to become a court jester. He admonishes the Chancellor to convert writer's word into Chancellor's deed. The next day an amazed world learns that Chancellor Erhard has resolved to demobilize the army, to recognize the German Democratic Republic and the Oder-Neisse line, and to expropriate all capitalists.

Encouraged by this feat, the humanist author Peter Weiss journeys from Sweden to the recently recognized German Democratic Republic and leaves his card at the office of Walter Ulbricht, Chairman of the Council of State. Like Erhard at a loss for good advice, Ulbricht receives the humanist writer at once. Advice is given, embrace rejected, word converted into deed; and next day an amazed world learns that the Chairman of the Council of State has countermanded the order to fire on those attempting to cross the borders of his state in either direction and transformed the political sections of all prisons and penitentiaries into people's kindergartens. Thus counseled, the Chairman of the Council of State apologizes to Wolf Biermann the poet and ballad singer and asks him to sing away his—Ulbricht's—Stalinist past with bright and mordant rhymes.

Of course court jesters, should there be any, cannot hope to compete with such accomplishments. Have I exaggerated? Of course I have exaggerated. But when I think of the wishes, often stated in an undertone, of committed and humanist writers, I don't think I have exaggerated so very much. And in my weaker moments I find it easy to see myself acting in just such a well-intentioned, or rather, committed and humanist, manner: After losing the parliamentary elections the opposition candidate for the Chancellorship sends, in his perplexity, for the writer here addressing you, who listens, gives advice and does not allow himself to be embraced; and the next day an amazed world learns that the Social Democrats have discarded the Godesberg Program and replaced it with a sharp, sparkling, and once again revolutionary manifesto encouraging the workers to discard hats for caps. No, no revolution breaks out, because for all its sharpness this manifesto is so much to the point that neither capital nor Church can resist its arguments. Without a blow the government is handed over to the Social Democrats, etc. The United States of America, I should think, offers similar possibilities. Why, for example, shouldn't President Johnson call on the preceding speaker, Allen Ginsberg, for advice?

These short-winded utopias remain—utopias. Reality speaks a different language. We have no special advisers or court jesters. All I see—and here I am including myself—is bewildered writers and poets who doubt the value of their own trade and avail themselves fully, partially or not at all, of their infinitesimal possibilities of playing a part in the events of our time—not with advice but with action. It is meaningless to generalize about "the writer" and his position in society; writers are highly diversified individuals, shaken in varying degree by ambition, neuroses and marital crises. Court jester or special adviser, both are disembodied little men—five six lines and a circle—such as the members of a discussion panel draw in their notebooks when they get bored. Nevertheless they have given rise to a cult which, especially in Germany, is assuming an almost religious character. Students, young trade-unionists, young Protestants, high school boys and Boy Scouts, dueling and nondueling fraternities—all these and more never weary of organizing discussions revolving around questions like: "Ought a writer to be committed?" or "Is the writer the conscience of the nation?" Even men with critical minds and a genuine love of literature, such as Marcel Reich-Ranicki, who will speak to us in a little while, persist in calling upon writers to deliver protests, declarations, and professions of faith. I don't mean that anyone asks them to take a partisan attitude toward political partics, to come out for or against the Social Democrats, for example; no, the idea is that speaking as writers, as a kind of shamefaced elite, they should protest, condemn war, praise peace, and display noble sentiments. Yet anyone who knows anything about writers is well aware that even if they band together at congresses they remain eccentric individuals. True, I know a good many who cling with touching devotion to their revolutionary heirlooms, who make use of Communism, that burgundy-colored plush sofa with its well-worn springs, for afternoon reveries. But even these conservative "progressives" are split into one-man factions, each of which reads Marx in his own way. Others in turn are briefly mobilized by their daily glance at the paper and wax indignant at the breakfast table: "Something ought to be done, something ought to be done!" When helplessness lacks wit it begins to snivel. And yet there is a great deal to do, more than can be expressed in manifestoes and protests. But there are also a great many writers, known and unknown, who, far from presuming to be the "conscience of the nation," occasionally bolt from their desks and busy themselves with the trivia of democracy. Which implies a readiness to compromise. Something we must get through our heads is this: a poem knows no compromise, but men live by compromise. The individual who can stand up under this contradiction and act is a fool and will change the world.

Translated by Ralph Manheim

LITERATURE AND POLITICS

Previously unpublished address delivered in March 1970.

Ladies and Gentlemen:

When I write a poem about lost buttons, I can hardly hope to avoid naming the political reasons, along with all the private and embarrassing ones, that might have led to the loss of the buttons. Which is to say: Politics is part of reality, and literature—which always seeks out reality—can neither leave politics out nor suppress it.

I've never found politics and literature to be mutually exclusive. The language I write in has been infected with politics. The land I write in is burdened with the consequences of its politics. The readers of my books are as circumscribed by politics as I, their author, am. Searching for politics-free utopias no longer makes much sense, now that even metaphors about the moon have suddenly become macabre.

In order to rectify literature's political dilapidation, writers have been encouraged, and have encouraged themselves, to be "engaged."

And so with each injustice that occurs—and injustice is a daily occurrence—they attach their famous names to manifestos and petitions. Morality has become a hot commodity. A dubious fiction, this attempt to suggest that bad politics might be cured by the humane slogans of literature.

Literature has no reason to elevate itself over politics and the crimes of politics. It has its own role in them.

From the eighteenth century on, European literature has had equally useful roles to play in both political enlightenment and enlightened politics. The tradition that began with Diderot and Lessing continues to this day: It is my own tradition.

To me, being a politically active writer means above all being a politically informed one; for if a writer seriously wishes to put his professed desire to be engaged into practice, then he should know that the everyday life of politics demands a certain tenacity.

Over the past ten years or so, I have devoted a growing and rather labor-intensive portion of my time to politics. I haven't succeeded in preventing any wars. Nor have I been watched and exploited on television as I proclaimed the revolution atop the barricades. At most, I have assisted my country in mitigating the legacy of National Socialism and in strengthening parliamentary democracy.

My participation has been biased. I support the Social Democrats, because to become politically active involves taking a stance. Writers who float above the various parties represent, at most, that part of the left-wing elite that pursues socialism as a sort of fashionable and exclusive neoscholasticism.

Generally I find pigeonholing writers according to a left vs. right political schema utterly nonsensical. Thomas

Mann and Saul Bellow share a conservative skepticism that allows them to recognize even in its infancy our age's blind trust in progress. The myths of irrationalism never stood a chance against their razor-sharp, enlightened minds.

Having attempted to report something of a writer's daily life to you, ladies and gentlemen, I would like to try to tease out of this topic, "Literature and Politics," a few theses — in spite of the fact that theses, even those I've cobbled together myself, beg to be refuted.

Since Trotsky has come back into fashion, this topic has been more vigorously formulated as "Literature and Revolution." But now that we're all postrevolutionary again, without the much demanded revolution ever having taken place, I think I'm justified in understanding politics not as the sensational result of earthshaking events, but rather as something laboriously slow. Progress has nothing to do with speed.

My children often ask me what my interest in politics is. Their questions are pointed, and my answers are elaborately muddled. For brevity's sake, I'll try here to present this otherwise endless game of question and answer in ten theses:

1. When I try to explain to my children the difference between literature and politics, I tell them: When I'm at home, I'm usually making literature; as soon as I go on a trip, it's politics I pursue. Sitting means writing. Standing means talking. Lately, in order to contradict myself, I've taken to writing at a lectern.

2. When my children continue to ask me questions, I tell them: Literature lives in the present while feeding

on the past; politics has an eye on the future, but mostly breaks down in the present as a result of the past.

3. My children won't let up their questioning. So I say: Politics knows what it wants, and wants what it knows; literature wants to know what it does not yet know.

4. My children ask what has happened to morality. I defend myself: Literature follows the laws of aesthetics, politics follows those of power. Nonetheless, both writers and politicians like to claim that only they, or they primarily, follow the laws of morality. Which we should understand as meaning that a writer's morality is aesthetic and a politician's morality lies in the exercise of power. Don't believe the pharisees! Neither aesthetics nor power is inherently bad.

5. My sons want to know why I'm not fighting for the revolution. I concede that pursuing reforms is more tiring and tell them: The word *revolution* has often been put into play on writing desks that would be confiscated after the revolution's completion. Writers like to underestimate the appetite their fictions have for reality.

6. My children have their doubts. They say: You don't believe in anything anyway. I admit to my unbelieving life, and tell them: As soon as belief gets ahead of reason you can count on the demise of both politics and literature. Examples include the belief in one God, the belief in Germany, and the belief in true Socialism. —At most, dear children, I believe in doubt.

7. My children want to know more about reason and doubt. Reason enlightens. Literature and politics join

forces once they begin to enlighten. Politics, of course, enlightens by encouraging conviction, whereas literature enlightens by pursuing doubt. Politics is born of compromise; we owe our lives to political compromises. But compromise is anathema to literature. Which is why it makes as little sense to arrange medium-term financial planning or the Mansholt Plan into free verse as it does to reach a majority ruling on the staging of a tragedy by casting votes. Politics is beholden to parliamentary control; literature is responsible above all for itself.

8. So that means literature and politics have nothing to do with one another, my children respond. I admit: Literature and politics mostly talk past each other, mixing only in their echo, cultural politics.

9. But you have politicians for friends, my sons exclaim. I respond: Friendship between writers and politicians is sustained by mistrust—each party thinks the other is too one-sided. But on one thing they agree: The pill will change society more drastically than either literature or politics can, especially because the pill will also change politics—and literature too, of course.

10. Finally, my children want to know why I, as a writer with a decent income, squander so much of my precious time on politics. In my bourgeois, egotistical way I tell them: So that I may go on writing what I must write.

Translated by W. Martin

A Father's Difficulties in Explaining Auschwitz to His Children

Address delivered at the opening of the exhibition "People in Auschwitz," in Berlin, May 26, 1970.

THIS EXHIBITION DISPLAYS DRAWINGS AND COLOR IMages. It communicates visually, yet it cannot be understood within the aesthetic framework in which most graphic and chromatic work is exhibited — unless we break open that framework of modern aesthetics and expand it, with some help from the aesthetic made graphic here.

Adorno's dictum about our no longer being able to write poems after Auschwitz has resulted in so many misunderstandings that one must at least try to modify it with an interpretation: Poems written after Auschwitz will have to get used to having Auschwitz as their standard.

At this point I have to pause and listen to the word *Auschwitz,* and to try to judge this word *Auschwitz* by the impact of its echo.

We're all familiar with that commonest of responses: What, Auschwitz again? Are we still talking about Auschwitz? Is there no end to it? Won't it ever stop?

I certainly hope not. But neither do I agree with that

other, restrained and genteel, echo that the response to Auschwitz can only be silence, ought to be shame and speechlessness. There is nothing mystical about Auschwitz, nothing that requires the awe of reserved and inward-looking contemplation. It was a reality; it was something that humans created, and as such it bears examining.

We did not start following a new calendar with Auschwitz, but something like a new calendar is reflected in our thinking — rarely consciously, but certainly unconsciously. After Auschwitz, people think differently; we force ourselves to think differently, and wherever Auschwitz is repeated, we have to think of Auschwitz as the established measure.

What took place before Auschwitz is judged — insofar as it is judged — by the standards of other categories. It makes no difference that a mechanism of destruction has always existed: its perfection is what put Auschwitz in a category of its own. The unspeakable cruelty of individuals was not new, but the sleek anonymity and what one might call hard work of pushing paper was new: the patently human invention that we, in distancing ourselves from it, call inhuman. Reducing the reality of Auschwitz to a historical turning point has invested the former concentration camp with symbolic meaning: Auschwitz stands for Treblinka and Mauthausen, for a multitude of former concentration camps and death camps. This symbolization makes it difficult to explain the everyday workings of Auschwitz, because the name of this place has become synonymous with every genocide.

When I try to explain Auschwitz to my children today— and they do demand an explanation, coolly suspecting something and openly curious: "So what was that about?" —my explanations soon become long-winded and circuitous and complicated, and I stop making sense altogether. It's as if with each step I take toward Auschwitz I have to take two steps back. Again and again in the middle of a halfway adequate explanation I see other reasons that have to be mentioned. And before I even get to those reasons, yet more reasons turn up: It was we, too. It wasn't something we wanted. But whatever we did and said and wrote led indirectly to that place called Auschwitz, a place that could just as well have been Treblinka.

Germany's children will grow up in peace. What with their games and homework and plans for vacation, they're influenced more by consumer goods and the vagaries of fashion than they are by their traumatized parents. What chance do I have, after the third playing of a Jimi Hendrix record and the enthusiastically itemized features and components of a Land Rover, to use this abstract number *six million* —a number that seems as if it will never be anything but abstract— to explain something that for children becomes meaningful, or, to put it trivially, exciting, only when it is presented as a private, individual case, like that of Anne Frank?

We still do not know how contradictory later generations will find the results of that tentatively mitigated education they've inherited. The death of 1.5 million Biafrans, which for more than two years we watched on television and grew accustomed to, provided a temptingly superficial occasion to substantiate the German past by comparing it with the immediate present. But the answer to my children's alert probing—"Who's doing it?" —opened up a whole new historical can of worms. With every mention of the British, Soviet, Chinese, or Swiss arms shipments that made these contemporary mass killings possible in Biafra, Auschwitz, Germany's clear and singular responsibility, was pushed further into the depths of history, the region of "That was long ago."

Today's youth, however, who have grown up in peacetime, are tired of history. And when I make such a conscious generalization about this peacetime generation, I do so based on my experience of it, and must even emphasize my point: This generation is nauseated by history, because what they've been taught and will go on being taught as history in school—this German idealist logicality galloping in on Hegel's world spirit—will, increasingly, reveal itself to be absurd. History—so they say—will teach us nothing. I fear that this flight from history, a flight that I have barely touched on here, will result more and more in the rejection of Enlightenment reasoning. Each day we experience how this younger generation of peace has created with its high moral ideals a new linguistic environment, one whose debt to the Enlightenment, when examined more closely, reveals the threat that a new irrationalism awaits us in the future.

Such irrationalism, I know, is hard to overcome through appeals to reason. Reason's failures are too self-mockingly numerous for the simple invocation of the rational to have any effect as a panacea for this new irrationalism.

If what I've been talking about here is merely the difficulties of a father who wants to explain Auschwitz to his children, then I'd like to ask you to consider the possibility that these difficulties could acquire dimensions that may no longer be subsumed under the traditional category of "learning disability." Auschwitz must be comprehended in the context of its historical past, be recognized when it happens in the present, and not be ruled out blindly for the future. Auschwitz is not only behind us.

Translated by W. Martin

WHEN FATHER WANTED TO REMARRY

(1968)

WHEN FATHER WANTED TO REMARRY, WE SAID NO.
Not on account of Mama—just because. After all, Gitta
had spent two years cooking for him—and of course for
me, her brother Peter, as well. Quite a feat for a girl who
was only fourteen years old at the time. Even so, after the
year of mourning was over we left Father all the freedom in
the world, at home or anywhere else. He could bring home
whomever he wanted. What I didn't understand at first was
why Gitta would get up in the morning and serve him and
his lady friends breakfast in bed. Admittedly she brought it
a little early, around seven o'clock or so, since she had to get
to school. When I told her, "You're overdoing it," Gitta an-
swered, "Let them see who runs things in this house." But
apart from that I kept away as much as I could, especially
because none of the ladies were my type—not Fräulein
Peltzer or Fräulein Wischnewski or even Frau von Wollzo-
gen. His taste in women was ridiculous. And Gitta, who

knew more than I did, would come down to the kitchen the minute she had finished serving them breakfast upstairs, and laugh herself silly. The first time Father brought Inge home, I thought: *Well, well, something different for a change.* In the first place, Inge was younger—three years and two months younger than I was, to be precise; second, she didn't presume to be on a first-name basis with me or even with Gitta; and third, I liked her right away, and not just because of the way she looked. Things were best in the beginning. Sometimes she'd help me out with my Latin, but never condescendingly—more as if I were her equal. Inge never stayed overnight. And Gitta didn't have to serve her breakfast. Father was so crazy about her he probably didn't notice a thing when I treated myself to a long night. Gitta had a different opinion. She smelled a rat right away and said, "You'd better stop fooling around. If you get into trouble Father will use it against us and present us with a done deal." After that I pricked up my ears, and rightly so. Inge started taking over the kitchen, first because Gitta ostensibly had too much on her slate, what with homework and all; second, because Inge really knew a lot about cooking; and third, because that was Inge's plan. Of course, she still didn't stay overnight, but that actually made us more suspicious: she was trying to make an impression on us. She admitted it, too, when I dropped in on her in Bockenheim once on the spur of the moment. At first she tried playing the grown-up: "I'll just pretend I didn't hear that, Peter." Then, after the usual necking, she started in about her landlady: "And what if I'm evicted?" I stood firm: "Then you'll just move in with us." Inge wasn't evicted. I serviced her two or three times a week out there in Bockenheim, passing as her private student when the landlady asked; I was pretty convincing, too, and Father remained clueless. When about four weeks ago he mumbled something about "Getting married to Inge,"—not without a childlike embarrassment— we said no. I had to promise to visit her on the weekend, and so on.

Translated by Philip Boehm

Isn't It Nice to Be Rich and Famous?

from From the Diary of a Snail (1972)

When I was thirty-two, I became famous. Since then, Fame has been with us as a roomer. He's always standing around, he's a nuisance, hard to get away from. Especially Anna hates him, because he runs after her, making obscene propositions. Inflated and deflated by turns. Visitors who think they've come to see me look around for him. It's only because he's so lazy, and so useless when he besieges my writing desk, that I've taken him with me into politics and put him to work as a receptionist: he's good at that. Everybody takes him seriously, even my opponents and enemies. He's getting fat. He's beginning to quote himself. I often rent him out at a small fee for receptions and garden parties. Amazing the stories he tells me afterward. He likes to have his picture taken, forges my signature to perfection, and reads what I scarcely look at: reviews. (Yesterday, in Burghausen, shortly before the meeting, a not untalented crook tried to sell him his life story—twenty years in Siberia.) My Fame, children, is someone I ask indulgence for. . . .

"But aren't you rich when you're famous?"
"How rich?"
"Isn't it nice to be rich and famous?"
"What can you buy with it?"

Since I've been famous, neckties, caps, handkerchiefs, and whole sentences complete with instructions for use have been stolen from me. (Fame is someone it seems to be fun to piss on.) The more famous a man gets, the fewer friends he has. It can't be helped: Fame isolates. When Fame helps you, he never lets you forget it. When he hurts you, he says something about the price you have to pay. I certify that Fame is boring and only rarely amusing. (Recently, when Laura wanted six autographs to trade for one of Heintje's, we all decided to be pleased with her deal.)

But I am fairly rich. By scraping everything together I could buy one of the smaller, as good as deserted churches here in Berlin, and convert my church into a hotel, which might, in emulation of the papal bank, call itself the Holy Ghost Hotel. It would serve all the dishes that I myself cook and eat: leg of mutton with lentils, veal kidney on celery, green eel, tripe, mussels, pheasant with weinkraut, suckling pig with lima beans, fish, leek, and mushroom soups, on Ash Wednesday hashed lung, and on Whit Sunday beef heart stuffed with prunes.

For this much can be said: I enjoy life. I'd be glad if all those who so persistently try to teach me how to live enjoyed life too. The betterment of the world ought not to be the monopoly of embittered people with stomach trouble.

Aside from that, children, I'm an accident, who has accidentally survived, accidentally manages to write something, but might also, just as accidentally, have founded an expanding industry—shipyards, for instance. Well, maybe next time. Then you can be my partners and look on at launchings, to see my ships founder. Anna could say: "I baptize you. . . ." I could write (what?) a book about it. . . .

"Is that all? Isn't there some more about you?"
"Ships—I can see that. But all that other stuff . . ."
"Come on, tell us some more."
"Short stuff. What you like. What you don't like."

All right. Short sentences to remember and forget.
I smoke too much but regularly.
I have opinions that can be changed.
I usually think things over beforehand.
In a devious way I'm uncomplicated.
(For the last four years I've been putting words and sentences between parentheses: it has something to do with growing older.)
I like listening from a distance when Laura keeps hitting the same false notes at the piano.
When Raoul rolls me a cigarette, I'm pleased.
When Franz says more than he meant to admit, I'm surprised.
When Bruno tells jokes wrong, I can laugh the way I used to.
I particularly like to watch Anna starting to make over a dress she has just bought.
What I don't like: people armed with the word "trenchant." (Those who don't think but think trenchantly also take trenchant action.)
I don't like bigoted Catholics or orthodox atheists.

I don't like people who want to bend the banana straight for the benefit of mankind.

I am repelled by all those who are able to prestidigitate subjective wrong into objective right.

I fear all those who want to convert me.

My courage is confined to being as little afraid as possible; I do not give demonstrations of courage.

My advice to all is not to make love in a hurry like cats. (That goes for you, too, children, later on.)

I like buttermilk with radishes.

I like to bid high at skat.

I like broken old people.

I, too, repeat my mistakes.

I was pretty well badly brought up.

I am not faithful—but attached.

I've always got to be doing something: hatching out words, chopping up herbs, looking into holes, visiting Doubt, reading chronicles, drawing pictures of mushrooms and their relatives, alertly doing nothing, driving to Delmenhorst tomorrow and the day after to Aurich (East Friesland), talktalktalking, nibbling at the dense blackness wherever I see gray spots in it, marching forward with the snails and—because I know war—resolutely keeping the peace, which, children, is another thing that I like.

"Can I ask a question?" says Franz in conclusion.

Bruno refers to grown-ups as "blown-ups."

They're boring, says Laura.

In a not unfriendly kind of way Raoul calls me "old-timer."

Translated by Ralph Manheim

A Call to the Special Unit

from My Century (1999)

I'M HE NOW. HE LIVES IN HANNOVER-LANGENHAGEN and is an elementary-school teacher. He—no longer I— never had an easy time of it. Unable to complete the secondary-school academic curriculum, he worked as an apprentice in business, but was forced to abandon that as well. He sold cigarettes, joined the army and rose to the rank of corporal, then enrolled in a private commercial school, but he was not allowed to take the examinations for the degree because he lacked the academic prerequisites. He went to England to improve his English and worked there in a car wash. He thought of studying Spanish in Barcelona. Finally a friend in Vienna tried something called success psychology on him and he plucked up the courage to go back to school in Hannover, where he managed to get into the teacher-training college without the formal academic prerequisites and eventually qualify as a teacher and where he is currently a member of the Union for Education and Research and even head of the Young Teachers Committee, a pragmatic leftist who believes in changing society step-by-step and dreams of doing so in a wing chair he picked up for a song in a junk shop. All at once he hears a ring at the door of his Walsroder Strasse second-floor apartment.

I—who is he—open the door. A girl with long brown hair asks to speak to me, to him. "Can the two of you put up two of us for a night?" She says "the two of you" because somebody must have told her that he or I live with a girl. He and I say yes.

Later, he says, I began to have my doubts, which my girlfriend echoed at breakfast. "We can only assume . . ." she said. But we went to school as usual. (She teaches too, but at a secondary school.) We had a class outing that day. We went to a bird sanctuary outside Walsrode. After school we still had our doubts. "They've probably moved in by now. I gave the girl with the long hair the key to the place."

So he talks it over with a friend—I too would certainly have talked it over with a friend—and his friend says what his girlfriend said at breakfast: "Dial 110 . . ." He dials the number (with my consent) and asks to speak to the Baader-Meinhof Special Unit. The Special Unit people prick up their ears, say, "We'll follow the lead," and do so. Soon their plainclothesmen and the janitor are keeping an eye on the front door. They see a woman and a young man enter. The janitor asks who they're looking for. The teacher, they say. "Right," says the janitor, "he lives on the second floor, but I don't think he's in." A while later the young man comes back down, goes out and finds a telephone booth; he is arrested as he is dropping coins into the slot. He has a pistol on him.

The teacher is politically to the left of me, I'm sure. Sitting in his junk-shop wing chair, he is wont to dream himself into a progressive future. He believes in the "emancipation process of the underprivileged." The Baader-Meinhof position of a Hannover professor who, in leftist circles, is nearly as well known as Habermas—"The signals they are sending with their bombs are will-o'-the-wisps"— more or less coincides with his own: "These people have given the right the arguments they need to discredit the entire spectrum of the left."

That corresponds to my view of the matter. That is why he and I—he as teacher and union member, I as freelancer—dialed 110. That is why detectives from the District Criminal Investigation Department are now in an apartment that is the teacher's apartment and has a junk-shop chair in it. The woman with stubbly, unkempt hair who opens the door when the police ring the doorbell looks in poor health; she is so emaciated as to bear no resemblance whatever to the photograph in her police file. Perhaps she is not the one they are looking for. She has been pronounced dead many times. She is said to have died of a brain tumor. "Pigs!" she cries upon being arrested. Not until the detectives in the teacher's apartment find a magazine open to the page showing an X ray of the wanted person's brain are the detectives certain who it is they have apprehended. After that they find more in the teacher's apartment: ammunition, guns, hand grenades, and a Royal cosmetics case containing a four-point-five-kilo bomb.

"No," the teacher says later in an interview, "I had to do it." I agree, because otherwise he and his girlfriend would have been mixed up in the affair. "Even so," he says, "I felt uneasy about it. After all, I often agreed with her before she started throwing bombs, with what she said in the magazine *konkret* after the attack on Schneider's Department Store in Frankfurt, for example: 'The general argument against arson is that it can jeopardize the lives of people who have no desire to have their lives jeopardized. . . .' Later, in Berlin, when Baader was released, she took part in an operation that left an innocent official severely wounded. After that she went underground. After that there were deaths on both sides. After that she showed up at my place. After that I . . . But I really thought she was no longer alive."

He, the teacher I see myself in, wishes to use the considerable reward which is legally his for having dialed 110 to ensure that everyone captured thus far—including Gudrun Ensslin, who attracted attention while making a purchase in a fashionable Hamburg boutique—has a fair trial, which, as he puts it, "will make the social interconnections clear."

I would not do that. It is a waste of money. Why should the lawyers—Schily & Co.—profit? I think he should put the money into his and other schools to help the underprivileged he has made it his mission to help. But no matter to whom he gives the money, the elementary-school teacher is troubled about being labeled "the man who dialed 110" for the rest of his life. I am troubled too.

Translated by Michael Henry Heim

Police Radio

(1968)

THE ONLY THING LEFT FOR ME IS TO REPEAT WHAT I said in my statement: I was not his mistress. At most his close friend, if there's such a thing as that. Our so-called confidences everyone keeps asking me about were exclusively professional. By that I mean that I learned a great deal from Professor de Groot—more than, say, Fräulein Manthey, who had come to Amsterdam on leave from the Kassler Museum just as I had come from the Wallraff-Richartz Museum, both of us here to finish our training with a semester on practical restoration techniques.

Professor de Groot was an internationally renowned expert. And all of his students, including Fräulein Manthey, who has testified that she felt unfairly treated, have a duty to be grateful to their teacher. I was in his private studio a total of two times, when I was allowed to help Professor de Groot remove a gesso undercoat; otherwise, we all worked together in the large restoration lab, as Dr. Jonk has already testified. Nevertheless it's true that, out of all his students, I was the only one he took along when his scanner alerted him to a fire in the old part of the city, which wasn't very far away. I can't say I was always thrilled to be pulled away from my work, which is of great interest to me. My colleagues can confirm how much I despise any kind of preferential treatment, although of course there's no cause for anyone to hold a grudge against Professor de Groot on that account.

It's common knowledge that our teacher listened to his police scanner all the time while he was at work. I had been told about this quirk even before I left Cologne. The word was that the professor was good at what he did, but a little off-the-wall. The majority of the reports coming over the police band didn't distract him in the slightest: car accidents, Saturday night fistfights, even jewelry-store heists— at most they would prompt a sarcastic comment that we indulged with smiles. But if within this constant stream of gibberish—which we had all got used to, and which Dr. Jonk could imitate perfectly—there was an attic fire somewhere, then nothing, not even the most engrossing job, could keep Professor de Groot from going. I still see him reaching into his coat pocket and rattling the car keys like a little boy: "Are you coming, Fräulein Schimmelpfeng?"

Within just half a year I was witness to four large-scale blazes: two on the Heerengracht, one by the old church near the whores, and one at Waterlooplein—as well as some two dozen middle-sized fires and minor incidents: Amsterdam has a lot of fires. Professor de Groot would go and watch these fires, calmly and composedly, often with visible disappointment but always with the same scientific

curiosity I knew from the lab. I have to confess, however—
and this can also go on record if necessary—that the same
fires made me uneasy or even anxious, although I didn't
mean to react like that, and I often wondered whether Pro-
fessor de Groot might be playing some kind of game with
me, for some particular purpose. But this was absolutely
not the case; these suspicions were unfounded; I, and only
I, was to blame for my behavior. Immature, and lacking the
necessary backbone, I failed to maintain my scientific disci-
pline. Professor de Groot's, on the other hand, seemed ex-
emplary, as he stood by, practically cheerful, looking on as
the fires were being fought. He hardly ever said anything,
and when he did, it was about Turner, his favorite painter,
and particularly about the conflagrations he painted around
1835—the fire in London, the fire in Rome—in other
words, what Turner had been inspired to paint after having
seen the burning of the Houses of Parliament with his own
eyes. For that reason, and for that reason alone, I had no
hesitation in saying yes when Professor de Groot so kindly
invited me last May to accompany him to London for a
three-day outing. We spent whole days inside the Tate
Gallery. Looking through Turner's sketchbook, we found
several impressions of the abovementioned fire that de-
stroyed the Parliament, spontaneously set down for all
time. And if I now say that my teacher Professor de Groot
and I grew closer during this brief time, which I assume
was as pleasant for him as it was for me, I can only hope
that I am not adding any more fodder to the rumors which
the high court still seems inclined to maintain.

I did not know that Professor de Groot also listened to
the scanner at home. He very seldom spoke of his home at

all, and never mentioned it when we were in London. Twice last year, in June and at the beginning of July, I was invited—at his wife's request—to Sunday dinner at their home. While Frau de Groot did indeed strike me as rather shy, or even distraught—she seemed tired and exhausted— I never imagined that the same police radio, which all of us students viewed as a quirk that had developed into a habit, had so undermined her health. Because it appears—as I must now believe—that Professor de Groot left the device running throughout the night, at full volume. And while he was able to sleep, his wife was not. Moreover—as I have just learned myself—any notice of a fire, and nothing else but a fire, would apparently wake him up right away, where-upon he would force his wife, often against her will, to get dressed and accompany him to the scene of the fire. As much as I have to condemn such behavior as utterly incon-siderate, I feel obliged to stress that it was only his profes-sional, that is to say, his scientific, curiosity—and especially the study of Turner that I mentioned earlier—that drove Professor de Groot to such unusual behavior.

Today, now that I know how my teacher, Professor Henk de Groot, wound up burning to death in his own cramped gabled house, I have to assume that he heard the dispatcher announce that fire, too. And I keep trying to imagine how he must have tried to save himself and his pa-pers from his bedroom high in the building, which, like most of the houses in the old part of town, burned from the bottom up. Today, as Frau de Groot stands here accused of a willful act of arson with intent to commit murder, I cannot forget a remark she made several times over dinner, seemingly out of context, a remark that will not allow me to testify to her innocence: "Some day," she said, "you're going to get your fingers burned. . . ." And from this day on I shall blame myself for not having tried to exert some moderating influence on my teacher, especially considering that I was assured of his trust, even if I never was—contrary to all assertions—his lover, not even in London, during our outing, which lasted a mere three days.

Moreover, my own alibi could not be clearer, as on the night of the fire I was at the movies with my colleague Fräulein Manthey, watching the late feature.

Translated by Philip Boehm

ISRAEL AND ME

In June 1973, Grass traveled to Israel with the German chancellor Willy Brandt. This essay first appeared in the *Süddeutsche Zeitung* (Munich), December 31, 1973.

AS SOON AS I STARTED PUTTING DOWN MY THOUGHTS about this outgoing year (according to the Christian calendar) in an essay, those thoughts began to swirl around the most recent Middle East war and the future of the state of Israel. Not that I wouldn't be thinking of these grave matters otherwise. And although I began by grouping my vacillating views under the heading "Israel and Us," the matter is in fact too upsetting to be left to the plural.

The fulcrum, the trauma? Three times I have visited Israel; not once have I traveled to an Arab country. None of my books has been free or nimble enough to elude the crime that continues to tag Germans today: the annihilation of six million Jews. I mean Germans in the Federal Republic—how they've done their grudging best not to forget. I mean Germans in Austria—how they've managed, with the blessing of politics, to excuse themselves from the matter. I mean Germans in the GDR—how they've been prevented by the state from bearing their part of this collective guilt.

In June of this year, on my last visit to Israel, I was a guest of the prime minister. Four jam-packed days. News of the imminent war was vague at best. We followed an official program, with its security issues. As the first German chancellor to visit that endangered small nation, Willy Brandt was wise to avoid the territories occupied during the Six Days' War. Brandt's standing formula on each occasion was that Israel's right to exist could be guaranteed only by a peace treaty. The formula remains valid today, but how it should be interpreted is more debatable than ever, now that the negotiations in Geneva might actually succeed.

In Israel, I talked with friends and acquaintances and heard contradictory things: How a people persecuted for centuries was suffering from having to be an occupying power; how now that they were confirmed by their success in the war, people responded to critical questions by referring to military security; how the dream of a Greater Israel (coupled with the issue of military security) was beginning to gain ground; and how incompatible Israel's political logic (which is not unlike that of Western Europe) was with Arabic ways of thinking, which we dismiss too hastily as irrational.

The war begins in the fall. I sit at my work and in front of the television. I smoke and draw and write and smoke; I see the twofold material expenditure, see how on each side the "just cause" is being defended; I listen to relativizing commentaries and learn that the superpowers' interest in this war, too—a war that would have had different dimensions, i.e., none, without their weapons—is primarily military. I call up friends, and am called up and written to and goaded for my opinion, and am incapable of standing by the Israelis as unreservedly as I did following the Six Days' War.

My friends in Israel don't understand. They want me to make myself clear, to take a stand. They feel abandoned, betrayed. In their disappointment, they make sloppy comparisons. But the misconduct of both sides makes taking either position impossible. Not only the Arabs, but also the Israelis (both those in the government and those of the opposition) have made mistakes resulting from their insecurities (really, this is all terribly normal: like any other state, Israel has the right to be entangled in political errors).

If, on the one hand, Arab states made no sign of being willing to enter into peace negotiations with Israel, weren't even willing to recognize Israel's existence, or else offered to negotiate under conditions they knew would never be accepted (a simultaneous withdrawal from the occupied territories, for example), Israel, on the other hand, squandered its reputation by increasingly setting up house in both the occupied territories and the already annexed ones. Israelis began to buy up land, defense settlements were established, and Arabs in the occupied territories were treated like colonial subjects.

Just as Egypt, when it sent its troops into the border zone of the Sinai Peninsula in 1967, offered Israel a pretext for starting the preventive Six Days' War, so has Israel given the Arab states a pretext for attack with its gradual annexation of the occupied territories.

Even if the last war was halfway successful for Israel militarily, the Arab states' position has grown stronger in terms of political value. What they did not achieve on the battlefield, they're managing now with the help of the oil boycott.

Multinational corporations, free from democratic control and recklessly pursuing profit, add to the Arabs' extortion a capitalist Western one. The first was to be anticipated; the second calls into question the feasibility of parliamentary democracy. We can no longer speak of a free West with conviction if it can be shown that Western politics is being steered by multinational corporations.

But what do I still support after all of this? Can we continue to speak of a this side or a that side? When I fall back on Willy Brandt's formula, "Israel's right to exist could be guaranteed only by a peace treaty"—and this formula is reasonable and the sole practicable one—then I support Israel's withdrawal from the occupied territories following the acceptance of such a treaty. But what if (as Israel rightly fears) the relinquished territories should be used as deployment zones by the Arab states? There has been little sign that those states intend to give up their goal of reclaiming Palestine and wiping Israel off the map. In that case, if Israel's right to exist is to be guaranteed by a peace treaty, then the relinquished territories would have to be demilitarized. But what if—and so begin the entirely justified objections—what if even in spite of these demilitarized buffer zones (the Golan Heights, the Sinai Peninsula, the West Bank), Israel remains subject to attack by mid-range missiles? Such an attack would elicit nothing more than obligatory protests from the international community, and a UN resolution that would probably conclude by blaming the victim. These fears will be quelled only if, as part of this peace treaty, the superpowers and the nations of Western

Europe commit to military protection of the newly established borders.

And cautiously I add the Federal Republic, too. For if it weren't for the Germans, there would be no state of Israel. And if we claim that our relations with Israel will always have this special status, no matter how much they otherwise may have normalized, then the Federal Republic and its government must realize that it cannot simply opt out of these new negotiations for Israel's security.

The occupation of Czechoslovakia by the Warsaw Pact forces, and the fascist military coup in Greece and its counterpart this year in Chile have all taught us how ineffective protest is, how shaking one's head with regret only makes moral protest ludicrous, and how easy it is to come up with so-called political facts. The destruction of the state of Israel (with or without a peace treaty) would only unleash similar protests and appeals to morality, as long as other nations—including, for the reasons I mention above, the Federal Republic—fail to make clear that they are prepared to defend Israel by using military means.

That is, if a militarily backed peace treaty fails to materialize, then the risk of Israel's destruction will be more of a threat than ever. Each of us in Germany would then be marked by a crime that began with Auschwitz and has continued to the present day. The fact that the Arab countries are not prepared to put an end to the ruthless murders committed by Palestinian terrorists only bolsters my fear.

All of us, myself included, have become susceptible to our own immediate, everyday concerns—the specter of economic stagnation, the threat of unemployment. The rate of inflation and the return of rising prices, the oil boycott and its unforeseeable consequences have tempted us into the tactless expectation that Israel will accept conditions that, upon closer inspection, could threaten its existence. Neutrality, however, which would presumably affirm Israel yet be subject to the Arab states' extortion, would be a false position and only make us despicable.

We might as well ask the cynical question: What degree of room temperature in winter, what rate of inflation, and what percentage of unemployment will we continue to endure and still stand, however shakily, by Israel and our guarantee of its existence? At what point do we become the helpless victims of our own politics of economic growth— incapable of bearing the responsibility we've inherited, committed only to the political superstition that charity begins at home? Already we're checking to see—and I do this, too—if a word in favor of Israel might not bring danger, if not terror, to us or to whomever utters it. Reason cannot exist under the rule of fear.

While the outgoing year was checking its political and moral defeats off on the calendar, I found myself in the visitors' gallery at the United Nations in New York a few weeks before the military coup in Chile, sitting behind the representatives, including, for the first time, representatives of our "most efficient of nations." There up in front was Willy Brandt giving a speech. He left out the name Allende, he avoided mentioning Chile; but it was clear when he spoke of a crime what crime he meant and what share of the blame belonged to Western capitalism. A strong, futile speech. All too familiar statements ("Hunger is war, too!") met with understanding nods all around. Even representatives of the German states found themselves, briefly, the subject of applause. And yet in its tacitly despairing plea for

rationality, Brandt's speech only made explicit the bank-
ruptcy of political reason.

I fear we no longer recognize how absurd our rational
strategizing (or strategizing that seems rational to us) has
become, and how irrational its consequences are. Kissinger
and Le Duc Tho's laboriously negotiated truce in Vietnam
was considered a victory of reason, but its participants have
all had a good laugh over its "reasonable outcome": the war
goes on.

A year paved over with good intentions. Too scattered in
its contradictions to be sobering. Western parliamentarism
gone threadbare with corruption and capitalist hubris. East-
ern communism turned utterly petrified, incapable of reform
and ready at the drop of a hat to seek salvation in Stalinist
terror. The left fraught with contention, the right riddled
with calluses. The churches impotently pleading impotence.
More than a hundred thousand victims of starvation in
Ethiopia, more than fifteen thousand murdered in Chile, an
estimated twenty thousand casualties in the latest Middle
Eastern conflict, the countless dead of Vietnam and Cambo-
dia, the terror in Greece, the terror in Czechoslovakia. A
fresh-faced question: Has anything positive come out of this?

How about: Fat business deals made possible by the
energy crisis? Or this: Rising copper prices following Al-
lende's assassination? Or, at a pinch, scientific progress: The
space mission succeeded in something, I'm no longer sure
what, something to do with Venus, Saturn, or Mars . . . ?

Or maybe only this: There's less traffic now, fewer fatal-
ities on the street.

Translated by W. Martin

IMMURED

(1957)

I DIDN'T BUILD JUST ANY HOUSE. AND THE SITE WASN'T the sort of place so many people spend their hard-earned savings on simply to get a roof—any roof at all—over their heads.

I took the longest side of my private study and had a five-year-old bull set in the wall; the bare masonry was carefully plastered over, given two coats of paint and some cheery wallpaper, and right over the spot that would be in front of the bull's head, I hung an empty baroque picture frame.

You know I used to be one of the most respected toreros around; you could hear my name being announced at various corridas, but after I injured my hip in the arena I had to hang up my beloved sword and cape.

No doubt you've guessed as much: I mounted my good old weapons on either side of the baroque frame, put up a few photos, and turned the study into a kind of trophy room. I had a good life. Instead of fighting bulls I tended flowers in the garden. Yellow, white, tender blue, even violet—but one color was conspicuously absent. I surrounded myself with caution and fences. But a fence can hardly hold all on its own. How can you keep out the mail? Every day this friendly man showed up, wearing his uniform. Greeting me as if I were his superior officer—he knew me from my glory days—he would hand me a lightweight envelope.

Naturally I was careful not to open these letters, not to read them. Even without any return address, I could tell it was my ex-fiancée dipping in the inkwell again. No, I thought, whatever she might be sending me, it couldn't be anything good. I would be foolish to read her letters—it would be better to write to her.

You should know I considered my breakup with Elvira permanent. Like every great love, ours had come to an utterly banal end. One day she could no longer tolerate the sound that apples make when a person with decent teeth bites into one and proceeds to devour it in solemn tranquillity down to the hard core. She didn't like the crunching. To her it sounded like bones splintering, like some violent force shattering against the knee; in short, this very digestible dessert was to her nothing but another noise from the bullfight, and she refused to hear any more of that. Even if the hip injury was the real reason for my retiring from the corrida with all its dangers, it was Elvira who gave me the final push. Bulls or love, she said. I chose love. And soon I had neither bulls nor love, but only the garden, where I simplemindedly tended my flowers—and the study, where I would sit in front of the empty baroque frame and lose myself in thought.

The mail. It came every day. And every day I answered the letters without reading them. I piled up stack after stack of her letters and bundled them with string every six months. Always assuming that Elvira's attitude toward letter openers was like my own, I was industrious in my own epistolary efforts. I defended the loud eating of apples, and I have no doubt that she railed against the same fruit in her pretty, upright handwriting.

But, of course, the best laid plans . . . One day I wrote that it might be possible to find a compromise. From now on, I said, I could limit my dessert to soft pears, plums, and peaches; perhaps she ought to come over and hear how that would sound. And she came. Elvira came. It turned out that she had read every single note; her letter opener had daily bared my soul to her, and now she wanted to hear how pears sounded—she had even brought some yellow Bartletts.

We never made it to the meal. The second she set foot in my trophy room I shouted: "Elvira, your skirt! Take it off, I beg you, you don't know what you're doing." But my warning came too late. The poor girl, no, my own true love, couldn't get the tomato-colored material off. It was horrible; the wall burst apart, right in the middle of the baroque frame, and the five-year-old bull came tearing out, ripping the gilt rectangle off its mounting with his shoulders, snorting mortar and broken brick, stamping with its hooves so that I feared the worst. Oh, no, Elvira cried, cursing her garish clothing. The mighty head was lowering, the eyes already shot with blood; in two bounds I was at the wall, where I pulled down what had been on display; I thrust through the air of the room, assumed the proper position, danced back and forth around the agitated animal, and tried with all my art to lure those horns, which were still shredding wallpaper, away from Elvira's holy parts. There—I saw the forehead, the animal's eye; it all looked so familiar—the terrible triangle. I let him pass. O Elvira, your skirt. I got down on my knees and waited. Your cape like a bloody nose, Elvira. A feather couldn't bend the way I bent out of his path, the way I grazed him. Even if the room is small, Elvira. Doesn't your heart rejoice to hear his knee crack? Are you still thinking about those miserable apples? His beautiful eye is overflowing, his chest is heaving its last, he is framed in baroque gilt, gold leaf is springing from his groin and swimming in the river of which he is the font.

The girl took just a tiny step toward the mountain that had now come to rest: "How many more bulls do you have stashed behind that wallpaper?" She was hardly breathing as she pointed at the other walls. "A hundred!" I replied. "Take off your skirt, Elvira. Because there are a hundred angry triangles waiting to charge, and you're waving that cape of yours right in their eyes."

She undressed quickly, taking off more than the fashionable material in question—partly to escape the wall-sundering force and partly to be able to feel in me her savior.

Today Elvira is my wife. She tends the garden and holds my son's hand. We had the wall repaired. There's no more bull dreaming behind the wallpaper. No empty baroque frame waiting for a portrait. But I'm back in the ring. Posters shout my name and anyone who wants to catch me has to look for a hotel room in the harbor. There, in a dingy, damp hole-in-the-wall, sitting on a rough chair, I sink my teeth into one juicy apple after the other. I check the marks after every bite, and keep finding proof that my gums are bleeding.

Translated by Philip Boehm

By a Rough Estimate

Address delivered in New Delhi before the Council of Cultural Relations, February 1975.

Ladies and Gentlemen:

At the end of 1974 I found myself rereading George Orwell's utopian novel *1984* as a way of reexamining my original experience of the book, which I first read long ago. I said: At the end of the year. Or to be more precise: Over Christmas. In Europe, Christmas is a time of greater consumption.

While I was reading Orwell's terrifying account of oligarchic collectivism, I had beside me (I had only just started it) the second "Report to the Club of Rome," published in book form under the title *Mankind at the Turning Point*. In my breaks from Orwell, I'd turn to the scientists Mesarovic and Pestel and follow their predictions up to the year 2000. They had many rows of statistics, numbers laden with zeroes. I would jot down the most important ones for South Asian infant mortality, and decorate the scientific jargon—phrases like "mortality pattern" and "protein deficiency"—with exclamation marks. Then I'd turn back to Orwell to read about the permanent war of a world divided into three blocs: Atlantic, Eurasian, and East Asian.

Between two future worlds, between two horrors. On one side, the fictional Big Brother, his omnipotence synonymous with the totalitarian pattern of any ideology. On the other, the dizzying statistics of the population explosion to come, or rather, the one already upon us: by the year 2000, the number of human beings will have doubled. And in the middle, myself—a Central European writer wanting to tell his stories with the whispering voice of history, a skeptical Social Democrat searching for a third way between communist dictatorship and rampant capitalist exploitation, a father whose children are growing up in a world notorious for giving false hopes, or more precisely, for offering no hope.

Back in West Germany, when I received the Indian ambassador's invitation to deliver this speech before you here today, I wasn't sure at first that I should accept. It makes little sense to advocate cultural interaction and to give the impression of mutual understanding, when all we know about one another comes out of school textbooks. Naturally I took some time to inform myself about India. India's culture, religions, and history, its constitution and unemployment rate, its corruption, foreign debt, and exceptional press—wherein one can read all about the degree of corruption, the consequences of unemployment, and the violence with which social tensions in the Indian federation have begun to erupt. It is not my place to talk about these things, the contrast between rich and poor being hardly specific to India, but, rather, international.

I decided to come here in order to see India for myself and possibly to learn something—never mind that we all think we already know everything and that the facts lie in great heaps all around us. I come bearing not a message but my own helplessness, which I would like to explain. But first my thesis: I am convinced that human beings have been overwhelmed by the results of their own expertise. While they may be able to extract wonderful discoveries out of their knowledge, their technological skills, and their investigative curiosity—they split atoms, they see infinitely far in any direction, they've been to the moon, etc. —these milestones of human progress stand in the midst of a society that is eminently barbaric, albeit in a sense that can be illustrated brilliantly with advanced statistics. They, the atom-splitters and sky-stormers, feeding their computers at regulated intervals, collecting, saving, and examining the data they provide, are still incapable of feeding the world's children.

Children make up half of the world's population. I have no idea how many million of them die each year of hunger. "By a rough estimate," which is what I've titled this talk, eleven million children will shortly go blind from a deficiency of vitamin A. Human science is capable of directing the reentry of a space capsule and its happy astronaut passengers down to the square mile where it will land, but we can only "roughly estimate" the millions of famine victims who die each year.

In Ethiopia there are between three and four hundred thousand victims of starvation; in Bangladesh, depending on which newspaper you read, there are between three hundred fifty thousand and as many as a half-million. We no longer think of this in precise terms, no longer want to know the precise details. Precise numbers are tallied up only for airplane crashes and robberies and the taking and freeing of hostages, after mine disasters, and for weekends with particularly heavy traffic.

These things are interesting, too. They're horrible to us because they're comprehensible. Where the dead are concerned, we can only count up to a hundred. Anything more than that becomes abstract, can no longer be identified; it gets repressed or shunted out of the way with religious hairsplitting, and is not addressed.

To come back to my thesis: Humans are great perpetrators; in most cases, they're undeniably brilliant in action. But the consequences of their actions usually leave them bewildered, as if they had had no idea what those would be. They behave like children; that is, they act irresponsibly.

But there is really no reason to be surprised, as if something unforeseeable had taken humanity unawares and forced chaos upon us. For years we've had figures and statistics showing overpopulation around the world, along with the malnutrition that goes with it. Unemployment and the stagnation of a gross national product followed by its decline are calculated well in advance. For years, a commonplace of developmental politics, declared in various air-conditioned congressional halls and affirmed with a general nodding of heads, has been that the rich will continue to get richer— even if somewhat less quickly than they once did—while the poor, even if somewhat richer, will always grow poorer.

For the past year and a half, the oil crisis has made the pattern of rich and poor a little less black-and-white. Along with the rich superpowers, the United States and the Soviet Union, which are not only rich but control their own energy resources, we have a group of wealthy industrial nations in both the Western and Eastern blocs that lack natural resources of their own and are therefore dependent on both the US and the USSR. There is also a third group: poor nations rich in natural resources.

What's left over is a group that has come to be known recently as the Fourth World. It includes those countries that are doubly deprived: not only poor in terms of gross national product but also without natural resources of their own, and thus dependent on wealthy industrial nations and their overpriced goods and on oil-producing countries that are otherwise as poor as themselves.

This impoverished Fourth World cannot make up for the increase in oil prices by raising prices on their own industrial products. Twice hit by inflation, these countries bear the brunt of political power struggles in which, needless to say, they take no active part. To give one example: The price of chemical fertilizer, an oil product, has tripled for all of the primarily agrarian nations of the Fourth World; chemical fertilizer plants have had to shut down or reduce their capacity by half. The vicious circle remains a closed one.

Four worlds. A pretty rough framework, I know. Where does the People's Republic of China fit in, for example? Although it is certainly overpopulated, China successfully put an end to its chronic famines two decades ago, and its power does not depend on natural resources. And where do we put India, a country in which the contrast between technological expertise and ongoing malnutrition is alarmingly entrenched?

Even the giants I mentioned at the beginning, the United States and the Soviet Union, don't really fit into this unintentionally rough assessment. In the United States, unemployment, the hopeless impoverishment of broad sections of the population, and continuing racial discrimination all belie the country's wealth and complacent self-image. In the Soviet Union, the potential power of a strong military and a top-heavy industrial sector contrast with the permanent lack of both consumer goods and guarantees of personal freedom. Authoritarian Communism wanted with all its might to legislate justice and was defeated by its own compulsions.

Until a few years ago the United Nations created hope around the world. Everywhere people realized that global problems—uneven growth, overexploitation of natural resources, overpopulation and malnutrition, and the permanent threat of military confrontation and the arms race—could not be solved from the standpoint of national interests, but only from that of a world government. This hope, too, has come to nothing. It looks as if European nationalism is going to be staged all over again in the new countries of Africa and Asia, as if historical experience were nontransferable.

At the beginning of this talk, I mentioned the report by Mesarovic and Pestel to the Club of Rome, published under the descriptive title *Mankind at the Turning Point.* Both scientists, after examining all their statistics, come to the conclusion that the pernicious economic growth of rich industrial nations needs to be replaced by an organic, worldwide economic growth that benefits developing nations. A concrete utopia. Only a world government, based on the United Nations, would be able to implement it. But even if the wealthy industrial nations are prepared to renounce their privileges—which is unlikely—and to adjust their production and consumption patterns to international necessity, it remains more than doubtful that the new Third and Fourth World nations will permit any needed infringements on their sovereignty.

During a visit to New York in September 1973, I had the opportunity to hear, as an audience member, the inaugural address to the United Nations given by Chancellor Willy Brandt of West Germany. It was the first time that representatives of both German states had sat in the plenum. Brandt's speech was an appeal to reason. He spoke for rapprochement and détente as components of an international politics of peace, a peace he did not wish to see ensured by military means. His categorical statement "Hunger is war, too!" met with unanimous cheering. The decibel level of those spontaneous cheers would have been enough to drown out the effect of any vigorously applauded rebuttal.

Precisely because Brandt's appeal to human reason was so urgent, I sensed in it a trace of disillusionment. He undoubtedly recognized that the instruments of reason are insufficient for staving off imminent catastrophe. Human action is too often undergirded by irrationality, even when it thinks itself guided by reason. Too often irrationality uses the language of reason and so disguises its own murderous influence. Rational insight into social realities is by no means the deciding factor in human action; compulsion, mistaken for motivation, steers in the opposite direction and opens the door to chaos. Whether nations are prone to communism or capitalism, compulsory self-interest prevents them from practicing that international domestic policy that politicians like Brandt have frequently called for as a condition of solidarity. The enmities seem irreconcilable: Arabs against Jews, Hindus against Muslims, Russians against Chinese, Christians against Christians, Germans against Germans.

In that building on the bank of New York's East River in the fall of 1973, did Willy Brandt sense the futility of his appeal when once again he called on reason and pleaded with the United Nations to demonstrate its power as a unified force rather than exposing the force of its factions? Even then, he had not given up. And there are many who today, like Brandt, will not allow themselves to be cowed by the general resignation, who refuse to stop pointing out injustices when they see them. Only recently, Brandt repeated his appeal on behalf of UNICEF, attesting to the emergency conditions of millions of starving children and invoking the well-known, roughly estimated numbers. But who's listening?

At the moment it's the hardened pragmatists who are working on this. They make deals and threats and take rain checks. Absorbed in the hardships of everyday politics, they've lost sight of the bigger picture. In general they're only focused on interests, which they weigh against other interests at the expense of yet further interests. What they've achieved is a hooked rug of quickly woven successes: whether in Vietnam or Israel, the truces won't hold, and the treaties signed yesterday can all be terminated tomorrow. The superpowers, the United States and the Soviet Union, the world's self-appointed police officers, have been defeated by their own ambitions. Without direction or prospects for the future, humanity clings to residual structures; for the more visibly social justice is lacking, the more fanatically will religious and nationalistic differences be acted upon.

Yet all the great religious ideas are declarations of peace. Hinduism and Buddhism both teach tolerance. Christ's Sermon on the Mount urges the love of one's neighbor. Even the secular religions—capitalism and communism—once saw themselves as the Enlightenment's children: they intended to make mankind happy and freedom universal.

Nothing is left of this. Tolerance has become impatience; neighborly love has degenerated into bigoted self-righteousness. Capital yields its return in abuses of power. And all that has survived in communism is the revolutionary slogan. Everywhere people who believed and were betrayed are suffering. Nameless and crammed into narrow spaces, held without rights, given over to fear, to hunger, and, if not to religious superstition, then to hopelessness—they do not understand what is happening to them. Their misery is too synonymous with anonymity to be portrayed in tragic, individual parts. They are not players; they are played with. Kept in the dark, these many hundreds of millions of roughly estimated illiterates cannot see through the corruption, recognize the misuse of power, or disprove a single lie. Where there is no strong hand to oppress them, they are mollified instead by pious promises and the clever assessment of their inconsiderable wants and needs.

Well outside of this growing misery, a privileged international elite spends its time in carefully demarcated security zones. It may not possess political power itself, but the politically powerful are the guarantors of its petty freedoms. It is not as if this intellectual elite did nothing at all: thousands of equally correct expert opinions, drafts, and plans for the future all contradict and neutralize each other. Specialists debate the correct method for remedying poverty worldwide, thereby filling libraries and providing future specialists with specious examination problems.

I don't wish to be unfair here, especially since I belong to this elite and share in its arrogance and impotence. But isn't it true? Even as we're predicting the imminent catastrophe and hating each other's guts, we still wink at each other and exchange comforting phrases: *Don't worry, we'll survive. We most definitely will survive.*

Born in 1927, I belong to a generation that although it may not have directly participated in the German crime — the genocide of six million Jews — bears to this day the responsibility for it and is neither able nor willing to forget it. I said: *Six million Jews murdered.* Once again, a rough estimate. The too-immense abstract number.

After 1945 the whole world believed that this, the gravest crime in history, would act as a curative shock, would have its causes plumbed and brought to light, and that restitution for it would be necessarily cathartic. Nothing of the sort has occurred. Just as before, minorities are discriminated against and murdered in the hundreds of thousands. Instead of shocking us, the abstract number has simply been suppressed. Even worse, six million may not be the final number in the genocide of the Jews. If the small state of Israel, which was created in the crucible of anti-Semitism, should once again be threatened and thus find itself reacting to terror with counterterror, to injustice with injustice, then the crimes of Auschwitz and Treblinka will be resumed in another war of extermination. A logically deduced insanity that seems alarmingly inevitable.

The world watches from the sidelines or involves itself in the preparations with only a mild sense of shame. With their arms shipments, the superpowers — the US and the USSR — ensure that the conflict will be a military one. The countries of the Third World, along with Europe's industrial nations, submit to being blackmailed by a few oil-rich Arab states. The Pope puts on a worried face and expresses concern over Jerusalem's Christian pilgrimage sites. Led by wrongdoing into wrongdoing, Israel is ostracized. And I feel absurd standing before you now, in India, speaking for this small, continually threatened and therefore unhappy nation, this roughly estimated remainder.

I said, roughly estimated, six million. German guilt and German responsibility, which cannot be cleared. Without wanting to diminish the crime of genocide even a little, I would like to say something now about this current genocide, about how it takes place in day-to-day life and has become something ordinary.

The majority of Germans knew nothing about the Final Solution's bureaucratic organization in the concentration camps. The roughly estimated number *six million* was revealed to them, in all its abstractness and inconceivability, only after the war. They doubted it out of self-defense, and repressed it. Yet many of my compatriots have endured it, willingly or unwillingly, as a lifelong burden.

Today there is nothing we don't know. Thanks to an unbroken network of information, we always learn punctually, between various daily news reports, where starvation and death have occurred. Then, at the end of the year, the roughly estimated numbers are added up. Television takes intrepid aim. Glossy magazines deliver high print runs of thoroughly photographed exposés of destitution. Suffering has become telegenic, photogenic. Even science no longer has to grope in the dark. Official almanacs are filled with irrefutable statistics. We know what vitamins are lacking, and where. Discussion of global protein deficiency has become routine for European high-school and university students. It is as much a part of our general education now as the theory of relativity. Even more horrible in its thoughtlessness and impotence is the widespread pedagogical practice of encouraging children who are not hungry to eat by invoking the starving children of India and who knows where else. Hunger has become a commonplace. No one can say he didn't know, that he never heard about it. And it isn't a tidal wave or some other natural disaster that is responsible for this scandal, but human action, or, rather, human inaction. Nothing can acquit us.

And still the growing misery gets relativized away. Cynicism celebrates the survival of the fittest. Indifferent fatalism ignores the growing catastrophe. Countries and peoples are written off as bad planning. And an image of the future is emerging with which Orwell's dystopia seems idyllic by comparison.

I am by vocation a writer. I try to write against the passing of time so that what is past does not remain unspoken. Lately I have been working on a manuscript, making words that range far back to the Middle Ages and, even further, to prehistory, and that have to do with people who eat and cook and starve. The history of food and feeding is one that begs to be told. Past famines and past starvation still seek expression. But the future has already caught up with us. Finally, we've done it. It's as if history had been leveled: Past barbarism appears before us as a mirror image. We think we're looking back and instead we're remembering a future we already know. Progress, it would seem, has been left in the dust.

I am here as your guest, and so in conclusion I would like to express my gratitude by not overlooking you and your own domestic problems. Though we may be strangers, we all live at close quarters. And soon those quarters will become even more cramped.

From the European perspective, India is a land that resists being romanticized or suppressed as something "ungraspable and mysterious." Today people talk about the Indian trauma. India? Shockingly up-to-date. We know the growing population figures. Is it five hundred seventy or already six hundred million? We hear news of so-called unrest in the states of Bihar and Uttar Pradesh. Rough estimates vary in their multiple-digit numbers. We have young people who enthusiastically follow the Hare Krishna sect and seek nirvana. We can buy sumptuously illustrated books that tell us how beautiful India's culture is. Our newspapers, full of our own scandals, always have room for the less pressing stories about India's corruption. We've had enough, but we don't want to have a bad conscience about it. People say, casually or maliciously, Only Mao can help.

Is India's poverty unchangeable because it is fated, a matter of destiny or karma? I've been wondering about this, and pose the question to you. If it is, then I will go home with this bitter knowledge. But what if it isn't? What if Indian poverty, like all other poverty, is merely the result of class and caste power, of mismanagement and corruption? Then there should be a way to end it, this poverty, because that is humanity's work.

Translated by W. Martin

ASKESE   (1960)

Die Katze spricht.
Was spricht die Katze denn?
Du sollst mit einem spitzen Blei
die Bräute und den Schnee schattieren,
du sollst die graue Farbe lieben,
unter bewölktem Himmel sein.

Die Katze spricht.
Was spricht die Katze denn?
Du sollst dich mit dem Abendblatt,
in Sacktuch wie Kartoffeln kleiden
und diesen Anzug immer wieder wenden
und nie in neuem Anzug sein.

Die Katze spricht.
Was spricht die Katze denn?
Du solltest die Marine streichen,
die Kirschen, Mohn und Nasenbluten,
auch jene Fahne sollst du streichen
und Asche auf Geranien streun.

Du sollst, so spricht die Katze weiter,
nur noch von Nieren, Milz und Leber,
von atemloser saurer Lunge,
vom Seich der Nieren, ungewässert,
von alter Milz und zäher Leber,
aus grauem Topf: so sollst du leben.

(continued on p. 158)

ASKESIS

The cat speaks.
And what does the cat say?
Thou shalt draw with sharpened pencil
brides of shade and shade of snow,
thou shalt love the colour grey
and be beneath a cloudy sky.

The cat speaks.
And what does the cat say?
Thou shalt be clad in the evening paper,
clad in sackcloth like potatoes,
and thou shalt turn this suit year out year in,
and in a new suit never be.

The cat speaks.
And what does the cat say?
Thou shouldst scratch the navy out;
cherries, poppy, bloody nose
thou shalt scratch out, that flag as well,
and daub geraniums with ash.

Thou, the cat goes on to say,
Shalt live on kidneys, spleen and liver,
lung that's out of breath and sour,
on urine of unsoaked kidneys,
old spleen and tough liver
out of a grey pot: live on that.

(continued on p. 159)

Und an die Wand, wo früher pausenlos
das grüne Bild das Grüne wiederkäute,
sollst du mit deinem spitzen Blei
Askese schreiben, schreib: Askese.
So spricht die Katze: Schreib Askese.

And on the wall, where earlier without pause
the ruminant green picture chewed its green,
thou shalt write with thy sharp pencil
this: Askesis; write: Askesis.
That's what the cat says: write Askesis.

Translated by Christopher Middleton

But What Is My Stone?

from Headbirths or The Germans Are Dying Out (1980)

Albert Camus published his essay in 1942, in the middle of the war. I read *The Myth of Sisyphus* in the early fifties. But even before that, with no knowledge of the so-called absurd, stupid as the war left me, I was on intimate terms with all the questions of being, hence with existentialism. And later, when the concept of the absurd became personified for me, when (fed up with the Christian-Marxist muck about hope) I saw the cheery stone-roller as a man who encouraged us to roll stones in vain, to scoff at punishment and damnation—so then I found myself a stone and was happy with it. It gives me purpose. It is what it is. No God, no gods can take it away from me; unless they capitulate to Sisyphus and leave the stone on the mountaintop. That would be boring and not worth wishing for.

But what is my stone? The toil of piling words on words? The book that follows book that follows book? Or the German uphill task of securing a bit of freedom for stone-rollers (and suchlike absurd fools). Or love, with all its epileptic fits? Or the fight for justice, that boulder so hard to push upward and so ready to tumble?

All this makes my stone round and jagged. I see it tipping, in thoughts I anticipate its fall. It never disappoints me. It doesn't want to be freed from me nor I from it. It is human, in my measure. It is also my God, who without me does not exist. No heavenly Jerusalem can take its place, no earthly paradise make it useless. Therefore I scoff at any promise that my stone will reach the top and rest there once and for all. But I also laugh at the stone, which wants to make me the hero of its overandoveragain. "Look, stone," I say. "See how lightly I take you. You are so absurd and so used to me that you've become my trademark. Sisyphus is a good advertisement. You are a good traveling companion."

Translated by Ralph Manheim

DER STEIN   (1996)

den ich wälze, ist nicht mein Eigentum.
Auf Zeit und gegen Gebühr
verleiht ihn die Firma Sisyphos
in verschieden gewichtigem Format;
      und neuerdings gehören faltbare Steine,
          die bei Bedarf aufzublasen sind,
             günstig zum Angebot.

THE STONE

I roll does not belong to me.
Sisyphus Inc. rents it
in various sizes and weights
by the clock and for a fee.
    Lately, well-worn stones,
        which can be blown up if need be,
           are offered at reasonable prices.

Translated by Charles Simic

THE ARTIST'S FREEDOM OF OPINION
IN OUR SOCIETY

Address delivered on June 29, 1973, in Florence.

Ladies and Gentlemen:

The Council of Europe and its Commission for Culture and Education are holding a symposium devoted to the far-reaching topic of freedom of opinion and the situation of the artist in our society. I thank you for asking me to participate. Quite rightly, you will expect to hear my opinion; but, much as the topic you have selected appeals to me personally, I must also speak in the name of those artists in Greece, as well as Czechoslovakia, whose freedom of opinion is restricted to the dimensions of a prison cell, and whose cold skepticism I seem to feel when it becomes necessary to discuss generally known facts in the pleasant atmosphere of this conference.

Since the task that has been set me is primarily political, and since the artists of all European countries are placed willy-nilly in political contexts, I shall start by elucidating my own political position, which is not tied to any ideology.

After the Second World War, hence burdened with the guilt-ridden consequences of German political actions, I was forced, in the course of my work as a writer, to recognize that (if only marginally) the creative artist's supposed freedom is a fiction, that the artist not only sets his stamp on society and gives expression to his times, but is in equal measure a product of society and a child of the times—a spoiled child, a stepchild, an illegitimate child, or a ward of the state. I therefore took it for granted that along with my writing I would do the share of the political work that seemed to be incumbent on me as a citizen.

Artist and citizen? Isn't that a contradiction in terms? Is the anticivic role of the artist an ideological must? Or can a sociopolitical attitude, which declares the citizen to be an adult—and which is also my attitude—regard the artist as a being apart, to be tolerated and assigned a special preserve where he can disport himself like a nineteenth-century genius—lest the bourgeoisie be deprived of its thrills of terror?

Yes, I'm a writer and nevertheless a citizen. My political work has not been confined to the unrisky business of writing and signing resolutions. I have busied myself, often to the point of exhaustion, with the ups and downs of day-to-day politics. Smitten by no faith, inspired by no doctrine of salvation, I resolved after dispassionate study of the alternatives to support the Social Democratic Party. I decided in favor of the slow, parliamentary way, of the inalienable right to opposition, and acted on the knowledge that there is more than one truth and one reality, that several truths and realities, which are therefore relative, must compete with one another and tolerate one another.

Despite this liberal attitude, I became increasingly certain, in the years-long practice of my political sideline, that democratic socialism is the system most likely to win for mankind the increase in social justice and the legal guarantee of free and equal development, which have thus far been denied it by the prevailing systems of Western private capitalism and Eastern state capitalism. I have, further, become convinced that freedom in the arts is possible only where social and individual human rights are respected; wherever artists have to pay for relative freedom or a privileged status by rising above social conditions that tend to be latent abuses, they become an isolated elite, contenting themselves with the freedom of the playground. Their art, by befuddling or concealing, then becomes window dressing for a state of affairs that makes for servitude, and the artist becomes the whore of one power or another.

You have probably noticed that I, though favored with the privilege of speaking freely, have no intention of festooning the stereotype of the "free West" with decorative phrases. Conditions in Western Europe offer no justification for pointing an accusing finger at the artist's situation—the regimentation, the lack of freedom—in the Communist countries, while saying nothing of our own camp. Spain, Portugal, and Greece are governed by dictatorships. In those countries the torture of political adversaries is daily practice. But even in Western countries whose constitutions guarantee freedom of opinion, reality is at variance with the constitution. In France and Italy, television is controlled by the state; in the German Federal Republic, the Springer interests still dominate the newspaper market. In all European countries, moreover, economic power is able to influence the so-called independent press by according or withholding advertising. The concentration of capital and the monopoly status of the giant corporations are largely removed from democratic control, thus highlighting the impotence of freely elected parliaments.

The relative freedom or lack of freedom prevailing in democratically governed countries may be bearable, but it certainly does not justify self-righteous talk about Western freedom of opinion as opposed to the slavery prevailing in the East. For what is daily practice in the Eastern-bloc states, the regulation of art in accordance with party-line orthodoxy and the stupid subordination of the artist to the views of the bureaucracy, is at least a latent danger in the West. Moreover, as détente develops, the coexistence of ideologies and power structures will come about more quickly and with graver consequences in the economic field than in any other. In other words, Western private capitalism will start doing business with Communist state capitalism a lot more quickly than the issue of "free exchange of information" can be talked to death by working groups in Helsinki. For fear of endangering the big business of East-West trade, there will be a tendency to turn a blind eye in matters of "freedom of opinion." A Metternich sitting in all the deliberative bodies of the East and West may well try to promote an all-European order based on authoritarian states which, because periods of détente require peace and quiet, would tend to be police states.

The instrument of regulation is ready at hand. It is a demonstrable fact, and not without a certain comic interest, that when the word "humanism" is used and misused in the East and the West, ideological indoctrination becomes a way of divesting art and artists of the striving for diversity and the tendency to contradict. Regardless of whether it is the fundamental values of the Christian West or the pure doctrine of Communism that is once again in need of being defended against subversion, decadence, nihilism, etc., whether Solzhenitsyn is being punished in the Soviet Union or whether government grants to artists in France are subject to restrictive conditions—the word "humanism" is made to stand at attention and practice an intolerance that's as ugly as it is absurd.

Though "humus," "humane," and "humor" have the same root and hark back to life-giving moisture, the political application of humanism, that still-valid concept of the European Renaissance, demands that it be invoked whenever administrative humorlessness plants its dry-as-dust decrees in sandy soil. Not only the artists in the Eastern-bloc states, but we too in the West have reason to take fright or to raise protests seasoned with contempt when the word "humanism" is abused.

When George Orwell returned to England disillusioned from the Spanish Civil War, a good many writers, not to mention his publisher, ignored and boycotted him. The most infamous attacks on Aleksandr Solzhenitsyn were made by Soviet writers. The East German poet and singer Wolf Biermann is avoided like the plague by such opportunistic magnates of literature as Hermann Kant and Peter Hacks.* In his book *The New State and the Intellectuals,* Gottfried Benn proved once and for all that racism too can have a literary spokesman; and even the resentment of a Josef

---

*Establishment figures in the German Democratic Republic's Writers' Union, which expelled the satirical poet Biermann. —ED.

Goebbels against culture and intellectuals found its expression in articles that could not conceal the author's intellectual ability. Thanks to their intolerance, whole artistic movements, such as Italian futurism, were not only fellow travelers but actual pioneers of fascism.

In other words, popular as it is, the intellect-power antithesis doesn't hold water. Intellectuals have often been powerful enough to restrict freedom of opinion in the arts and to narrow it further in the realm of politics. And, on the other hand, democratic-minded politicians have often been obliged to impose tolerance on intolerantly warring artists and intellectuals, and to demand respect for freedom of opinion.

To enrich the confusion: the European Enlightenment, which in the eighteenth century gave birth to the ideas or concepts that still shape our lives—socialism, liberalism, and probably capitalism as well—also developed the notion of tolerance. And yet from the very start it demonstrated intolerance in clashes between its ideas. Anyone who is prepared to accept Michel de Montaigne as the father of the European Enlightenment may be amused to note how absurdly his descendants have reviled him as a reactionary or whipped him into line as an apostle of progress. Yet it cannot be denied that tolerance and intolerance, those twin scions of the early European Enlightenment, have been at war ever since—always in the jargon of the Enlightenment, sometimes with murderous outcome. Whether during the French Revolution the guillotine was made to serve progress and revolutionary virtue, or in the Soviet Union today undesirable artists and scientists are shut up in psychiatric hospitals, it has always been the language of the Enlightenment, with its appeal to freedom, that has cut back the human rights which are needed every day of our lives and, with a view to the perfect justice of the future, sown and perpetuated injustice.

I say all this without malice, just by way of dispelling illusions. For nowhere is it written that artists—or intellectuals, for that matter—are better, let alone more tolerant, than other citizens, endowed only with practical gifts.

To argue from another direction: even if accounts in the illustrated magazines show that Picasso was a wretched, hard-hearted father, his portraits of children lose none of their expressiveness; whereas the bank clerk Meier's (or Dupont's) wretched taste in art need not detract from his pedagogic tolerance—or, in old-fashioned terms, from his warmhearted treatment of his children.

One need only read the pamphlets, or the exhibition catalogues and their prefaces, that transpose the quarrels between artistic trends into ideological gobbledygook, and compare them with the indoctrination pamphlets of parties claiming the exclusive right to rule, or the tracts of churches claiming exclusive possession of the truth. Though intolerance may not have its Esperanto, it has certainly developed its characteristic style.

To come out for freedom of opinion—and that's what I'm doing here—is to plead for diversity, to protect the desperately blasphemous outburst, to tolerate the kitsch that blooms everlastingly, to grant admittance at all times to subversive doubt, even where faith has established an entrenched society, to live with the contradictions characteristic of man and human society.

Since I'm not addressing some vaguely benevolent academy, but representatives of the Council of Europe, West European parliamentarians who bear political responsibility,

I hope my plea for freedom of opinion won't just make you nod your heads; in some cases your opposition might be preferable. And because I'm not speaking to artists about the arts and their freedom—that is, confining myself to the intolerance of artists toward one another—I must now speak of political power and its abuse, a subject so vast that for fear of losing myself I shall concentrate on conditions in one West European and one East European country.

I am referring to the suppression of freedom of opinion under the Greek military dictatorship* and to the neo-Stalinist repression in Czechoslovakia following the intervention of the five Warsaw Pact powers.

You are aware that in Greece, as in Czechoslovakia, numerous artists, writers, journalists, and intellectuals have been imprisoned, along with many other citizens; that in Czechoslovakia they have been subjected to the vilest methods of interrogation and in Greece to torture. You are aware that in Czechoslovakia hundreds of artists and intellectuals are struggling to live without jobs or incomes. You have undoubtedly heard of the humiliating pressure put upon the students of Salonika and Athens. The methods of Stalinist and fascist terror are interchangeable; no ideological objective, no pragmatic motive—on the part of NATO or the Warsaw Pact, not to mention private-capitalist or state-capitalist big business—can justify their daily crimes. In Greece and Czechoslovakia the most repugnant aspects of the two bloc systems are revealed for all to see.

I'm not interested in rehashing familiar facts or in formulating cheap rhetorical pleas for freedom in Greece and

*Greece was ruled by the military from 1967 to 1974. —ED.

Czechoslovakia. I wish only to entreat you to give a thought, in the Council of Europe but also at the Helsinki Conference, to the conditions prevailing in Greece and Czechoslovakia, and to use your political clout in an effort to remedy them.

The eruption of neo-Stalinism in Czechoslovakia has brought shame on the Eastern bloc, and the perpetuation of the military dictatorship in Greece involves the responsibility of Western Europe. The number of political prisoners in both blocs is incalculable. The security requirements of neither bloc can justify a relapse into Stalinist and fascist barbarism. Tolerance must not become a cynical exercise in which, for reasons of immediate interest, each ideological bloc tolerates the injustice in the other's camp and, since birds of a feather tend to be nice to one another, may go so far as to laud such tolerance as a triumph of détente. Injustice and the absence of freedom in the Eastern-bloc countries do not excuse the attitude of the Western democracies toward the Greek dictatorship.

Until you loudly and repeatedly—at home as parliamentarians and here in the Council of Europe—demand the restoration of democracy in Greece, Western Europe will only be partly justified in singing a democratic tune in Helsinki.

The man addressing you is someone who has always condemned the Cold War, its friend-and-foe ideology and its military consequences, and who has actively supported the policy of détente.

This policy has been pursued in spite of resistance, thus far successfully. It is based on treaties. Bastions that were manned only yesterday are today overgrown with weeds because they have become useless. Both blocs have thrown off ideological ballast. They are still distrustful of the new experiment. Insecure, because bereft of the enemy image, the two blocs confront each other armed to the teeth; they are constrained to coo détente, when they would prefer to rattle their sabers. So they shut their eyes to antagonisms. They look for the common denominator, for shared interests; they come to an understanding about mutual difficulties and start forming a united front against all those who take a skeptical, critical attitude toward the new consensus, which, because it is superficial, has a leveling effect in practice. For instance: the hard-boiled pragmatists and technocrats of both ideologically opposed technocracies note to their amazement that in both systems the exalted principle of all-out achievement is no longer held sacred, but is being systematically questioned, first and foremost by the younger generation—either coyly because of surfeit, or on the basis of political foresight, or on ethical grounds.

Defying the catechism of private as well as state capitalism, a generation that has grown to adulthood in peacetime is daring to question the doctrine of all-out achievement. Today we are beginning to hear from a generation which, as is often the case with younger generations, has not achieved anything and for that reason is shamelessly innocent. So much innocence is upsetting. Concerned and feeling persecuted, capitalist and Communist fathers are beginning to join forces. There is reason to fear that the very pillars of the state in both blocs, who only yesterday carried their mutual hatred to excess, are now agreed that the primary task of a détente policy must be to uphold the achievement principle, by drastic means if necessary.

A second example of a possible perversion of détente resulting from an alliance of the basically authoritarian and intolerant elements is as follows. In both blocs there are artists and intellectuals who in the fifties and sixties were persecuted in accordance with divergent ideological principles, for refusing to participate in the Cold War and advocating peaceful coexistence. But now that these pioneers think they have done their bit and gained for artists the right to meet freely and to exchange information and experience (after all, the Cold War is over; irreconcilable enemies have been metamorphosed into respected opponents) —now, I say, that private capitalists and Communist state capitalists are hobnobbing and concluding business deals, there are sobering indications that détente will take on a primarily big-business character, which will cast its shadow on cultural policy.

When—the foreign offices of the two blocs ask, with much head-shaking and not without a menacing undertone—when will these Solzhenitsyns and Bölls finally realize that the vital interests of the two détente-seeking blocs are exclusively economic, and that it's futile and harmful to détente to keep harping on the unavoidable consequences of normalization in Czechoslovakia and on military dictatorship in Greece, which must be tolerated for security reasons?

It is undemocratic, we are assured, to disregard the need of the working population in both blocs for job security, for increased exchange of consumer goods, for law and order, or, worse, to sacrifice all this to the needs of a hysterical minority, who still believe that freedom of opinion is the beginning and end of all things and knows no frontiers.

Have I exaggerated? I don't believe so; if anything, I have not gone far enough. My aim has been to keep the wounds of Prague and Athens open. You statesmen have it in your power to dispel the fears I have expressed.

Thank you for your attention.

Translated by Ralph Manheim

THE LAST MEAL

from THE FLOUNDER (1977)

FIRST BUILT IN 1346 AS A BASTION TO THE HIGH GATE
and subsequently enlarged as the need for prison cells, tor-
ture chambers, and business premises increased, the Stock-
turm, whose dungeon keeps were reputed to be dry, was
rebuilt in 1509, when city architects Hetzel and Enkinger
added two stories and capped the tower. Thereafter it stood
empty and unused until King Sigismund of Poland, re-
sponding in April 1526 to the call of Mayor Eberhard Fer-
ber, occupied the city, posted Counter-Reformation statutes
in the seven principal churches, and haled all the leaders of
the uprising against the patrician council, except for the
fugitive preacher Hegge, before a court of aldermen, which
sentenced the six ringleaders to death by beheading, in-
cluding the blacksmith Peter Rusch, whose daughter had
recently been appointed abbess of Saint Bridget's—an im-
posing woman of controversial reputation who flattered the
taste of all parties with her conventual cookery, took her cut

on every transaction, and even in times of general ruin (war, plague, and famine) made a profit.

And because Mother Rusch was not without influence, she was able to obtain, if not her father's pardon, at least the right to cook one last meal for him. Highly placed persons accepted her invitation. Mayor Ferber, deposed and banished to his starosty in Dirschau by the rebellious guilds but now restored to office, and Abbot Jeschke of the Oliva Monastery repaired to the Stockturm in fur-trimmed brabant, quite willing to join blacksmith Rusch in spooning up his favorite dish. Executioner Ladewig was also invited, and came. The cooking abbess had put her full kettle on the hearth the night before in the kitchen of the executioner (and knacker), and the smell penetrated to every last dungeon of the now fully occupied Stockturm.

WHO WILL JOIN me in a dish of tripe? It soothes, appeases the anger of the outraged, stills the fear of death, and reminds us of tripe eaten in former days, when there was always a half-filled pot of it on the stove. A chunk of the fat paunch and the limp, honeycombed walls of the second stomach—four pounds for three fifty. It's the widespread distaste for innards that makes beef heart and pork kidneys, calf's lung and tripe cheap.

She took her time. She pounded the pieces and brushed them inside and out, as though some beggar's sweaty rags had found their way to her washboard. She removed the wrinkled skin, but she spared the belly fat, for tripe fat has a special quality—instead of hardening into tallow, it dissolves like soap.

When a last meal was prepared for blacksmith Rusch and his guests, seven quarts of water seasoned with salt, caraway seed, cloves, ginger root, bay leaf, and coarsely pounded peppercorns were set over an open fire. The limp pieces, cut into finger-long strips, were added until the pot was full, and when the water came to a boil the scum was skimmed off. Then the daughter covered her father's favorite dish and let it boil for four hours. At the end she added garlic, freshly grated nutmeg, and more pepper.

The time it takes. Those are the best hours. When the tough has to be made tender, but can't be hurried. How often Mother Rusch and I, while the billowing tripe kept the kitchen stable-warm, sat at the table pushing checkers over the board, discovering the sea route to India, or catching flies on the smooth-polished table top, and telling each other about the tripe of olden times, when we were Pomorshian and still heathen. And about older than olden times, when elk cows were the only source of meat.

Later on, after the daughter had cooked her father's last dish of tripe, she cooked for rich coopers at guild banquets, for Hanseatic merchants who cared about nothing but Öresund tolls, for fat abbots and King Stephen Batory, who wanted his tripe sour and Polish. Still later Amanda Woyke, in her farm kitchen, cooked up tripe with turnips and potatoes into a soup that she seasoned with lovage. And still later Lena Stubbe taught the patrons of the Danzig-Ohra soup kitchen to enjoy proletarian cabbage soups made with (cut-rate) tripe. And to this very day Maria Kuczorra, canteen cook at the Lenin Shipyard in Gdańsk, makes a thick soup once a week out of *kaldauny* (tripe).

When you are feeling cold inside — try the walls of the cow's second stomach. When you are sad, cast out by all nature, sad unto death, try tripe, which cheers us and gives meaning to life. Or in the company of witty friends, godless enough to sit in the seat of the scornful, spoon up caraway-seasoned tripe out of deep dishes. Or cooked with tomatoes, Andalusian-style with chickpeas, or à la Portugaise with kidney beans and bacon. Or if love needs an appetizer, precook tripe in white wine, then steam it with diced celery root. On cold, dry days, when the east wind is banging at the windowpanes and driving your Ilsebill up the wall, tripe thickened with sour cream and served with potatoes in their jackets will help. Or if we must part, briefly or forever, like the time I was a prisoner in the Stockturm and my daughter served me a last meal of peppered tripe.

BECAUSE THE execution was to take place next day in the Long Market, in the presence of the king of Poland, of the seated and standing councils, of the aldermen and various prelates and abbots, the abbess of Saint Bridget's had invited the guests to her father's dungeon for an early evening meal. Torches on the walls provided light. A basin of coals under the barred window hole kept the pot of tripe warm. Margarete Rusch tasted for seasoning, and after that she didn't touch another mouthful. She said grace, appending a prayer for the condemned blacksmith, then served her father and his guests. But while the men were spooning up their tripe out of earthenware bowls, and while she was pouring black beer into mugs, she spoke. She spoke and her words passed over the autocratic head of the patrician, over the sleek, round head of the abbot, over the bald pate of the executioner, and over her father's head, which he had lowered into his bowl. She spoke without paragraphs or punctuation of any kind.

Margarete Rusch was known for that. When the soup was too hot, while the men were gnawing at goose drumsticks, before fish was served on Friday (mackerel bedded on leeks), but also over tables eaten bare, the abbess spoke to all those she cooked for, with a broad accent that brooked no interruption. She could reel off several stories (or instructive disquisitions) at once without dropping a thread. From sheep raising on the Island, from the sewage sludge in the Mottlau, she would ramble on to Councilor Angermünde's daughters, but without failing to bring in price increases that the Danes had clapped on Scania herring, to get the latest joke about Preacher Hegge off her chest, to mention the continued interest of the Brigittine nuns in certain Old City real estate; yet with it all she found breath to spin out her favorite topic—larded with pious invocations of all the archangels from Ariel to Zedekiel—namely, the necessity of establishing a pepper depot in Lisbon (with a warehouse on the Malabar Coast of India), spinning out every detail of the commercial law involved.

Regardless of whom she cooked for, her table talk was thrown in—a subliminal mumbling with subplots as intricate as the politics of her time. She spoke as if to herself, but loud enough for the bishop of Leslau, who was dipping his bread into Margarete's hasenpfeffer, or for Councilors Angermünde and Feldstadt, who were shoveling in her beef hock with millet, to detect the purpose behind her chatter, although it was never certain whether Mother Rusch favored the patrician council or the lower trades, whether she was agitating for the Hanseatic League and against the Polish crown, and whether or not she was outwardly Catholic but contaminated through and through with Lutheranism. And yet her table speeches captured all ears with their ambiguities. They put this one in the right, injected that one with doubt, supplied tactical pointers, and in the long run brought benefit only to the Abbey of Saint Bridget, which obtained profitable fishing rights (Lake Ottomin), indentured leases (the Scharpau, the sheep farms of Schiedlitz and Praust), and property in the Old City (on the Rähm, in Peppertown), and an episcopal letter safeguarding the abbey against Dominican snooping.

And so, when the abbess Margarete Rusch served up the last dish of tripe to her father and his guests, her tongue wagged as usual. That was her way. Always, along with her cookery, she apportioned her subtly balanced interests.

AT FIRST THE MEN at the table sat silent. The only sound was the jangling of Peter Rusch's irons, for the blacksmith ate in fetters. And outside the barred window hole, the tower pigeons clamored. Guzzling and gulping. The executioner's Adam's apple bobbed up and down.

Yet it was not at all certain that the king of Poland had intended so harsh a sentence. Jeschke and Ferber had worked on the judge and on the aldermen. Ferber, who spoke first, admitted as much; law and order, he said, must be manifested visibly. True, the abbot conceded, the blacksmith might have been spared (and merely blinded) if Hegge, that minion of Luther, had not escaped. He had a pretty good idea, said the wealthy Ferber, bending over his tripe in his fur-trimmed broadcloth, who had helped Hegge escape from the blocked-off city. That, said the abbot, all the while plying his spoon, was known to all, though no one could prove it. Executioner Ladewig gave assurance that the scrawny neck of the escaped Dominican would have been far more welcome to him in the morning than that of a blacksmith. When Peter Rusch lifted his head out of the bowl and said, more in resignation than in protest, that he, too, was not unaware who had helped Preacher Hegge, spiritual head of the burghers' uprising, to escape from the beadles of the patrician order, Ferber said harshly, while holding out his bowl to the abbess to refill, "Then you also know whom you can thank for your death sentence." "Yes, indeed," said Jeschke. "Things have come to a pretty pass when a father can expect no mercy from his child. That's what happens when the pulpit is opened up to heresy." Here he threw in a bit of information, namely, that Hegge had apparently escaped to Greifswald and was going right on with his preaching.

Then Mother Rusch laughed so resoundingly, with every ounce of her flesh, that the walls expanded, and, pouring black beer, said casually: Yes, yes, she supposed all these insinuations were aimed at her. And maybe there was some truth in them. For one night in April, after it had pleased His Polish Majesty to occupy the city, she had seen a man in a woman's skirts clinging to the town wall, in a place where it's low, not far from Jacob's Gate. Trying to climb over it, but he didn't have the strength. His misery had cried out for help, and she had helped. She had reached under his skirts, and when all her pushing and puffing had gone for nothing, had bitten off his left or right testicle. After that he had literally flown over the wall. Maybe the man had been Peter Hegge. But how could one be sure? Because, in her fright, she, Margarete Rusch, had swallowed this left or right ball. To tell the truth, she had been feeling pregnant ever since — this was the third month. But by whom? That was the question. If he was so inclined, Ferber could go to Greifswald, taking Jeschke with him, and they could reach between the still-eloquent Hegge's legs. Then they'd know more.

At that blacksmith Rusch and the bald-headed Ladewig laughed. Then, apart from the chains, nothing could be heard but the spoons in the bowls, the sound of chewing and swallowing, and the pigeons in the window hole. And when she saw the men so deeply immersed in their tripe, Mother Rusch started in again with her ambiguous mumbling; for the abbess spoke freely and frankly only in the refectory of Saint Bridget's, where at vespers and in the evening hours the nuns and novices forgathered around the long oak table.

IN TROUBLED TIMES—everywhere monks and nuns were escaping from their cloisters to risk the perils of secular life—it was often difficult to hold pious girls to their vows. They fidgeted, they wanted out, they wanted a man in breeches, wanted to be married, to bear children by the dozen, to walk in silk and satin and try to keep up with the town fashions.

And so, while the sweet millet porridge diminished on the long table, the abbess told her little nuns, whose asses were itching for life, what life is and how quickly it crumbles away. She listed the freedoms of the nunnery and, in the debit column, the arduous duties of the married woman. While buckwheat piroshki filled with bacon and spinach were being enjoyed on both sides of the long table, the abbess explained the male build to her man-crazy women with the help of the vegetable course, buttered (and parsleyed) carrots, which with their varied shapes provided a graphic illustration of what a man is good for. How deeply penetrating he can be and how knobby. How soon he gives out and starts drooping pathetically. How brutal he becomes when he can't get it up. How unprofitable this quick fucking is to women. How all he wants is children, especially sons. How soon he looks for variety in other beds. But how his spouse must never wander, never lust for other carrots. How hard his hand strikes. How suddenly he withdraws his favor and gets his carrot cooked soft away from home.

But when the nuns, and especially the novices, kept squirming on their stools and persisted in seeing harder and more lasting promise in their buttered carrots, the abbess gave them permission to receive visitors through the back door of the convent, and also to range freely outside the cloister, thus acquainting them with the pleasures of the flesh and making them better able to resist the seductions of married life.

Before saying grace and dismissing her charges, the abbess gave them further bits of advice: Let no quarrel over a codpiece ever disturb their monastic tranquillity. Let them always remain good sisters to one another. Let them not content themselves with holding still, but ride with and against. A man's thanks should always be weighable in silver. And never, never, never, must they succumb to weepy, gushy love.

THOUGH NOT yet thirty, Mother Rusch had been abbess of Saint Bridget's for over a year, having, as nun in charge of the kitchen, shown accomplishments of many kinds. And the accomplished abbess succeeded in holding her nuns, whereas the monks and nuns of the Dominican, Beguin,

Franciscan, and Benedictine orders were running away to Luther. The consequence was unrest, uprisings of the guilds, iconoclast riots, alarums, and excursions, followed by little change or at the most by Royal Polish punitive expeditions. Preacher Hegge, to be sure, had managed to escape, but blacksmith Rusch and five other artisans, all poor devils, members of the lower trades, were condemned to death. And that is why a daughter served her father his last dish of tripe, which, since beginning to feel pregnant—most likely the work of Hegge shortly before his flight—she had taken to peppering excessively.

And after she had filled her guests' bowls for the third time, pepper kept cropping up in her talk.

THAT WAS her obsession. Fat Gret had a thing about pepper. It sharpened her wit, she thought, it did wonders. It tormented her to think that all the new sea-borne pepper—the overland pepper that traders had been bringing in from Venice as long as anyone could remember was so fearfully expensive—passed through Lisbon. True, the Augsburgers maintained a depot there, where they hoarded pepper to keep the price up, but the Hanseatic towns let the trade slip through their fingers. Which explains why for some years Mother Rusch was impelled, by political ambition as well as the normal concerns of the kitchen, to take a hand in international politics. Much as she hated the patrician Ferber, she was determined to harness the experienced merchant and still actively seafaring admiral to her plans.

After dishing out a third helping of tripe for her father and his guests, she let her table talk drift overseas. It wouldn't do to leave the New World to the Portuguese and

Spaniards. The Dutch and English were already coming in on a large scale. The only bankers engaged in the pepper trade were the Fuggers. But the Hanseatic League was shortsightedly confining its operations to the lesser seas, squabbling to no effect (as it had done only last year) with the Danes over Öresund tolls and herring silver, spitefully competing with one another (witness Lübeck and Danzig), sticking to wood, cloth, grain, dried codfish, and salt, refusing to take over the pepper trade, and neglecting to fit out ships for the longer voyage, too small-minded to establish a trading post on the pepper coast of India, as the Portuguese had done in Goa and Cochin, and preferring to engage in divisive religious quarrels and chop off the heads of good men like her father.

She went on to discuss the principal pepper varieties most knowledgeably, their moist and dry weight, how stored and marketed; undertook, if an overseas expedition should be organized, to lure certain Arab helmsmen away from the Portuguese caravels; predicted spice wars between Spain and England; and even professed her eagerness—provided Jeschke would come along—to embark her own full weight on a vessel bound for India, there to propagate the Catholic faith, if only Ferber would consent to throw off his weariness, stop toadying to the Polish court, and at last start commissioning navigation charts.

But Ferber remained indifferent over his tripe. Jeschke only sighed: pleasing as such a mission would be to God, he feared the Indian climate. Blacksmith Rusch said nothing. Executioner Ladewig had other dreams. And when the patrician leaned back, after spooning up the last bowl of tripe, his answering speech was uncompromising.

He knew the world. He was a humanist and spoke five languages. Everywhere things were the same as in the Baltic area. Trading posts and warehouses in distant places could never be maintained for long; great losses were a certainty. Novgorod was giving them trouble enough. Falsterbo cost more than it brought in. Goa! It would cost the Portuguese dearly one of these days. As for the English, they seemed to have no inkling of what a burden India might well become to them. Trading posts in India. Ridiculous. Now, after last year's futile war, did we want to pay the Danes pepper fees along with their herring silver? Hamburg in a pinch could afford such an undertaking. To maintain colonies you need an open coast. Danzig's motto remained: Moderation in all things. No, he had no use for adventures. And speaking of his weariness: despite the ingratitude of the local rabble, he had earned the right to rest. Immediately after the morrow's execution, he would divest himself of his chain of office and retire to his starosty for a quiet old age. Yes indeed! He would collect paintings from Antwerp. Musicians would play the lute for him and sing Italian songs. If the abbess wished, she could follow him to Dirschau, but not—by God! —to India. What was to keep him from financing a branch of the pious Brigittines in Dirschau? There'd always be plenty of pepper for her kitchen.

Thereupon Mother Rusch, for the fourth time, filled first her father's bowl, then the bowls of the guests with tripe. Even as she wielded the ladle, she cursed men for hopeless stay-at-homes. Then she fell silent, and the executioner spoke his mind. Ladewig complained about the wretchedness of his job. Luckily horse flaying brought in a little extra money. They wouldn't pay him to kill stray dogs. And the city was drowning in shit and piss.

Ladewig, whose meticulous, unhurried methods in the torture chamber allowed of no premature confessions, outlined an exemplary system of sanitation for the walled city, but only the blacksmith was listening. Here again Ferber was shortsighted, or he might have commissioned the executioner to keep the city clean, catch ownerless dogs, take measures against the plague, and, for suitable fees, clean out the sludge boxes of all premises adjoining the Mottlau (thereby anticipating the "Newly Revised Ordinance" of 1761 by a good two centuries).

Sensibly as Ladewig spoke and hard as he tried to win the patrician's approval, Ferber's mind, as he spooned up tripe, was already on his retirement in Dirschau. Still deeply immersed in his tripe, Abbot Jeschke dreamed himself and his benefices into a perfect world, undarkened by heresy. But though reacting with resolute silence to the cleansing of the city, Mother Rusch would not desist from Indian pepper. And because she was pregnant, her hope grew and grew.

IT WILL BE a girl! And a girl it was. She was named Hedwig, brought up by Fat Gret's aunts in the Wicker Bastion, and seventeen years later married the merchant Rodrigues d'Evora, a Ximines of the big Portuguese spice-trading family, who opened a trading post in Cochin on the Malabar Coast of India. Twice a year, for the feasts of Saint John and Saint Martin, the son-in-law honored the marriage contract (for Hedwig's body was beautiful, in a Baltic sort of way) by sending a keg of ginger, two bales of cinnamon, a ship's pound of saffron, two crates of bitter orange peel, a sack of almonds, a sack of grated coconut, specified amounts of cardamom, cloves, and nutmeg, five barrels containing Mother Rusch's weight (at the time of the marriage contract) in black and white pepper, and one barrel of moist green pepper.

After merchant d'Evora, his wife, and four of his daughters died of the fever in Cochin, the one surviving daughter, who later married the Spanish pepper magnate Pedro de Malvenda, is believed to have kept up the pepper shipments to Mother Rusch as long as she lived. Isabel de Malvenda lived in Burgos, then in Antwerp, from where, after her husband's death, she corresponded with Martin Enzesperger, the Fuggers' pepper agent, and established her contractors as far afield as Venice.

By then London and Antwerp had taken a hand in the trade. Hamburg, which like all the Hanseatic towns was hostile to anything foreign, maintained a pepper trading post for only a few years. Several spice wars contributed dates to history, and in one of them Spain lost its Armada.

EVEN WHEN the bowls were empty for the fourth time, the blacksmith and his guests had not yet spooned up sufficient peppered and caraway-seeded tripe. Accordingly Mother Rusch ladled fifth helpings out of her deep kettle and poured black beer into mugs. She also went on mumbling her table talk: hints smothered in local gossip, threats stirred into her usual nunnish chatter. But if patrician Ferber and Abbot Jeschke had not been too stuffed to listen, they might have had something to think about, for Mother Rusch quite transparently detailed her plans for settling accounts with both of them. Which plans she also carried out, for three years later she smothered the rich Eberhard Ferber in bed under her double hundredweight; and fifty years later—for Fat Gret lived to a ripe old age for her vengeance—she fattened Abbot Jeschke to death: he died over a bowl of tripe.

Blacksmith Rusch may have gathered the gist of his daughter's projects from her table talk and understood how she meant to avenge his death, for the poor devil grinned broadly over his empty bowl. Indeed, something more than the warm feeling of having filled his belly one last time may have accounted for his satisfaction. He sang his daughter's praises, and there his talk became rather confused, for he brought in a fish, whom he referred to as the "Flounder in the sea," and thanked him for having advised him, at a time when his hair was still brown, to send his youngest daughter, whose mother was dying of the fever, to a convent, for there, so the Flounder had assured him, she would become shrewd and crafty, so as to manage her female flesh independently and have hot soup in daily readiness for her father in his old age.

Then he, too, fell silent, replete with tripe. After that, belches were accompanied only by an occasional word or half sentence. Ferber dreamed of his life in the country; far from all strife, he would live in the midst of his art collection, culling wisdom from books. After eating so much tripe, Abbot Jeschke could think only of the tripe he hoped to spoon up in the future, peppered just the way the abbess did it. But by then Lutheranism would—by drastic measures if necessary—have been eradicated from the world. Executioner Ladewig anticipated several articles of the "Newly Revised Ordinance." He would have liked to place with the local coopers an order for the barrels needed to clean up the city. For every barrel emptied he would charge only ten groschen. Blacksmith Rusch, on the other hand, predicted that the patrician council would be faced forever and ever with unrest and insurrectionary demands on the part of the guilds and lower trades, and his prophecy came true in December 1970. The lower orders have never ceased to rebel against patrician authoritarianism and to risk their necks for a little more civil rights.

THEN, FULL FED, the guests left. Ferber said nothing. Jeschke delivered himself of a Latin blessing. Ladewig took the five emptied bowls with him. The pigeons in the window hole were silent. The torches had almost burned down in their holders. Peter Rusch sat in his chains and shed a few tears for his last supper. Laden right and left with the kettle and the empty beer keg, his daughter resumed her mumbling on her way out: "You'll soon be out of your misery now. You'll soon be a lot better off. They'll give you a nice cozy place in the heavenly guildhall. And you'll always have plenty of tripe. So stop worrying. Your Gret will settle up with them. It may take time, but I'll fix them good."

Then Mother Rusch admonished her father to hold his curly gray head erect the next day and not to fling curses at anyone whomsoever. He should kneel unbowed before the executioner. He could rely on her vengeance. The taste of it would linger in her mouth like Indian pepper. She wouldn't forget. No, she wouldn't forget.

Peter Rusch did as his daughter had bidden. He must have had a goodly portion of tripe half digested in his innards when, next day in the Long Market, facing the Artushof, where the patricians and prelates stood as though painted around Sigismund, king of Poland, he (fourth of the six candidates) silently let his head be severed from his shoulders. No bungling. You could count on executioner Ladewig. The abbess looked on. A sudden shower of rain made her face glisten. And addressing the Women's Tribunal, the Flounder said, "In short, dear ladies, vigorously as Margarete Rusch pursued her aims, perseveringly as she raked in her gains, slow as she was in settling her account—on June 26, 1526, when blacksmith Peter Rusch was executed along with the other ringleaders, a daughter wept for her father."

Translated by Ralph Manheim

LITERATURE AND MYTH

Address delivered in June 1981, at a writers' conference in Lahti, Finland.

ASKED TO SPEAK ON THE TOPIC OF LITERATURE AND myth, I find myself a bit embarrassed, because the subject really presumes a literary critic's certainty and faith in concepts. A presumption I'd much rather decline: I am not certain, and prevalent concepts serve best as coffin lids. Also, my experiences with the vocabulary of myth, mythos, and the mythic have made me mistrustful, since we in Germany still bear the consequences of a politics that tried to create a new mythos and ended up with Auschwitz.

These experiences with irrationalism and its actual excretions, which remain with us today, have made us greater adherents of reason than "we can bear," to use a common phrase. The cost of every miracle has been accounted for. We've divvied up and parceled out to the point of chaos. The darknesses have all been illuminated with the lanterns of statistical method. We've helped ourselves to reason as if it were an antitoxin. We've sniffed, inhaled, and injected each other with reason to make ourselves immune to recent enticements in which the words *mythos, myths,* and *mythic* have flickered inside the fuzzy collective concept "irrationalism."

The result is already clear. An ever-narrower concept of reason, increasingly immune to challenge, has created, under cover of rationalistic language, a kind of homemade irrationalism that reaches its peak in the myth of progress. Which is why even the underbrush of this new, reason-saturated irrationalism is seeded with all manner of myths originating in this or that ideological greenhouse. As a result, success (with its myths of superachievement) has become the overriding idea shared by supposedly classless and presumably pluralistic societies.

Even Reason is tired of going about in sackcloth and ashes. Ever since she was deified, long before the French Revolution, as the alpha and omega of European Enlightenment, and set up in the course of the Revolution in her own temples and shrines, Reason has become as much a myth as has our notion of progress: Reason transcends. And now, because she can't bear her saturnine condition any longer, she gazes forlornly and asks for pills to make her happy.

The antitheses have been nullified. Two sides that one thought had been cleanly and unimpeachably distinguished in terms of ideology—illuminating, enlightening reason on one side, its pace matched to that of progress, and on the other side unreason, condemned as irrationalism—have proven to be hopelessly intertwined. Modern shamans no longer capable of acting on our own, we lurch and speculate and give ourselves over to computers. Fairy tales are still good for a truth or two, while the so reasonably articulated material conditions of our day cheat us out of knowing anything. Technically precise — that is to say, unambiguous and purged of any dubious mystery — the apocalypse has been programmed for us in advance.

Whether John's Revelation on Patmos was written down under the influence of delirium or with the diligence of a writer always searching for the most precise, the perfect, word, this ambiguous work of literature, overgrown with mysteries as it is and fraught with the number seven in numerous playful configurations (seven lights, seven angels, seven trumpets), has repeatedly inspired not just theological hairsplitting but also new and creative interpretations. (I'm reminded of Albrecht Dürer's series of woodcuts, in which the literalness of John's Revelation is illustrated to the minutest detail.) And yet this showpiece of literary illumination and darkening, this seven-times-sealed myth of apocalypse, promises today to get cashed in flat out. Bring on your Seventh Seal! Mankind, that is, technology, is what's behind it. We can unseal anything. Nothing is hidden from us. We will not tolerate any missing information.

If a present-day John, a writer, say, were to set his revelation down on paper, it would come out as some doom-and-gloom dime novel, a trivial science-fiction brew. We can imagine John as Stanislaw Lem. He'd put a sarcastic or ironic spin on both old-fashioned and new-fashioned myths. He'd let his Professor Donda get to the Donda Barrier, the limit of knowledge increase beyond which any civilization that endeavors to know everything, to break every seal, including the seventh — any civilization that has absolute knowledge for its objective — necessarily proves science's total ignorance, neutralizes itself, and falls into nothingness. And this nothingness, this emptiness—yet another myth! — makes room for literature's reverberating laughter.

Actually we should be glad that divine Reason has started to display the leaks in her roof, damage as obvious as it is irreparable. Now she no longer holds us so strictly to our promises. With regard to her categorical imperatives, she's become a bit of a clown, jumping like Candide from one frying pan to the next and allowing us, too, finally, a few leaps and insinuations. She practically begs to have her shabby gray academic gown, worn-out as it is, patched up, to have her trembling scantiness enriched.

Isn't literature, the Enlightenment's wayward child, especially suited to invoking the beginnings of our modernity— Montaigne and his essays—and to freeing Reason of both its puritanical confines and grouchy dogmatism? Couldn't writers impart to Reason the actually quite rational insight that fairy tales, myths, and sagas are not products of another reality outside of our own, inhabiting the peripheries and calling up reactionary eclipses, but are part of our reality, and have retained enough force to represent us more clearly —in spite of their exaggerations—than Reason, which has become increasingly reticent and now murmurs only in jargon, is able to?

After the end of the Second World War, when I, an ignorant young man with a boundless curiosity, had like many of my generation embraced the fashion for existentialism, I read Camus' *Myth of Sisyphus* for the first time, not understanding exactly why it fascinated me. Today, buffeted by my experiences and circumscribed by the futility of heaving political stones, I feel, once again, close to Camus, to the tale of that impetuous stone pushed over and over up the mountain, always refusing to stay put; to the heroic absurdity of Sisyphus, faced with the gods' mockery and a stone he could only say yes to. It is a daily occurrence. This image of a man cheerfully pushing stones is not only a more complex but a more sensuous image of human existence than our contemporary desert of information or even our overproduced sociology could ever provide.

Perhaps it is the archaic severity of our myths, and their complexity, both concentrated and made simple, that always stops us in our tracks and makes us—in spite of our temptation to split apart into countless statistical particularities—coherent again and recognizable to ourselves. That is the way we recognize ourselves in fairy tales, too, and, since time immemorial, have seen ourselves preserved in myths. We are Echo and Narcissus. Three wishes have been granted to us. Bread and wine mean more than eating and drinking. We seek the Fountain of Youth promised us by television commercials. Every Goliath has his David. Our everyman's dream: finally to catch the fish that can talk to him.

It should be clear from these examples, which I cannot elaborate upon here, that my own work, at least, would be unthinkable without the style-shaping power of fairy tales. It permits insight into a broader reality, one that enlarges human existence. That is my understanding of fairy tales and myths: as part of, or rather, as the false floor of, our reality. The not merely childish, human wish to be able to fly, to remain small, to be invisible, even to be able to work good or evil at a distance through the power of will or by speaking a command aloud, and the desire to stop time, to travel backward or forward to any moment of what we take to be the past or future — these strange and extravagant desires are neither unreal nor outside our reality; rather, they determine our reality, in dreams and daydreams and even in our everyday, often unconsidered speech. Achilles' Heel and the Oedipus Complex, Eden and the Land of Nod, the Trinity and the Seven Deadly Sins, all are relics of a world of images, signs, and meanings that we've inherited and ought not to defame as irrational.

Literature lives on myth. It creates and destroys myths. It tells the truth differently each time. Its memory saves what we should remember.

Perhaps some day, one that won't come too late, I hope, we will succeed in thinking once again in images and signs by allowing our reason to believe in fairy tales, to play like a fool with numbers and meanings, to grant free rein to fantasy, and to realize that if we do survive it will be in myths, just possibly with the help of literature.

Translated by W. Martin

The Hare and the Hedgehog

(1993)

Rensch was tired of racing. He had plenty of oomph, but no clear purpose. And no delight in the simple goals he did set for himself, those short sprints of dreams. Despite his good start he had always managed to come in second. Bumbling on. Tugging at his tie. Learning jokes for every occasion. Laughing before the punch line. But Rensch wanted to do right by himself, and so he decided to take a trip. He didn't think it would be very nice to end things at home, for instance on a Tuesday—his one free evening—just as the Little Sandman was summoning the family to the television. He also had the business to take into account. So he booked a flight, packed more than he needed, dawdled at the newsstand, and was shocked to hear his name echoing up and down the hall—although he actually enjoyed the words "Last call for . . ." He did what he was told; he extinguished his cigarette and fastened his seat belt, all the while snickering to himself, and was there before the plane lifted off the runway—along with the excess baggage.

A hotel in Frankfurt that he'd cleverly reserved between conventions had a room with a private bath. He checked in as Ewald Nöldichen, which was the first name that popped into his head. He'd tossed all his personal items—the official Rensch—into the river Main on his way to the hotel. So Herr Nöldichen took his time over dinner—brisket with horseradish sauce; he had a good appetite and didn't forget to take his pills. Then he went back to his room, which he suddenly took a liking to. Being first for once: Here I am. I'm already here. Actions long considered and quickly carried out. Because so many things fall through at the planning stage. That's why there wouldn't be any farewell note—everything there was to say had already been said, and always just a split second too late. I don't like to repeat myself. There comes a point . . .

But as the water in the tub was rising, the gun called out to him again, asking him to put things off. Nöldichen teased Rensch, recounting all the failed attempts: the sailboat during that week in Kiel, when the boat close to them had capsized and he'd had to play the rescuer; the electric shock that never happened because the kids caused a short circuit with their train set; the time he broke into the big-cat house at the zoo and discovered that the Siberian tigers had just been fed. Rensch gave in and locked the gun away. And Nöldichen, overconfident about winning, didn't look back. Meanwhile, even the unmelodic whistle of the razor being pulled out of its sheath signified nothing more than the habit of a man once known as Rensch who'd been shaving the old-fashioned way for twenty-seven years.

Why did he brush his teeth after getting undressed? Why did he answer the telephone after the second ring? Why didn't he hang up when he heard a chummy voice announcing, "I'm already here, Nöldichen, old buddy!"? Why did he say, "How are you?" and not "Wrong number"? Why did he accept that invitation at such short notice? Why did he agree to meet Nöldichen's pal, who was already there and eager to share some new jokes? Why did he promise to meet the man at some bar by the train station? "See you soon, old buddy!"

I confess: The tub was already full, so I went ahead and took a warm bath. It's also true that I took care getting dressed; I fussed over the tie; I memorized two jokes I had reason to hope were new—but I didn't shave. With prickly cheeks—how nice not to be the hare just this once—I found the bar in the Kaiserstrasse and met my old friend, who was already there. We talked about old times, laughed at the right moments, and boozed our way into the early hours. The city of Frankfurt is well-known for its nightlife.

Translated by Philip Boehm

The Destruction of Mankind Has Begun

Address delivered on November 25, 1982, in Rome.

Chairman, Ladies and Gentlemen;

I shall try to express the thanks of all those who have been
honored with the Antonio Feltrinelli Prize. This should be
easy, since honors of this kind not only acknowledge work
done, but are also encouragements to remain active in the fu-
ture. Optimism is expressed at all award ceremonies, as
though one could take it for granted that life will go on as it
is. Up until now this attitude and pose have supported our
concept of progress, for somehow life has gone on.

My message of thanks obtrudes doubt into traditional
expectations. Our present makes the future questionable
and in many respects unthinkable, for our present pro-
duces—since we have learned above all to produce—
poverty, hunger, polluted air, polluted bodies of water,
forests destroyed by acid rain or deforestation, arsenals that
seem to pile up of their own accord and are capable of de-
stroying mankind many times over.

Apart from its past and present historical significance, Rome, the city in which I am trying to give thanks, has come to be identified with the reports issued by the Club of Rome. These reports are our down-to-earth Revelation. We are not threatened by any judgment of the gods or of the one God. No Saint John is sitting on Patmos, penning obscure images of doom. No book of the Seven Seals has become our oracle. No, realistically and in the spirit of the times, we derive our vision from columns of figures assessing starvation; from the statistics of pauperization; from tables summarizing the ecological catastrophe—numbered madness, the apocalypse as balance sheet. The exact figures may be a matter for controversy, but the conclusion is inescapable that the destruction of mankind by man in a variety of ways has already begun.

On the assumption that scientists have also begun to question, if not to deny, the likelihood of a future as a field for further development, I hope to be speaking in the name of all the prize-winners if I now report briefly on my work as an author and call literature as well as myself into question.

Even more than the other arts, literature presupposes an assured field of action—that is, a future. It has outlived absolute rulers, theological and ideological dogmas, dictatorship after dictatorship; time and again censorships have been lifted and the word set free. The history of literature is in part a history of the victory of books over censorship, of writers over potentates. Thus, in the worst of times, literature has always been sure of one ally: the future. Silone and Moravia, Brecht and Döblin outlived fascism, just as Isaac Babel and Osip Mandelstam outlived Stalinism—though it killed them.

Literature has always had superior staying power. Sure of its aftereffect, it could count on time even if the echo to word and sentence, poem and thesis might take decades or even centuries to make itself heard. This advance payment, this provision of time, made the poorest writers rich. Even in the most loathsome times, these free spirits, whose growth rate went by the name of "immortality," were unconquerable; they could be imprisoned, executed, or driven into exile, as has been customary throughout the world down to our own day—but in the end the book won out and with it the word.

This was the case until today—or, rather, until yesterday. For with the loss of mankind's future, the "immortality" of literature, taken as a certainty until now, has ceased to be anything more than wishful thinking. The book, formerly made to last forever, is beginning to resemble a nonreturnable bottle. It is not yet certain whether or not we still have a future, but already we have stopped reckoning with one. The same hubris that enables man to destroy himself is now threatening, before night falls, to darken the human spirit, to extinguish its dream of a better tomorrow and make a laughingstock of every utopia—including Ernst Bloch's *The Principle of Hope*.

A glance at the relation of forces in political and economic life shows that—against better knowledge—the over-exploitation of natural resources is on the increase, that shameless justifications are offered for the pollution of air and water, that the potential for destruction of both superpowers and their satellites has long overstepped the threshold of madness. Despite all shouts of warning, no idea has managed to take on political reality. With all the display of force and with so many musclemen around, there is no force ready and willing to call a halt to already existing catastrophes and those that lie ahead. The holders of power engage in meaningless bustle and adjourn their responsibility from conference to conference.

All that remains is protest, enfeebled by abject fear, which soon, for want of words, will turn to speechless dread, because, in the face of the void, all sounds will have lost their meaning.

It may be, ladies and gentlemen, that my words of thanks frighten you and mar the sedately festive atmosphere to which this sort of day can reasonably lay claim. I suspect that my fellow prize-winners think my view of the situation unduly black, whereas they see it, at the worst, in tones of gray, since, after all, trite as it may sound, life does go on. New discoveries to be made, new inventions perfected, more and more books to be written. And I too, because I can't help it, shall persist in lining up words, in writing. Yet I know that the book I am planning to write can no longer pretend to certainty of the future. It will have to include a farewell to the damaged world, to wounded creatures, to us and our minds, which have thought of everything and of the end as well.

Everything that has thus far become a book for me has been subservient to time or has chafed under it. As a contemporary, I have written against the passage of time. The past made me throw it in the path of the present to make the present stumble. The future could only be understood on the basis of past made present. First and foremost, I found myself harnessed to German time, constrained to steer a course cutting obliquely across the epochs, disregarding the convenience of chronology. Epic moraines had to be cleared away, reality sloughed off again and again. There's no end to it. So many dead. And everywhere, even where life might release joy and pleasure might take its fling, the great crime casts its shadow, which time cannot efface.

Between books I have given politics what excess energy I could. Now and then something stirred. After all my experience with time and its contrary course, I inscribed a slow-moving animal in my escutcheon and said: Progress is a snail. At that time many wished—and so did I—that there could be jumping snails. Today I know, and recently wrote as much, that the snail is too quick for us. Already it has passed us by. But we, fallen out of nature, enemies of nature, still imagine that we're ahead of the snail.

Can human beings stop thinking about themselves? Are they—godlike creative beings endowed with reason, creators of more and more total inventions—capable of saying no to their inventions? Are they prepared to forgo the humanly possible and show some humility toward what's left of ruined nature? And lastly: Have we the will to do what we can do—namely, feed one another until hunger ceases to be anything more than a legend, a once-upon-a-ghoulish-time story?

The answers to these questions are overdue. I myself have no answer, either. But in my perplexity I know that a future will only be possible again when we find an answer and do what, as guests on this orbiting chunk of nature, we owe to one another; namely, stop frightening one another, relieve one another of fear by disarming to the point of nakedness.

Translated by Ralph Manheim

In Posthuman Times

from The Rat (1986)

In olden times we were better informed; but during the first phase of the posthuman era, which was longer than can be expressed in counted calendar years, we heard next to nothing about the rat nations that had dug themselves in elsewhere. We were sure we existed all over, and that made us all the more avid for news. But when the first immigrants came from the East and were assigned to districts outside the city, in the Kashubian hinterland and on the still-swampy Island, the immigrants didn't know much, just that conditions were worse in Russia, a lot worse than here at home, and almost unbearable even for rats. This wasn't news. Nothing concrete, only complaints and rumors; we'd had enough of that.

It was different in the human era, said the She-rat of my dreams. From time immemorial we had traveled from continent to continent in ships of all sizes, as long as they didn't give off that sinking smell that sometimes pervaded particular ships or whole fleets. The Spanish Armada sank without us. We steered clear of the *Titanic*. There were no rats on board the *Wilhelm Gustloff,* a Strength-Through-Joy ship, which in January 1945 was torpedoed in Gdynia, then called Gotenhafen, soon after leaving Danzig Bay; the same goes for the *Steuben,* carrying four thousand wounded, the *Goya,* and other ships that ran into mines, turned turtle, or sank stern-first. Some admiral had sent them all to Courland to bring as many soldiers and civilians as possible to the West. We know that, because some of us had traveled west on ships that did not sink. Seven times we sailed on the *Cap Arcona;* in fact we doubled in number before going ashore in Danish and North German ports, but we denied ourselves the former luxury liner when it was loaded with inmates of the Neuengamme concentration camp and thus marked for sinking.

Anyone who doesn't believe me, said the She-rat, who just wouldn't stop talking about avoided sinkings, should remember how, when we had a premonition of the naval battle of Tsushima, we fled from the armored cruisers and battleships of the Russian Baltic fleet. . . .

On and on she went, losing herself in her favorite topic. She listed the cruisers *Svetlana* and *Zhemchug,* the flagship *Ostjaba,* the armored cruiser *Admiral Nakhinov,* the battleships *Borodino* and *Suvorov.* Forty-two black tubs in all, which on the night of October 14, 1904, were abandoned by all the naked of tail.

But, friend, she cried, why do we talk about sinkings when there are so many ships to be remembered that we boarded without a qualm and from which we landed safe and sound, though occasionally deep-frozen, like those

New Zealand rats who were so dead set on traveling from the antipodes to Europe that they stowed away on freighters carrying a cargo of mutton? Yet they survived the cold shock. It had no lasting effect on the deep-frozen New Zealand rats, who recovered their full mobility on reaching the London docks. Refrigeration hadn't impaired their rat memory in the least. Far from inducing atrophy, freezing kept it fresh. They brought news and, leaving again by the next ship, carried news somewhere else.

The She-rat praised the intercontinental info-system of the rat nations, deplored the newslessness of the post-human era, and waxed positively lyrical about the techno-logical perfection of the late human era, as she called it. She spoke of airborne rats, who traveled in passenger as well as cargo planes. Not an airline, she cried, that we didn't pa-tronize. Always up to date, we were always better informed than humans. A pity that next to no news comes our way nowadays.

But, She-rat, I said, what do you need news for, why do you need information? At peace, free from the pointless headlines that cancel one another out from day to day, free from daily reports of catastrophes, you are able at last to live ratworthy lives, to live for yourselves. Now that you've put an end to the hectic bustle of human existence, you shouldn't give a damn about news and sensations.

In a way, she conceded, you're right. You live more serenely if you don't know what's coming from behind the Seven Mountains. All the same, we're curious to know how rats in other places are dealing with a development that alarms the nations settled here — nay, more, that endan-gers — nay, more, that might ruin us. . . .

I saw her scurrying nervously back and forth, then blurred and tripartite, but unanimous. Of course, she cried, it's understandable that the old, old woman in the armchair, who would like to die but can't, should be worshipped by country rats; of course, in the cities, numerous intact churches are available for collective use. But must the worship of an old woman, must the gatherings of our nations in the cities degenerate into idolatry in the country, and into irrationality in the cities? It can't be denied. We're getting religion. No sooner has the human race perished than we start looking behind things, searching for meaning, fashioning images. All this would be bearable, if not understandable, if it were one unifying faith that was making us rats pious. But far from it: just like humans, we go in for deviations. Outward indications mark trends and creeds. Even now there are grounds for an irreconcilable conflict—as though we were doomed to walk in the footsteps of man.

Sharper in her contours and more sharply tripartite, including her whiskers, the She-rat said: By and large, we can distinguish three denominations. The origin of a rat nation may have something to do with it. We in this region are old settlers, but some of our number immigrated from the West via the so-called underground railway, and still others trickled in shortly before the Big Bang from the vast Russian land mass. These three nations are basically identical in character and even in the zinc-green coloration of our posthuman hair; only in our pieties are we at odds. . . .

When she said that, I couldn't tell which of them had said *pieties* and *at odds,* because in my dream three she-rats enlivened the screen. They kept out of one another's way or glared at one another ferociously. They scurried restlessly back and forth. One she-rat chased the second, who was chasing the third. I never knew which was speaking to me in my dream. They shouted one another down, vilipended one another. I heard absurd accusations; the first she-rat cursed the second, wishing her back where she had come from, in far-distant Russia, excoriated the third for Polish disorder, and was in turn damned as a Prussian by the Russian and Polish she-rats who, God knows, viewed each other with mutual hatred.

But essentially the three she-rats, each of whom may have been mine, were arguing about questions of faith. Their disputation had a Christian ring. When they invoked charity in their mutual recriminations, they sounded human. While one fulminated with Protestant zeal, the second remained stubbornly Catholic, and the third—but which one? —tried with orthodox zeal to outdo the obstinacy of the others. Crouching to leap or confronting one another with bare-toothed fury and bristling whiskers. Then for a time each hissed to herself; I had difficulty in disentangling their embattled knot.

Apart from theological hairsplitting and other human claptrap, the question was largely territorial: who was entitled to assemble when in what churches? Those rats who had immigrated from Russia and were reduced to living in the marshes of the Lower Vistula, claimed exclusive rights over the mud-slide-enclosed Church of Saint Barbara. The rats who had immigrated from Germany shortly before the finale laid claim to Saint Mary's and demanded a share in other religious premises. On no account would the Polish Catholic rats cede the former Dominican church to the

Protestants. And the German rats were no less quarrel-
somely intent on Saint Bridget and Saint Catherine.

But, I shouted into the fray, what about Christian charity,
damn it all? A little more tolerance, if you please.

After that I had all three of them against me: A pretty
pass things have come to if this last human thinks he can
teach rats how to behave. His space capsule isn't enough
for him. He should mind his business. The gall! One thing
the human race was never any good at was tolerance. Then
the three of them went back to quarreling among them-
selves and seemed to enjoy it.

But when they went on with their religious controversy,
there were four, then five female rats going at it hammer
and tongs. As far as I could make out, the Protestants had
split and among the Orthodox there were Early Christian–
Communist deviations. This was just what the Polish-
Kashubian—but which was the Catholic? —wanted. She
demanded restitution of Saint Barbara's in the Lower City
and, it goes without saying, of the former Royal Polish
Chapel next door to Saint Mary's, which the fourth she-rat
quite absurdly claimed for Calvinist meetings, while the
Communist Early Christians wanted the Church of Saint
James beside the former Lenin Shipyard as a meeting place.

Oh well, I said, there are plenty of churches around,
damn it. But wouldn't it be nice if even pious rats could
manage to preach, perhaps not tolerance in every church,
but at least common charity?

Again I have them all, now five in number, against me.
My situation seemed familiar. I'd had experience and to
spare. I looked for comparisons, tried to drive the woman-
manned ship into my dream, but I was hopelessly beratted,

and all I could do was shout: Charity, dammit, a little more charity!

The answer was scornful laughter. No need to preach charity to rats. We've practiced it from time immemorial. Only humans have had to make it a commandment, which, as it transpired, they were incapable of keeping. Instead they devised murder and torture and kept perfecting them. It was high time this last man in his space capsule learned to keep his trap shut.

When I nevertheless protested and threatened them with dreams that would be true in a different way—our Herr Matzerath still has a surprise in store, the ship is still anchored over Vineta, the chancellor and his retinue are still imprisoned in deep Brier Rose sleep—I heard all five she-rats laugh, but only one, probably the Catholic one, cried out: Scram! Buzz off into your stories! What do we need you for? The old, old woman is still alive in her armchair. She mumbles and mumbles and she can't die. . . .

And again they quarreled. But this time it was not over the use of unscathed churches in the preserved city. No longer as though preaching from pulpits, but in wild confusion, atop a mound of porcelain shards, toy-sized figurines, and heedlessly rejected coins, they were fighting over the old woman who wanted to die but couldn't, who struck me as familiar, adamantly as I refused to name the old woman by name. Only if you speak to her, I said to myself, will she really be lost.

Translated by Ralph Manheim

BIKINI ATOLL

(1993)

On June 12, 1946, Matthias Törne left his farmstead, a broad acreage that even though it lay a good ways off was officially part of the village of Lötsch, a small spot between Breyel and Venlo on the Dutch border.

Törne raised a lot of asparagus. His people had been picking and sorting the spears that very morning.

At the toolshed he cut diagonally across a beet field that was carefully set apart. When he had gone some two hundred paces he stopped abruptly, took a compass out of his left jacket pocket and a watch out of his right. With the help of the compass he turned toward the southeast, readjusting his position several times. Then he consulted his watch, first following the minute hand, then the second hand, until he finally looked up, past the land marked with hedges, poplars, single farmhouses, villages, burned-out tanks, telephone poles . . . all the way to the horizon and the monochrome sky.

But what the radio had promised would appear in the southeast—what the announcer had called a mushroom-shaped cloud—did not. And so Matthias Törne slipped compass and watch into their pockets, turned around, crossed through the beet field once again, stooping twice to pull up weeds, and didn't look back even when he reached the gate.

Translated by Philip Boehm

BERLIN—A PROJECTED FICTION

In 1983 Grass, along with a number of prominent writers, was asked to reflect on the literary scene in Berlin.

WHEN I MOVED TO BERLIN FROM WEST GERMANY, IN 1953, my motives in doing so were less those of a sculptor in search of a new teacher (Karl Hartung) than those of someone who needed a fundamental change of location, a turning away from the West German "economic miracle" that was then taking off so quickly. Despite the many political and economic changes Berlin has undergone since then, my original impression of it remains: This city is a wound that will not heal, that is permanently open—a proof of the broken course of German history. All the international crises that elsewhere only confuse us in their variety are concentrated and given definition here, as if Berlin were using this heap of problems to show how paradigmatic it is.

Maybe it is the city's openness and shamelessness in showing off its injuries and deformations that fascinates and still captivates this writer. While I often need to put some distance between myself and Berlin, it doesn't matter what topic I choose as my vehicle for doing so. At the end of every manuscript it is apparent that this city is where I've stacked and carted and tossed out my material, that Berlin remains the vanishing point of my fiction.

That said, the place is unwieldy. Anyone who wants to have it all at once will quickly be apprised of what's missing. Rash judgments—Berlin is sick, is dying off, or is dying out—have no effect on the condemned city, because Berlin's illnesses are the sources of its vitality. Anyway, its dying off or out is just a part of its brittle charm. In general, I'm talking about the whole city. Of course, we have the Wall here, that naked and brutally honest and apparently permanent dividing line. But one cannot overlook the fact that the city's two halves live for each other, and never more obviously than when they are at pains to ignore each other.

Throughout the seventies, a number of writers, including myself, periodically convened in East Berlin, without an audience and entirely focused on our manuscripts, from which we would read passages aloud to one another. It still amazes me that this critical mass of literati, whose conventions went on for over four years and affect us even today, attracted little attention aside from that of the state security apparatus, and that our activities remained undisturbed by the curiosity of the public: one more proof that Berlin's literary life takes place in two distinct scenes that have almost nothing to do with each other. On the one hand, there is the silent, consciously solitary process of production that creates books. On the other hand, there is the fast-paced literary industry that takes books and authors as a pretext but would continue to function even if authors ceased to exist.

Books written here are stigmatized. They bear the scars of this city—often unrecognizably because they hide them, often unmistakably because they show them off: Look how injured I still am! Like any pilgrimage site, Berlin is a great place for living out hysterical excesses. Only here are miracles—of whatever kind—everyday occurrences. If there were no Berlin, it would have to be invented. On closer inspection, Berlin—in all its striking reality—is a projected fiction.

Translated by W. Martin

ALEXANDER AND ALEXANDRA

from THE CALL OF THE TOAD (1992)

CHANCE PUT THE WIDOWER NEXT TO THE WIDOW. OR maybe chance had nothing to do with it, for the story began on All Souls'. Be that as it may, the widow was already there when the widower tripped, stumbled, but did not fall.

He stood beside her. Shoe size ten beside shoe size eight. Widow and widower met facing the wares of a peasant woman: mushrooms heaped in a basket or spread out on newsprint, and three buckets filled with cut flowers. The woman was sitting to one side of the covered market in the midst of other truck farmers and the produce of their small plots: celery, rutabaga the size of a child's head, leeks, and beets.

His diary confirms "All Souls'" and makes no mystery of the shoe sizes. What made him stumble was the edge of the curbstone. But the word chance does not occur in his diary. "It may have been fate that brought us together that day on the stroke of ten o'clock . . ." His attempt to give body to the third person, the silent intermediary, remains vague, as does his bumbling attempt to pin down the color of her head scarf: "Not exactly umber, more earth-brown than peat-black . . ." He has better luck with the brickwork of the monastery wall: "Infested with scab . . ." I have to imagine the rest.

Only a few varieties of cut flowers were left in the buckets: dahlias, asters, chrysanthemums. The basket was full of chestnuts. Four or five boletus mushrooms with slight slug damage were lined up on the title page of an ancient issue of the local paper *Głos Wybrzeża*. Also a bunch of parsley and a roll of wrapping paper. The cut flowers looked bedraggled: leftovers.

"No wonder," writes the widower, "that this and other stands in St. Dominic's Market seemed so poorly supplied. Flowers are much in demand on All Souls'. Even on All Saints', the day before, the demand often exceeds the supply . . ."

Though dahlias and chrysanthemums are showier, the widow decided in favor of asters. The widower was hesitant: Even if "the surprisingly late mushrooms" and chestnuts may have lured him to this particular stand, "I'm certain that after a moment's dismay—or could it have been the ringing of the bells? —I gave in to a special sort of seduction—no, call it magnetism. . . ."

When from the three or four buckets the widow took a first, a second, then hesitantly a third aster, exchanged this last for another, and pulled out a fourth, which also had to be put back and replaced, the widower began to take asters from buckets and, no less picky-and-choosy than the widow, to exchange them; he chose rust-red asters just as she had chosen rust-red asters, though white and pale-violet ones were still available. The color harmony went to his head: "What gentle consonance. Like her, I am especially fond of the rust-red, how quietly they smolder. . . ." Be that as it may, they both concentrated on rust-red asters until there were no more left in the buckets.

Neither widow nor widower had enough for a bouquet. She was ready to shove her meager selection back into one of the buckets when the so-called plot set in: The widower handed the widow his rust-red spoils. He held them out, she took them. A wordless surrender. Never to be reversed. Inextinguishably burning asters. That made for a bond between them.

STROKE OF TEN: that was St. Catherine's. What I know about the place where they met is a combination of somewhat blurred but also ultradistinct knowledge about the locality through the widower's assiduous research, the product of which he has confided to his notes in dribs and drabs, for instance the fact that the octagonal seven-story-high fortress tower constitutes the northwest corner of the great town wall. It was nicknamed "Kiek in de Köck" (Peek in the Kitchen) after a smaller tower, which had been so called because it was next door to the Dominican monastery and offered an unobstructed view of the pots and pans in the monastery kitchen, which toward the end of the nineteenth century had fallen into such disrepair that trees and shrubs took root in its roofless interior (for which reason it was known for a time as "the flowerpot") and was torn down along with the rest of the monastery. Beginning in 1895, a covered market in the neo-Gothic style was built on the site. Named St. Dominic's Market, it survived the First and Second World Wars and under its broad vaulted roof it still offers sometimes abundant, more often scant wares in six rows of stands: darning wool and smoked fish, American cigarettes and Polish mustard pickles, poppy-seed cake and pork that is much too fat, plastic toys from Hong Kong, cigarette lighters from all over the world, caraway seeds and poppy seeds in little bags, cheese spread and Perlon stockings.

Of the Dominican monastery nothing remains but the gloomy Church of St. Nikolai, its interior splendor resting entirely on black and gold: an afterglow of past atrocities. But the memory of the black-robed monastic order lives on only in the name of the market, as it does in that of a summer holiday named St. Dominic's Day, which since the late Middle Ages has survived all manner of political change and today attracts natives and tourists with street musicians, sausage stands, and all kinds of baubles and trumpery.

There between St. Dominic's Market and the Church of St. Nikolai, diagonally across from Peek in the Kitchen, widower and widow met at a time when the name "Kantor" on a handwritten sign identified the street floor of what was the former fortress tower as an exchange office. Teeming with customers spilling out through the wide open door; a blackboard at the entrance, brought up-to-date every hour, bore witness to the deplorable situation by indicating the steadily increasing number of zlotys obtainable for one American dollar.

The conversation began with "May I?" Wishing to pay not only for his own asters but for the whole now-unified bouquet, and somewhat bewildered by the look of a currency so rich in zeroes, he drew banknotes from his wallet. The widow said with an accent, "You may nothing."

Her use of the foreign language may have lent additional sharpness to her negative reply, and if her next remark— "Is now pretty bouquet, yes?"—hadn't opened the door to conversation, the chance encounter between widower and widow might have begged comparison with the diminishing rate of the zloty.

He writes that while the widow was still paying, a conversation had started up about mushrooms, especially the late, belated boletus. The summer that had seemed endless and the mild autumn were cited as reasons. "But when I said something about global warming, she just laughed."

On a sunny to partly cloudy November day, the two of them stood face-to-face. It seemed as though nothing could separate them from the flowers and the mushrooms. He had fallen for her, she for him. The widow laughed frequently. Her accented sentences were preceded and followed by laughter that seemed groundless, just a little prelude and postlude. The widower liked this almost-shrill laugh, for it says in his papers: "Like a bellbird, sometimes frightening, I have to admit, but I enjoy the sound of her laughter and never ask what seems to amuse her. Maybe she's laughing at me. But even that, even for her to think me laughable, gives me pleasure."

So they stood there. Or rather: they stand there a while and another little while, posing for me, to give me a chance to get used to them. If she was fashionably dressed—he thought her "too modishly done up," his tweed jacket and corduroy trousers gave him the look of shabby elegance that went with his camera case — a traveler for educational purposes, the better type of tourist. "If you won't accept the flowers, suppose we go back to the subject of the conversation we had just started, namely, mushrooms; will you permit me to select this one and perhaps this one, and make you a present of them? They look inviting."

She would. And she watched carefully to make sure that he wouldn't peel off too many bills for the marketwoman. "Here is all so crazy expensive," she cried. "But cheap perhaps for a gentleman with deutsch marks."

I wonder if he succeeded by mental arithmetic in interpreting the multidigital figures on the zloty bills, and whether he seriously, without fear of her laughter, thought of mentioning the reference to Chernobyl and global warming in his diary. It is certain that before buying the mushrooms he photographed them with a camera identified in his diary as a Japanese make. Because his snapshot is taken from above at a sharp angle, so sharp that it takes in the tips of the squatting marketwoman's shoes, this photo bears witness to the astonishing size of the boletus mushrooms. The stems of the two younger ones are wider than their higharching hats; the wide brims of the older ones, now curled inward, now rolled outward, shade their fleshy, convoluted bodies. Lying together, the four of them turn their tall wide hats toward one another, but are so placed by the photographer that there is little overlap. Thus they form a still life. The widower may have made a remark to that effect. Or was it she who said, "Pretty, like still life"? In any case, the widow reached into her shoulder bag and found a string bag for the mushrooms, which the marketwoman wrapped in newspaper, throwing in a small bunch of parsley.

He wanted to carry the string bag. She held on tight. He said please. She said no, "Pay then carry is too much." A slight battle, a tussle, taking care, however, not to harm the contents of the string bag, kept the two of them in place, as if they were unwilling to leave the spot where they had met. Back and forth they pulled the string bag. Nor was he allowed to carry the asters. A well-rehearsed battle—they might have known each other for years. They might have done a duet in an opera; to whose music I can already guess.

They didn't lack an audience. The marketwoman looked on in silence, and there were witnesses all around: the octagonal fortress tower, with its latest subtenant, the overcrowded exchange bureau, and next to it the broad-beamed covered market that seemed bloated with mist, and the gloomy Dominican Church of St. Nikolai. And the peasant women in the adjoining stands, and finally the potential customers, all making up an impoverished crowd, driven only by their day-to-day needs, their scant funds diminishing in value by the hour, while widow and widower looked upon each other as money in the bank and showed no desire to separate.

"Now I go to different place."

"May I come with you, please?"

"Well, it's far."

"It would be a pleasure, really. . . ."

"But it's cemetery where I go."

"I'll try not to bother you."

"All right, come."

She carried the bunch of asters. He carried the string bag. He gaunt and stooped. She with short percussive steps. He inclined to stumble, dragging his feet a little, a good head taller than she. She with pale blue eyes, he far-sighted. Her hair tinted Titian-red. His mustache salt-and-pepper. She took the scent of her aggressive perfume with her, he the mild counterpoint of his aftershave lotion.

They merged into the crowd outside the market. Now the widower's beret was gone. Shortly before the stroke of eleven from the top of St. Catherine's. And what about me? I have to follow the two of them.

Translated by Ralph Manheim

MADNESS! SHEER MADNESS!

from MY CENTURY (1999)

DRIVING BACK TO LAUENBURG FROM BERLIN, WE tuned in as usual to the Third Program, so we got the news late, but when it finally came I cried out in joy and in panic—like thousands of others, I'm sure—"Madness! Sheer madness!" and then—like Ute, who was at the wheel—sank into thoughts running both forward and back. Meanwhile, an acquaintance who lived on the other side of the Wall and worked in the archives of the Academy of Arts, keeping watch then as now over literary estates, was likewise late in receiving the glad tidings, which reached him like a time bomb.

The way he tells it, he was jogging home from the Friedrichshain—nothing out of the ordinary, because even East Berliners had taken up that American-inspired form of self-castigation by then—when at the intersection of Käthe-Niederkirchner-Strasse and Bötzowstrasse he came upon an acquaintance who was likewise panting and sweating from his jog. Bobbing up and down, they agreed to meet for a beer that evening, and that evening he repaired to the acquaintance's spacious flat, where, since his acquaintance was employed in what the East called "material production," my acquaintance was not particularly surprised to find a newly laid parquet living-room floor, an achievement utterly beyond the means of an archival paper-pusher in charge of nothing more than footnotes.

They had a Pilsner, then another, and before long a bottle of Nordhäuser schnapps appeared on the table. They talked about the old days and their children and the ideological constraints at parent-teacher meetings. My acquaintance — who comes from the Ore Mountains, on whose slopes I had sketched dead trees the year before — told his acquaintance he was planning a ski trip there that winter with his wife but was having trouble with his Wartburg — the tires, both front and back, had hardly any tread left — and hoped his acquaintance could put him on the track of some snow tires: anyone who could have a parquet floor laid by a private person under the conditions of "actually existing socialism," as the regime was called at the time, would have an idea of how to get hold of so precious a commodity.

As we arrived home in Behlendorf with the good news from the radio now in our hearts, the volume on the television set in the living room of my acquaintance's acquaintance was turned down low so the two of them could go on undisturbed about the tire problem, and the man with the parquet floor said the only way to get snow tires was to come up with some "real money" but he could find him some carburetor jets. Glancing over at the silent screen, my acquaintance thought the program must be a feature film of some kind because it showed young people climbing the Wall and sitting astride it while the border police stood idly by. When my acquaintance's acquaintance was made aware of the flagrant disregard for the Wall's protective function, he muttered, "Typical," and the two men quickly dismissed the tastelessness of "yet another Cold War product" so as to get back to the subject at hand—the bald regular and unavailable snow tires. The subject of the archives and the papers of the more or less important writers housed there never came up.

As we switched on the television set, deep in thought by then over the coming post-Wall period, my acquaintance's acquaintance had not yet decided to take the few steps over the newly laid parquet floor to turn up the volume, but when he finally did there was not another word about tires: it was a problem the new period and its "real money" could solve instantly. Stopping only to down the rest of the schnapps, they made their way to Invalidenstrasse, which was jammed with cars, more Trabants than the relatively expensive Wartburgs, trying to cross the—wonder of wonders—open border. And if you listened carefully, you could hear everyone, well, nearly everyone who wanted to cross over to the West on foot or in a Trabi, you could hear them all either shouting or whispering "Madness!" just as I had shouted "Madness!" outside Behlendorf before sinking into my reverie.

I forgot to ask my acquaintance how, when, and for which currency he finally managed to come by his snow tires. I never found out whether he and his wife, who'd been an ice-skating champion during the days of the German Democratic Republic, got to celebrate the New Year in their Ore Mountain retreat. Life just kept moving on.

Translated by Michael Henry Heim

THE WALLPECKERS

from TOO FAR AFIELD (1995)

ON A FROST-CRACKLING WINTER DAY, WITH A WATERY
blue sky spanning the now undivided city, on 17 December,
when the hitherto leading party was convening in Dynamo
Hall to adopt an assumed name, on a Sunday when folks
large and small were out and about, two figures entered
the picture at the corner of Otto-Grotewohl-Strasse and
Leipziger Strasse, striding toward their destination: tall and
thin beside short and squat. The outlines of their hats
and coats, of dark felt and gray wool blend, converged into
a unit that grew larger and larger as it approached. The
paired phenomenon seemed unstoppable. Already they had
reached the Ministries Building, or, more precisely, had
passed its northern flank. Sometimes the tall half gesticu-
lated, sometimes the short half. Then both would wax elo-
quent, arms poking out of wide sleeves, the one with a
long, swinging gait, the other with short, bustling steps.
Their puffs of breath coalesced into little white clouds and

floated off. Thus they remained ahead of and behind one another, yet grown together into a single form. Since this yoked pair never managed to march in step, it looked as though flickering silhouettes were moving across the screen. The silent film unreeled in the direction of Potsdamer Platz, where a gap as wide as a street had been opened in the wall once erected to secure a border. Traffic could now flow in both directions; yet this crossing point was so jammed that it allowed only a fitful stream of cars to pass from one half of the city to the other, between two worlds, Berlin and Berlin.

They crossed a strip that for many decades had been a barren no-man's-land and was now a vacant lot, panting for developers; already the first projects were underway, each striving to outdo the others; already the building boom was breaking out; already land prices were on the rise.

Fonty liked such walks, especially now that the Tiergarten's paths in the West gave him room to roam. Only now did his walking stick enter the picture. Hoftaller, tagging along, stickless but with bulging briefcase, was known to have in his possession, in addition to his thermos and sandwich box, a collapsible umbrella, which expanded to normal size at the touch of a button.

In its perfunctorily guarded condition, the Wall offered good buys on both sides of the opening. After a moment's hesitation they decided to strike out to the right, toward the Brandenburg Gate. Metal on stone: from far off they had already heard the peck-peck-peck. A sound like that carries especially far in the cold.

The wallpeckers were standing or kneeling cheek by jowl. Those working as teams took turns. Some wore gloves against the cold. With hammer and chisel, or in many cases only a cobblestone or screwdriver, they were chipping away at this bulwark, whose western side, during the final years of its existence, had been upgraded by anonymous artists to an artwork, with loud colors and hard-edged contours. It did not stint with symbols; it spat out quotations, shouted, accused, and as recently as yesterday had still seemed relevant.

Here and there the Wall already looked porous, exposing its innards: reinforcing rods that would soon begin to rust. And the vast expanse of the mural, stretching for many kilometers and still being extended until just before the end, was now yielding museum-ready swatches no bigger than the palm of a hand, wild daubs in tiny fragments: imagination set free, protest set in stone.

All this was supposed to serve as a form of historic preservation. Off to one side of the hammering, in what might be described as the second wave of dismantling by the West, business was already booming. Spread out on pieces of cloth or newspaper lay massive chunks or tiny chips. Some merchants were offering three to five fragments, none bigger than a one-mark coin, in Ziploc bags. Particularly impressive were larger details that had been painstakingly chiseled out of the mural—for instance, a monster's head with an eye in the middle of the forehead, or a seven-fingered hand—pieces with a hefty asking price, and yet there was no dearth of buyers, especially since a dated certificate— "Authentic Berlin Wall" —came with every souvenir.

Fonty, who could never let anything pass without comment, exclaimed, "Better in parts than whole!" Because he had only lightweight Eastern coin jingling in his pocket, a youthful merchant who had apparently already turned a tidy profit that day presented him with a gift: three penny-sized shards, whose traces of color—black clashing with yellow on the first, then blue jostling red, and finally three shades of green—were supposed to make them valuable: "Here you go, Gramps, only for my Eastern customers, and because it's Sunday."

Initially his day-and-night-shadow did not want to observe this popular pastime, which, although illegal, was tolerated on both sides of the Wall; Fonty had to tug him by the sleeve. He actually had to drag his companion past the arrayed pictures. No, this was not Hoftaller's cup of tea. This Wall art did not suit his taste at all; yet now he found himself forced to contemplate something that had always horrified him. "Chaos!" he exclaimed. "Sheer chaos!"

They reached a spot where the tightly joined concrete slabs with their crowning bulge allowed them to see into the East—a hole recently chopped in the border-guarding structure. There they stopped and gazed through the open wedge, from whose jagged edges reinforcing rods projected, some bent back, some hacksawed off. They saw the safety strip, the dog run, the wide field of fire. They stared across the death strip, saw the watchtowers.

From the other side, Fonty was visible through the widened fissure from his chest up. Next to him, Hoftaller entered the picture from the shoulders up: two men in hats. Had a soldier still been on patrol, out of the Eastern mania for security, he could have snapped a serviceable mug shot of the two for the files.

For a time they gazed in silence through the wedge-shaped crack, yet each kept his rush of memories to himself. Finally Hoftaller remarked, "Makes me sad, even though we've been predicting this dismantling ever since the *Sputnik Magazine* affair. It'll be published some day, our report on the collapse of government order. Wasn't taken seriously. The leading comrades refused to pay attention. No news to me: deafness always sets in when things start to fall apart. . . ."

More in a whisper than out loud, Hoftaller vented his professional dismay through the gap in the Wall. Suddenly he giggled. A fit of long-suppressed giggling, now dammed up to the point of overflowing, shook him. And Fonty, who had to stoop to hear his whispering, caught the words "Funny, actually. Typical case of power-weariness. Center can't hold. But wouldn't it be nice to know who unlocked the gate? I mean, who slipped Comrade Schabowski that script? Who let him use the PA system? Bellowing out sentence after sentence . . . 'From this day forward . . .' Well, Fonty, who do you think remembered the formula 'Open Sesame!'? Who do you think? No wonder the West practically had a stroke when the ninth of November rolled around and tens of thousands—what am I saying? —hundreds of thousands came over, on foot and in their Trabis. They were dumbfounded, they called the whole thing crazy . . . crazy! But that's how it is when you've been whining for years, 'Tear down this Wall. . . .' Well, Wuttke, who was it who said 'Go ahead, swallow us up'? Has the penny dropped?"

Fonty, who had stood in silence, his head cocked, did not want to play Twenty Questions. He countered with a question of his own: "So where were *you* the day they sealed this place up, smack down the middle?"

They were still there, framed by the gaping hole that caught them at chest and shoulder level: a dual portrait.

Because they both enjoyed submitting to the ritual of well-rehearsed interrogations, we assume that Fonty knew in advance the elements that would go into Hoftaller's litany: "Due to counterrevolutionary tendencies . . . Without the support of the Soviet Union . . . Purges soon followed . . ."

He enumerated neglected security measures, spoke of disappointments. He was still deploring gaps in the system. The seventeenth of June 1953 stuck in his craw: "Was punitively reassigned. Sat around at the State Archives. Slid into a depression. Had to get out of the Workers' and Peasants' State. Not a real crisis of values, though. No, Tallhover didn't call it quits, just changed sides, was in demand over there. Unfortunately, my biographer didn't want to believe that; he misjudged the freedom they take for granted in the West, saw me as boxed in, cooked up a death wish for me — as though my kind could ever call it quits. Our work, Fonty, it never ends!"

Hoftaller had stopped whispering. He was no longer posed in front of the gaping slab structure that forced confessions out of people, but was once more walking with bustling steps past the interminable mural. Now he sounded jovial: "All right to talk about it now: was received with open arms. Obviously: my special expertise! Went by a reversed name over there. I was on the books as 'Revolat.' The change of scenery did me a world of good. But no shortage of disappointments on the other side either. My warnings regarding the sealing of the border fell on deaf ears. I showed the agency in Cologne photocopies — bills of lading that documented all the large-scale purchases, stuff needed for the Peace Wall: cement, reinforcing rods, tons of barbed wire. Finally tipped off Pullach. Pointless. Eventually, when it was already too late, Agent Revolat realized that the West wanted the Wall, too. Made everything easier. For both sides. Even the Yanks were all for it. Couldn't get much more secure than that. And now it's coming down!"

"Nothing lasts forever," Fonty comforted him. In the diagonal rays of afternoon sunlight they strode and bustled toward the Gate. The sun, already low in the sky, cast a paired shadow on the Wall's painted surface. The shadow followed them, mimicking their gestures as they talked, hands poking out of wide coat sleeves. They assessed the recent breach in security either as a risk— "They'll want it back one day" —or as a "colossal gain": "Better without than with!"

A few wallpeckers were still practicing their handiwork with grim determination, as if for piece wages. One elderly gentleman was even using a rechargeable electric drill. He was wearing safety goggles and ear protectors. Children were watching him.

Lots of folks were out and about—Turks, too. Young couples were having their pictures taken with a backdrop, so that later, much later, they would be able to remember. Here long-separated families were meeting. Travelers from afar stared in wonder. Groups of Japanese. A Bavarian in lederhosen. A cheerful but not rowdy mood. And hovering over everything, that sound usually attributed to the woodpecker.

Two Western mounted policemen came toward them and proceeded to ignore the Sunday work scene. Hoftaller snapped to attention, but in response to his question as to the legality of the destructive goings-on, one of the patrolmen responded like a true Berliner, "It's not permitted, but it's sure as hell not prohibited either."

To comfort his day-and-night-shadow, Fonty gave him the three penny-sized chips off the Wall. And as he stowed the fragments with their one-sided color in his change purse, like pieces of evidence, Hoftaller continued his narrative: "At any rate, after August '61 it was time for a change again. My old department came calling. Didn't wait to be asked twice. You know, of course, that I was always pan-German. . . ."

Their ritual had nothing more to offer. They continued along the Wall in silence. Their breath floated away, carrying only puffs of steam. One step after the other, and then the yoke-fellows were standing in the crush by the Brandenburg Gate, or rather by the wide curve of the concrete barricade where the world had been waiting for weeks, the camera teams poised to capture its demolition.

MASSIVE, AS IF built for the ages. Only the embarrassment of several border guards, hanging around rather than showing their presence on the bulge atop the bastion, wide enough here to walk on, proclaimed the bulwark's imminent downfall. This much we are sure of: Hoftaller viewed the scene with mixed emotions. But Fonty was enjoying the sideshow to this Sunday idyll. Young women and children held up by their mothers were offering the soldiers flowers, cigarettes, oranges, chocolate bars, and of course bananas, the tropical fruit of the month. And wonder of wonders, these men in uniform, so quick on the draw until just the other day, allowed themselves to be showered with gifts. They even accepted Western bubbly.

And here—in the midst of the festive Sunday mood, surrounded by onlookers, including young folks shouting

"Open the Gate!" more beer-happily than aggressively, in that time of rapidly rising expectations and round tables, of big words and petty reservations, in that hour of toppled bosses and first hasty deals, on a windless, clear December day in the year '89, when stock in the word "unification" was rising hourly—Fonty suddenly began to declaim, at the top of his voice and refusing to be shushed by Hoftaller, that long poem entitled "Victory March" that had been printed on 16 June 1871, in the Berlin *Foreigners' and Classified Advertising Gazette*, specifically to mark the victorious end of the campaign against France and the founding of the Reich, as well as the coronation of the Prussian king as kaiser of all Germans, a poem whose many stanzas paraded all the returning regiments through the streets, the guard at the head of the procession— "And with them march, in closed ranks and coupled, / Their sabers in hand, fame and honor doubled, / The pale-blue riders of Mars la Tour, / But half of their number left, no more . . ." —and marched them through the Brandenburg Gate, then up the splendid avenue Unter den Linden in lockstep: "Prussians and Hessians in a welter of colors, / Also Bavarians and Badians and many others, / Saxons, Swabians, tall ones and short, / Spiked helmets, plain helmets, of caps every sort. . . ."

This was not the first such celebration, for after Prussia's victories over Denmark and Austria, the first wars of unification, there had likewise been parades and rhymed victory marches—an eagerness to pay tribute, of which Fonty's first stanza had reminded the throng of onlookers before the barricade: "And here they come, the third time of late, / Marching through the magnificent gate; / The Kaiser ahead, the sun high in the skies, / Everyone laughs, and everyone cries. . . ."

Despite the vigor with which he declaimed these verses, here out in the open the voice of the former lecturer for the Cultural Union, Theo Wuttke, whom everyone called Fonty, did not carry very far. Only a few laughed, and none wept for joy, and the applause remained sparse when, in the final stanza, he brought the victory parade to a close before the statue of the second Frederick, the monument to "old Fritz."

The echo of the verses had hardly died away when the two extracted themselves from the crowd. Fonty seemed in a hurry, and Hoftaller's voice hastened after him: "I assume this is your contribution to the coming unification? Nice spit and polish. Still have it in my ear: 'Down the Linden thunder their feet, / Prussia's Germany feels the beat. . . .'"

"No need to remind me! Done for the money, and precious little of that . . ."

"There's more in the same genre, sometimes ramrod-straight, sometimes sloppily rhymed."

"Alas. But there's better stuff, too — and that will last!"

MEANWHILE THEY were making their way along under trees stiff with cold. Their conversation on the value of occasional poetry soon petered out; we offer no comment. They walked along in strides of differing lengths, encountering Sunday strollers heading for the gate. The pair's destination was the Victory Column, whose crowning angel glittered in the evening sun, a freshly gilded monstrosity. Drawn to the intersection known as the Great Star, they struck out straight across the Tiergarten, which lured them to branch off to the left to Queen Luise Bridge, the Amazon, and Rousseau Island with its park benches. But they stayed on course. They barely slowed their steps at the Soviet War Memorial.

Seen from the Brandenburg Gate, they grew smaller and smaller. An unmatched pair. Now gesticulating again: one with his walking stick, which he called "my Brandenburg hiking staff," the other with the stubby fingers of his right hand, for in his left he was carrying the bulging briefcase. A silent film. One striding, the other bustling along. Seen from the Great Star, they were making headway. Coat merged with coat into a single silhouette, although they had not linked arms. At the end of the grand parade route, the two disappeared for a moment, for they had to duck under the ceaseless flow of traffic around the Victory Column, crossing by way of a tunnel built expressly for pedestrians.

Now that the couple is gone, we are tempted to utter some choice words about this Berlin landmark, which managed to preserve its full height through both world wars, but Fonty took the words out of our mouths, for they had barely surfaced and posted themselves at the base of the lofty column, which measured sixty-six meters to the tip of the victory pennant, when an opportunity arose for digressions into the field of history, undertaken either with the help of many-stanza'd poems or on the basis of a memory that reached back to Sedan Day and even farther down the steps of time.

It sounded as if they had been there for the unveiling of the column on 2 September 1873. At the time, the figure of Borussia as Victoria stood on a pedestal on Königsplatz, known today as Platz der Republik. Shortly before the

beginning of the Second World War she was moved, on or-
ders from on high, from the square in front of the Reichs-
tag to the Great Star.

A relief mounted on the column at eye level is said to be
worth seeing. It celebrates the wars of unification, one vic-
tory after another. Here a curly-headed lad brings his father
his gun, as his mother bids the father farewell with an em-
brace; there members of the *landsturm* have just fixed their
bayonets. A bugler blows the attack signal. The fighting
men rush forward over the fallen.

They paced off the pedestal. Because the column—with
its red Swedish granite, all-around metal casting, and crown-
ing goddess of victory—had been damaged in the last, so
wretchedly lost, war, Hoftaller's finger pointed out pock-
marks everywhere; impossible to tell whether shrapnel
had found its final resting place there, or, at the very end,
grenade fragments. The breast of an infantryman pierced.
Helmets chopped in half. This hand has only three fingers.
Here a dragoon's cast-iron horse is missing its right front
leg, there a headless captain storms headlong into the fray,
at Düppel, or perhaps at Gravelotte. Looking dismayed,
Hoftaller calculated the bottom line. He counted fifty and
more direct hits, not including the damage to the granite
base. But when it came to victories and the span of Prussia's
history, Fonty had more to offer than the monument did.

He cited Count Schwerin and his flag, old Derfflinger,
Generals Zieten and Seydlitz, and reeled off all the battles
from Fehrbellin to Hohenfriedberg to Zorndorf. He was
about to pin Prussia's victories and occasional defeats to
the standards of various famous regiments and present
Frederick the Great's fabled old troopers in terse quota-

tions— "Herr Seydlitz smashes bottlenecks / When he settles down to drink; / His foes would fear for their own necks / If they could pause to think. . . ." Suddenly Fonty— who was already gathering breath for the ballad, and had raised his arms, the walking stick in one hand—was nudged from behind.

A little boy, whom he later described to us as freckled, voiced a bold request like the little Berliner he was: "Say, sir, could you tie my shoelace? Don't know how yet. I'm only five, see."

Laying his hiking staff on the ground, Fonty bent down and tied, as requested, the right shoelace in a bow.

"There," he said, "that'll hold."

"I'll do it myself next time!" the boy exclaimed and ran off to join the other boys, who were kicking a football around the Victory Column as the traffic circled incessantly.

"There you have it," Fonty said, "that's what really matters. Battles, victories, Sedan and Königgrätz, are null and void. All balderdash, *ridicule*! German unification, pure speculation! But tying your first shoelace, that's what counts."

Hoftaller stood there in his down-at-heels buckled shoes. He did not wish to be reminded.

THEN THE SUN was gone. They ducked under the Great Star again by way of the pedestrian tunnel, walked down the long street renamed to commemorate the seventeenth of June, and headed for the Tiergarten S-Bahn station. Two old men deep in conversation. Their gestures more angular now. They no longer cast a shadow.

Translated by Krishna Winston

MEINE ALTE OLIVETTI   (1996)

ist Zeuge, wei fleißig ich lüge
und von Fassung zu Fassung
der Wahrheit
um einen Tippfehler näher bin.

———•—•———

MY OLD OLIVETTI

bears witness to how diligently I lie
and from version to version
one typo at a time
get closer to the truth.

Translated by Charles Simic

WILLY BRANDT AT THE WARSAW GHETTO

First published in 1995, this letter provided an occasion for Grass to reflect on a seminal moment in German history.

Dear Hartmut von Hentig:

Yes, it's true, I was there when Willy Brandt got down on his knees at the site where the Warsaw Ghetto used to be. But what does that mean— "I was there"? What kind of experience was that, standing in the crowd, forced to the side by the security personnel, who presumably were only following protocol? Something beyond the usual ceremonial rites did take place that December day in 1970. Suddenly an image was made. A German, a politician, a Social Democrat, knelt down. Did he act on his own behalf? Did Willy Brandt the emigrant have reasons to act on others' behalf? Was he aware of the dimensions of his action?

I'll briefly describe my experience. I remember being shocked momentarily, realizing that something unbelievable was happening. Then I heard only the clicking of cameras all around. The world was taking notice, and my heart was skipping beats. How would they take the chancellor's gesture back in Germany? Wasn't it bound to provoke yet another attack from the mob of his political enemies, publisher Axel Springer at the fore? Such fears were justified. Never mind that he had fought against Germany's return to barbarism ever since he was a child; whatever this man did turned into an opportunity for more slander. And this had been going on for years.

In order to explain my fears at that time, I'll have to call up some other experiences. Willy Brandt's visit to Warsaw was part of the politics of détente that he was pursuing and developing. It was a task voters had given him by voting for him the year before. His political canniness allowed him to avoid falling into the Cold War's various ideological traps. He took upon himself the consequences of the war that Germany had started and lost, and his actions bespoke that responsibility. This visit to Warsaw meant more than recognition of the Oder-Neisse line as Germany's eastern border, which was important enough in itself. It also expressed the even more important recognition of Warsaw as the place where Germany's genocide of the Jews had begun. A visit fraught with such a history was controversial from the start.

This is why I need to recall the hatred that Brandt's political opponents deliberately fomented and directed, if not against the chancellor himself, then in place of him against Egon Bahr, one of his closest aides. And this brings us right up to the present, because the recent attempts—now, after Willy Brandt's death—to trip up his trusted friend are really only a resumption of those other, failed efforts to trip up Brandt. Once again, it is Egon Bahr who serves as the bull's-eye of the real target: Brandt and Brandt's memory. Once again, Brandt's political position is being denounced, the same position that brought him to kneel down in Warsaw.

You see, dear Hartmut von Hentig, how difficult it is to confine this moment of German history within a single event. Several hours afterward, I spoke with Polish friends who were attempting, from their point of view and experience, to understand the broader dimensions of the chancellor's remarkable action. Until then, the war for them had always been about Polish suffering. But now (though it certainly was not Brandt's intention), the Poles' own prejudices and sins of omission became apparent. These had shown themselves recently at memorial ceremonies in Auschwitz, when the Polish president had difficulty adopting an appropriate stance.

I remember other things. A few days after the signing of the first German-Polish treaty, shipyard workers coordinated strikes in Poland's port cities. In Gdansk—formerly Danzig—the police fired on the workers; there were fatalities. At the same time, there were signs of the first independent workers' unions developing. This was the establishment of Solidarnosc, the Solidarity movement. The edifice of Soviet power was beginning to reveal its structural flaws. A new development was emerging that, helped along by Willy Brandt's politics of détente, would eventually lead to the end of the East-West conflict.

Yes, I was there. From the sidelines I caught a fleeting glimpse of the kneeling chancellor: a speechless event that left nothing unsaid. And now, in writing to you, my heart once more is skipping beats with the same fear I felt back then, a fear that has not gone away. For Willy Brandt's kneeling down in Warsaw that day is still, or is again, considered an offense.

Translated by W. Martin

Obituary for Helen Wolff

Eulogy on the (posthumous) award to Helen Wolff of the Friedrich Gundolf Prize in Leipzig on April 30, 1994.

HER DEATH HAS ALTERED EVERYTHING, MORE THAN I can say. And what I can say lies now on a different sheet of paper, for originally I had wanted to greet Helen Wolff with a jovial remark and brush aside all the formalities: Dear Helen, I'm so glad you could make it.

When the German Academy of Language and Literature invited me to deliver a eulogy at the Friedrich Gundolf Prize ceremony, I knew I had far more to say about the award's recipient than a short speech could encompass. Or perhaps it was the aura surrounding the name Gundolf that had me in a mild state of shock, or, rather, of paralysis. There was something of the high priest about that name, something otherworldly and unreal. And the distance to that other world was impassable; all I could do was demonstrate, along with my ignorance, respect, for I did not want to impose something slapdash on either the prizewinner or the ceremony's audience.

Then came the sad news. The final certainty. The loss. And yet it seems as if I could still talk to you, Helen, whom in my secret, one-sided conversations I've always called Helena, directly, as one friend to another, as an author to his publisher. It seems as if I could still act as if nothing had happened, as if I should still be expecting that bit of advice from you, as if the letter were on its way, as if I could still respond to your impatient requests for the next manuscript with all manner of prevarication.

What a publisher! Who ever heard of it? The immense, epically proportioned love she showered on writers, her leniency toward the chronic egotists among them, her frank and trustworthy criticism that always sought to know more precisely, not to know better. Then there was her abundant hospitality, the inviting backdrop of her home, to which, on more than one occasion, the exhausted writer on the stage, about to give up, was invited, offered refuge and a drink, or two.

This obituary may sound more like a eulogy, but I know that I speak for many writers—in particular, two who would have offered similar words of praise. For Max Frisch and Uwe Johnson were, like me, pups in the Wolff Breeding and Care Facility. She knew us down to our lowest dungeon and least perfidy. You couldn't fool her. Being published by her meant being looked after by her, through lean times and good.

We authors knew—and often said so to one another—that regardless of our own reputed achievements, it was Helen Wolff we had most to thank for our literary presence in America. This gratitude was doubtless shared by our translators, who could count on her critical advice or objections

right through the page proofs. Ralph Manheim, my transla-
tor, could tell you a thing or two, or three or four, about that.
For, ever since his *Grimms' Fairy Tales,* back when Kurt Wolff
was still alive, he has been subject to the strictest discipline.

Kurt Wolff—what a publisher! And his partner, who
never wanted to detach herself from his shadow, who never
needed to emphasize her independence, but instead sup-
ported her positions by appealing, even obliquely, to his. I
remember sentences like "Kurt would have done it this
way," or "Kurt would have been of a different opinion on
that. . . ."

Helen and Kurt Wolff Books, through the decades. It
was a mark of distinction. Their imprint is legendary. Like
Frisch and Johnson, I was proud my books were taken up
by that imprint. We were grateful for it, for no matter how
self-confident any of us were as authors, without the pub-
lisher Helen Wolff there would have been little chance
of German fiction getting very far in the United States.
She built the bridge. She spared herself no trouble in
order to bring even quite difficult works—I'm thinking
of Schädlich's *Approximation* —to American readers from
New York to San Francisco. She would have taken any risk
to publish Uwe Johnson's *Anniversaries.* Even if her work
should be continued, and I hope it will be, Helen Wolff's
are shoes that cannot be filled. With her death, I fear that
even in the field of literature the future will belong either
to the quick business deal or to the American love of
convenience.

From my European perspective, America seems impov-
erished without Helen. Suddenly there's nothing there any-
more. The bridge's column is gone. I'm saying this out of

panic, certainly, but with an understanding, too, of how much writers of my generation owe to the German émigrés. Those who were expelled from Germany did more for us than anyone could have expected or hoped. Those who remained in America saved us from the confines of provincialism: they made us open-minded.

This is something I learned during my early, *Tin Drum* days. In January 1960, a young author then, I was invited to a hotel in Zurich that in its haute bourgeois grandeur might have been oppressive had it not been for Kurt and Helen Wolff, who masterfully downplayed the concentrated pomp and made everything seem so easy. I had barely ordered my drink—I believe it was a Bloody Mary—when the Wolffs surprised me with a question, which Kurt asked: "Can you imagine *The Tin Drum* finding readers in America?"

I answered truthfully with a *no*, but wanted to support my negation with proof, so I admitted my recent surprise at learning that I even had readers in Bavaria. To make myself more clear, I pointed out that Oskar Matzerath's entire world was far away on the Baltic coast, and was largely limited to Danzig or, more precisely, to the unsightly suburb known as Langfuhr; that people there talked in their homey, earthy, gruff, and easygoing way and always about the Kashubians, a vanishing minority; that it stank of the provinces there.

When I finished, Kurt Wolff authoritatively declared that his mind was made up: The book would appear in America. My explanation was convincing, he said, even though I was against the idea, for he knew that all great literature was centered in the provinces, tucked away there, without being in the least provincial, which was why it had such international appeal. Helen agreed with him, posing questions about passages of dialect or jargon that might prove difficult to translate: "Can you please tell me, what is *Glumse?*"

And so it happened that two years later *The Tin Drum,* in Ralph Manheim's translation, was entrusted to American readers. Apparently the Texans are as receptive to Kashubian potato fields and that stuffy suburb Langfuhr as the Bavarians were before them. The leap over the big pond was successful, thanks to my publishers' foresight.

Not long after, Helen and Kurt Wolff moved from Random House to the publishing house of Harcourt Brace Jovanovich. I joined them. When Kurt Wolff died in an accident during a visit to Germany, Helen Wolff continued her husband's work. Her editorial solicitude was already the basis of my trust in them. We accompanied each other book by book. And every translation had to stand the test of her critical eye. It was to her persistence and clout—in dealing with the publisher William Jovanovich, for instance—that Uwe Johnson, as I mentioned earlier, owed the publication of his books in America. And it was she who set up the place on Riverside Drive where Johnson reminisced about his lost Mecklenburg. In a letter to the literary critic Roland Berbig, written in Hanover, New Hampshire, on June 6, 1991, Wolff remembers: "How strongly I felt his and his wife's nostalgia for the lost landscape of their homeland, the geography of which he so meticulously described, even the wind and the waves. That he was forced to go into exile, irrevocably, an innocent man yielding to criminals, was an eternal thorn in his side."

As fragile as Helen Wolff may have appeared to others, she was endowed with a power that, combined with her ed-

itorial courage, guaranteed the survival of the Helen and
Kurt Wolff Books imprint over the decades, even in times
of crisis, of which there were many: well-known publishing
houses everywhere were going under, following the laws of
the free market, of course.

Helen Wolff lived through it all. Born in Macedonia and
raised in Austria—albeit in the Prussian style, at a school
that may as well have had Theodor Fontane for a director—
she brought her delicate, quiet manner to bear on her hus-
band's editorial course, which was hers also, steering it
through unsteady seas and unsteadier markets. Any author
who had the opportunity, as I had, to be present for the
launch of each of his or her books will remember being sub-
jected to a taxing—but for all that no less stimulating—
program of events. And always one was sure to be con-
fronted with highly qualified critics. My encounters with
American literary criticism have again and again given me a
chance to recover from its German counterpart. In the
United States, I met with professionalism and passionate
practicality, with editors whose worlds weren't bounded by
their desks or limited to the alternating rhythms of pressure
and leisure. And during strictly timed interviews I found
myself sitting across from critics who had actually read
something and whose talk was anything but off-the-cuff.

Presiding over all of this, in person or at a distance, was
Helen Wolff. She made sure her European author did not
fall prey to the idle clutches of boredom, and at the same
time protected him from the heady and unfamiliar velocity
of American life. It was through her that I met Hannah
Arendt. Conversations around her table were never arbi-
trary. She never failed to give her guests their proper portion

of attention, whether in the form of respect or of another glass of wine. Helen Wolff the publisher never lost sight of the fact that authors are the very substance of publishing. She knew that no matter how beautiful and modern and multistoried it is, a publishing house is an empty house if the publisher and editors do not daily take care of their first priority, their authors. She deliberately adopted a mediating position in the service of others. Not a few German publishers would do well to study Helen Wolff's example; they might at least come to recognize thereby their own high-handedness.

Publisher of books, writer of letters. We kept up our correspondence over the course of many years. Oh dear Helena, how I shall miss it. How patiently you would listen to me go on at length about my work. You frequently had a better understanding of my many children than I did. Only occasionally, and never entirely, did we allow the clouds of American or German politics to darken our letters; you were both radical and conservative at the same time. In both our letters and conversations, we shared our worry over Uwe Johnson, who was beyond help. Our correspondence outlasted numerous presidents and several chancellors. Your comments on the German temperament were ironic, and informed by your indelible memory. And now and then we even managed letters of nothing but chatter; Fontane sent his regards.

I'll close this obituary, which should have been a eulogy, with a word of thanks. When I first started preparing the eulogy that I was invited to write, I realized that Helen Wolff's return to the city of Leipzig would close a long chapter in a long and very German history. Two years ago she wrote me a letter expressing her regret at not being able to make it to the book fair: "I don't feel up to all the commotion of the fair, especially in a Leipzig I would no longer recognize. . . ."

Helen Wolff would have wanted to be here today, in a city where not long ago many thousands of people raised their voices to their then rulers, shouting: *We are the people!* It wasn't long before some people started replacing one little word in that statement, apparently hoping "*one* people" would count for more than merely "*the* people." The complexities of German self-discovery aside, I think I speak for all of us in saying how much we would have liked to welcome Helen Wolff now, here, in Leipzig. How I would have liked to thank her: my friend, my publisher. I miss her.

Translated by W. Martin

Literature and History

Address delivered on the conferment of the Prince of Asturias
Prize in Oviedo on October 22, 1999.

Your Majesty, Your Highness,
Ladies and Gentlemen,
Esteemed Prizewinners!

Were I to attempt, on your behalf and my own, to give
thanks for the honors bestowed on us today in Your
Majesties' presence by the Prince of Asturias, then I should
begin, tentatively at first, by searching for something that
might provide us, although we represent the most diverse
disciplines, with common ground for the duration of an
ideally brief speech. All at once we are confronted by an
event for which the whole world has been waiting: the end
of a century and, with it, of a millennium. As prizewinners,
we represent the rear guard, so to speak, of the terrible pro-
gression of an era that even today remains dedicated to
dogma. But since the past will not end for any of us, no mat-
ter what country we belong to, but will overtake us again

and again, each individually in our respective societies, we may expect that the date marking the turn of the century will have little impact on the repressed or prematurely written-off contents of the past. History and its reverberations could not care less about the problem of the zero, which might wreck even the most intelligently devised computer systems. History derides numbers. It will throw its shadow far into the next century. We cannot escape it. It forces us to review everything. And what we leave behind, badly digested, will remain an obstacle for both current and future generations: excrement, the dried crusts of which are texts to be read.

And here I arrive at my topic: Literature and History. For as long as I have been a writer—going on five decades now—history, and German history most insistently, has stood in my way. It has been impossible to avoid. Even the cleverest artistic infidelities have led me again and again onto its meandering path. From my first novel, *The Tin Drum,* to the latest child of my whims, which bears the proprietary title *My Century,* I have been its rebellious vassal. The destruction and loss of my hometown, Danzig, unleashed an epic mass of material, and although this mass was clouded, down to the last narrative detail, with petit bourgeois circumstances and the fug of Catholicism, yet it constantly, through the torpor of daily life and at endless family get-togethers, gave voice to history: at first in announcements of victory, then in hushed admissions of retreat. No idyll, no matter how lovingly encapsulated, was safe from the incursions of current events. Private life took place on call, while history went on thunderously entering its data. And only thanks to literary trickery was it possible to pit a countertext against such a force: by abridging time on the one hand and drawing it out on the other, and by the stretto of simultaneous actions, changes in perspective, and the demonstrative peeling of onions.

Literature thus exposes history's undergrowth. It clears the view to those decomposing minor events that take place behind the grandstands of state. It makes the sublime ridiculous and great things small and, as in Andersen's fairy tale "The Emperor's New Clothes," it enables a child to see any majesty naked. What I am describing is a narrative perspective that begins below the table and leads up over its edge and beyond; the view is amoral and therefore uninhibited, and it cannot be fooled. Thus the supposedly meaningful course of history becomes an effluent from which the sea of absurdity is fed unimpeded.

Spiteful narratives like this have their tradition. Here in Spain, Moorish and Iberian cultures exhausted and enlivened each other over the centuries that their love-hate relationship endured, and that grotesque conflict of realities was the proving ground for a form of the novel that elevated the outsider to hero and that would later be termed "picaresque" by nomenclature-obsessed literary scholars. The picaro captured the world and its commotion in mirrors convex and concave. Through his lies he brought the truth to light. Nothing was sacred to him. His mockery rubbed the parchment of scholasticism so hard the wrong way that it crumbled apart. He unleashed a laughter so demonic, even the powers that were had to dance to it. And out of those many authors who, shuttling between Morocco and Andalusia, came out of this school—which, being unhoused, was altogether unacademic—was one named Cervantes, and his hero, Don Quixote, continues today to bring literary children into the world, children as fanciful as himself, who demonstrate to reality its absurd subtext and to absurdity its spoor of reality. He is the father of the European novel, and in his yard Voltaire's Candide picked apart "the best of all possible worlds," Laurence Sterne's Tristram Shandy attributed his conception to an inquiry after the well-being of a clock, Charles de Coster's Till Eulenspiegel played a trickster-fool in the Flemish struggle for freedom against the Spanish occupation, and Grimmelshausen's Simplicissimus fought to survive between the onslaughts of alternating armies. What would Germans know about the horrors of the Thirty Years' War if not for this picaro, who with his worm's-eye view recounted the events that the historians in their diligence, as lifeless as it is precise, arranged for us purely chronologically, date by date?

The evidence that literature's eyewitnesses provide is more substantial. They let the losers have their say, too: all those who failed to make history yet were unable to escape it, inasmuch as it dictated their being perpetrators or victims, collaborators or quarry. I would know nothing, or next to nothing, about the complex relations between friend and enemy during the Spanish Civil War had not George Orwell, in his book *Homage to Catalonia,* documented the system of terror established by the Communists, whose commissars had countless Anarchists and Socialists liquidated behind the front lines. Writers from around the world played a role in the Republic's struggle and downfall by telling its story. Hardly any event in this century has been so well preserved by so many voices, that it might be experienced again in the mirror of literature—even if the voices of Spanish authors, long suppressed by censorship, have been heard belatedly. For instance, it is only now, in conjunction with Germany's fall book fair, that publishers are issuing the first two volumes of the six-volume epic novel *The Magic Labyrinth,* written during his decades of exile, by Max Aub, a Spanish author of German and French origin. No, this history cannot end. It must be retold again and again. Perhaps one day this homeland of the picaresque obsession with narrative will produce a new young author, one who is no less an heir to the great Unamuno, who will endow his country with a dance of death comparable in its urgency to the sequence of images titled *The Disasters of War* that Goya left behind and that is permanently etched into our memory, just as Picasso did when he captured the terrors of the Spanish Civil War in his painting *Guernica.*

A good deal of literature, as far as I can tell, comes from loss. When systems, like the Soviet one recently, break down over their own history; when structures of power crumble and disappear; when the stupidity of the victors cries to high heaven; when freedom brings privation in tow and a flood of refugees mixes in with recent mass migrations; when history keels over into an ongoing state of catastrophe, and capitalism, as the last remaining ideology, dissipates into global irrationalism; when only the stock market yields meaning anymore and could well bring everything crashing down with it; and finally, when the guild of historians, weary of the quarrel over footnotes, gets lost in the fuzziness of the *posthistoire,* then literature enjoys a bull market. Crises are literature's bread and butter. It blossoms amid ruins. It hears the death rattle. Rifling through the pockets of the dead is its business. Paid or unpaid, it keeps watch over the body and always tells the survivors the old stories anew.

But if you look into the culture pages of the newspaper or listen to the murmurs behind the scenes, it appears that wherever the secondary has had the cheek to upstage the primary, literature is, to use the current jargon, out. At most it can be tarted up and brought out on stage, or fed, tidbit by tidbit, to the Internet. For fringe groups, advertising tells us, it can even be used to promote consumer spending.

I don't want to believe any of this. I'm confessedly ignorant. Progress that insists on my self-acceleration means nothing to me. I'm old-fashioned and I pursue an old-fashioned profession. I don't own a computer, nor do I monkey about on the Internet. I really do still write my manuscripts by hand and type up the second and third drafts with the help of a rickety manual typewriter. And all of this I do daily, standing at a lectern, walking back and forth, murmuring to myself, chewing apart sentences until, both written and spoken, they've either been thoroughly slimmed down or filled up to the brim. I know this much: history will continue, seizure by seizure, and along with it, always in opposition to it, literature, too, will have a future.

Driven to the margins, books will be subversive again. And there will be readers for whom books are a means of survival. Already I see children who are sated with television and bored by computer games; who isolate themselves with a book, captivated by the pull of told history, of stories; whose imaginations range across hundreds of pages and more; who read much more than what is merely printed, black on white. For this is what distinguishes humanity. No image is lovelier than the sight of a reading child. Utterly lost in the world between two book covers, that child is no less present in this one; she simply does not want to be disturbed.

And even if someday, whether soon or a long time from now, humanity should by means of one or another intelligently devised system destroy itself, this, too, being an option, after all, the book—I am certain of it, honored Ladies and Gentlemen, dear Prince of Asturias—will have the last word.

Translated by W. Martin

To Be Continued . . .

Nobel Lecture, December 7, 1999, Stockholm, Sweden.

Honoured Members of the Swedish Academy, Ladies and Gentlemen,

Having made this announcement, nineteenth-century works of fiction would go on and on. Magazines and news papers gave them all the space they wished: the serialized novel was in its heyday. While the early chapters appeared in quick succession, the core of the work was being written out by hand, and its conclusion was yet to be conceived. Nor was it only trivial horror stories or tearjerkers that thus held the reader in thrall. Many of Dickens's novels came out in serial form, in installments. Tolstoy's *Anna Karenina* was a serialized novel. Balzac's time, a tireless provider of mass-produced serializations, gave the still-anonymous writer lessons in the technique of suspense, of building to a climax at the end of a column. And nearly all Fontane's novels appeared first in newspapers and magazines as serializations.

Witness the publisher of the *Vossischen Zeitung*, where *Trials and Tribulations* first saw print, who exclaimed in a rage, "Will this sluttish story never end!"

But before I go on spinning these strands of my talk or move on to others, I wish to point out that from a purely literary point of view this hall and the Swedish Academy that invited me here are far from alien to me. My novel *The Rat*, which came out almost fourteen years ago and whose catastrophic course along various oblique levels of narration one or two of my readers may recall, features a eulogy delivered before just such an audience as you, an encomium to the rat or, to be more precise, the laboratory rat.

The rat has been awarded a Nobel Prize. At last, one might say. She's been on the list for years, even the short list. Representative of millions of experimental animals—from guinea pig to rhesus monkey—the white-haired, red-eyed laboratory rat is finally getting her due. For she more than anyone—or so claims the narrator of my novel—has made possible all the Nobelified research and discoveries in the field of medicine and, as far as Nobel laureates Watson and Crick are concerned, on the virtually boundless turf of gene manipulation. Since then maize and other vegetables—to say nothing of all sorts of animals—can be cloned more or less legally, which is why the rat-men, who increasingly take over as the novel comes to a close, that is, during the posthuman era, are called Watsoncricks. They combine the best of both genera. Humans have much of the rat in them and vice versa. The world seems to use the synthesis to regain its health. After the Big Bang, when only rats, cockroaches, flies, and the remains of fish- and frog-eggs survive and it is time to make order out of the chaos, the Watsoncricks, who miraculously escape, do more than their share.

But since this strand of the narrative could as easily have ended with "To Be Continued..." and the Nobel Prize speech in praise of the laboratory rat is certainly not meant to give the novel a happy end, I can now—as what might be called a matter of principle—turn to narration as a form of survival as well as a form of art.

People have always told tales. Long before humanity learned to write and gradually became literate, everybody told tales to everybody else and everybody listened to everybody else's tales. Before long it became clear that some of the still-illiterate storytellers told more and better tales than others, that is, they could make more people believe their lies. And there were those among them who found artful ways of stemming the peaceful flow of their tales and diverting it into a tributary, that, far from drying up, turned suddenly and amazingly into a broad bed, though now full of flotsam and jetsam, the stuff of subplots. And because these primordial storytellers—who were not dependent upon day- or lamp-light and could carry on perfectly well in the dark, who were in fact adept at exploiting dusk or darkness to add to the suspense—because they stopped at nothing, neither dry stretches nor thundering waterfalls, except perhaps to interrupt the course of action with a "To Be Continued..." if they sensed their audience's attention flagging, many of their listeners felt moved to start telling tales of their own.

What tales were told when no one could yet write and therefore no one wrote them down. From the days of Cain and Abel there were tales of murder and manslaughter.

Feuds—blood feuds, in particular—were always good for a story. Genocide entered the picture quite early along with floods and droughts, fat years and lean years. Lengthy lists of cattle and slaves were perfectly acceptable, and no tale could be believable without detailed genealogies of who came before whom and who came after, heroic tales especially. Love triangles, popular even now, and tales of monsters—half man, half beast, who made their way through labyrinths or lay in wait in the bulrushes—attracted mass audiences from the outset, to say nothing of legends of gods and idols and accounts of sea journeys, which were then handed down, polished, enlarged upon, modified, transmogrified into their opposites, and finally written down by a storyteller whose name was supposedly Homer or, in the case of the Bible, by a collective of storytellers. In China and Persia, in India and the Peruvian highlands, wherever writing flourished, storytellers—whether as groups or individuals, anonymously or by name—turned into literati.

Writing-fixated as we are, we nonetheless retain the memory of oral storytelling, the spoken origins of literature. And a good thing too, because if we were to forget that all storytelling comes through the lips—now inarticulate, hesitant, now swift, as if driven by fear, now in whisper, to keep the secrets revealed from reaching the wrong ears, now loudly and clearly, all the way from self-serving bluster to sniffing out the very essence of life—if our faith in writing were to make us forget all that, our storytelling would be bookish, dry as dust.

Yet how good too that we have so many books available to us and that whether we read them aloud or to ourselves they are permanent. They have been my inspiration. When

I was young and malleable, masters like Melville and Döblin or Luther with his Biblical German prompted me to read aloud as I wrote, to mix ink with spit. Nor have things changed much since. Well into my fifth decade of enduring, no, relishing the moil and toil called writing, I chew tough, stringy clauses into manageable mush, babble to myself in blissful isolation, and put pen to paper only when I hear the proper tone and pitch, resonance and reverberation.

Yes, I love my calling. It keeps me company, a company whose polyphonic chatter calls for literal transcription into my manuscripts. And there is nothing I like more than to meet books of mine—books that have long since flown the coop and been expropriated by readers—when I read out loud to an audience what now lies peacefully on the page. For both the young, weaned early from language, and the old, grizzled yet still rapacious, the written word becomes spoken, and the magic works again and again. It is the shaman in the author earning a bit on the side, writing against the current of time, lying his way to tenable truths. And everyone believes his tacit promise: To Be Continued . . .

But how did I become a writer, poet, and artist—all at once and all on frightening white paper? What homemade hubris put a child up to such craziness? After all, I was only twelve when I realized I wanted to be an artist. It coincided with the outbreak of the Second World War, when I was living on the outskirts of Danzig. But my first opportunity for professional development had to wait until the following year, when I found a tempting offer in the Hitler Youth magazine *Hilf mit!* (Lend a Hand!). It was a story contest.

With prizes. I immediately set to writing my first novel. Influenced by my mother's background, it bore the title *The Kashubians*, but the action did not take place in the painful present of that small and dwindling people; it took place in the thirteenth century during a period of interregnum, a grim period when brigands and robber barons ruled the highways and the only recourse a peasant had to justice was a kind of kangaroo court.

All I can remember of it is that after a brief outline of the economic conditions in the Kashubian hinterland I started in on pillages and massacres with a vengeance. There was so much throttling, stabbing, and skewering, so many kangaroo-court hangings and executions that by the end of the first chapter all the protagonists and a goodly number of the minor characters were dead and either buried or left to the crows. Since my sense of style did not allow me to turn corpses into spirits and the novel into a ghost story, I had to admit defeat with an abrupt end and no "To Be Continued . . ." Not for good, of course, but the neophyte had learned his lesson: next time he would have to be a bit more gentle with his characters.

But first I read and read some more. I had my own way of reading: with my fingers in my ears. Let me say by way of explanation that my younger sister and I grew up in straitened circumstances, that is, in a two-room flat and hence without rooms of our own or even so much as a corner to ourselves. In the long run it turned out to be an advantage, though: I learned at an early age to concentrate in the midst of people or surrounded by noise. When I read I might have been under a bell jar; I was so involved in the world of the book that my mother, who liked a practical joke, once demonstrated her son's complete and utter absorption to a neighbor by replacing a roll I had been taking an occasional bite from with a bar of soap—Palmolive, I believe—whereupon the two women—my mother not without a certain pride—watched me reach blindly for the soap, sink my teeth into it, and chew it for a good minute before it tore me away from my adventure on the page.

To this day I can concentrate as I did in my early years, but I have never read more obsessively. Our books were kept in a bookcase behind blue-curtained panes of glass. My mother belonged to a book club, and the novels of Dostoevsky and Tolstoy stood side by side and mixed in with novels by Hamsun, Raabe, and Vicky Baum. Selma Lagerlöf's *Gösta Berling* was within easy reach. I later moved on to the Municipal Library, but my mother's collection provided the initial impulse. A punctilious businesswoman forced to sell her wares to unreliable customers on credit, she was also a great lover of beauty: she listened to opera and operetta melodies on her primitive radio, enjoyed hearing my promising stories, and frequently went to the Municipal Theater, even taking me along from time to time.

The only reason I rehearse here these anecdotes of a petit bourgeois childhood after painting them with epic strokes decades ago in works peopled by fictitious characters is to help me answer the question "What made you become a writer?" The ability to daydream at length, the job of punning and playing with language in general, the addiction to lying for its own sake rather than for mine because sticking to the truth would have been a bore—in short, what is loosely known as talent was certainly a factor, but it was the abrupt intrusion of politics into the family idyll that turned the all too flighty category of talent into a ballast with a certain permanence and depth.

My mother's favorite cousin, like her a Kashubian by birth, worked at the Polish post office in the Free City of Danzig. He was a regular at our house and always welcome. When the war broke out the Hevelius Square post office building held out for a time against the SS-Heimwehr, and my uncle was rounded up with those who finally surrendered. They were tried summarily and put before a firing squad. Suddenly he was no more. Suddenly and permanently his name was no longer mentioned. He became a nonperson. Yet he must have lived on in me through the years when at fifteen I donned a uniform, at sixteen I learned what fear was, at seventeen I landed in an American POW camp, at eighteen I worked in the black market, studied to be a stonemason and started sculpting in stone, prepared for admission to art school, and wrote and drew, drew and wrote, fleet-footed verse, quizzical one-acts, and on it went until I found the material unwieldy—I seem to have an inborn need for aesthetic pleasure. And beneath the detritus of it all lay my mother's favorite cousin, the Polish postal clerk, shot and buried, only to be found by me (who else?) and exhumed and resuscitated by literary artificial respiration under other names and guises, though this time in a novel whose major and minor characters, full of life and beans as they are, make it through a number of chapters, some even holding out till the end and thus enabling the writer to keep his recurrent promise: To Be Continued . . .

And so on and so forth. The publication of my first two novels, *The Tin Drum* and *Dog Years,* and the novella I stuck between them, *Cat and Mouse,* taught me early on, as a relatively young writer, that books can cause offense, stir up fury, even hatred, that what is undertaken out of love for one's country can be taken as soiling one's nest. From then on I have been controversial.

Which means that like writers banished to Siberia or suchlike places I am in good company. So I have no grounds to complain; on the contrary, writers should consider the condition of permanent controversiality to be invigorating, part of the risk involved in choosing the profession. It is a fact of life that writers have always and with due consideration and great pleasure spit in the soup of the high and mighty. That is what makes the history of literature analogous to the development and refinement of censorship.

The ill humour of the powers-that-be forced Socrates to drain the cup of hemlock to the dregs, sent Ovid into exile, made Seneca open his veins. For centuries and to the present day the finest fruits of the Western garden of literature have graced the index of the Catholic church. How much equivocation did the European Enlightenment learn from the censorship practiced by princes with absolute power? How many German, Italian, Spanish, and Portuguese writers did fascism drive from their lands and languages? How many writers fell victim to the Leninist-Stalinist reign of terror? And what constraints are writers under today in countries like China, Kenya, or Croatia?

I come from the land of book burning. We know that the desire to destroy a hated book is still (or once more) part of the spirit of our times and that when necessary it finds appropriate telegenic expression and therefore a mass

audience. What is much worse, however, is that the perse-
cution of writers, including the threat of murder and mur-
der itself, is on the rise throughout the world, so much so
that the world has grown accustomed to the terror of it.
True, the part of the world that calls itself free raises a hue
and cry when, as in 1995 in Nigeria, a writer like Ken Saro-
Wiwa and his supporters are sentenced to death and killed
for taking a stand against the contamination of their coun-
try, but things immediately go back to normal, because
ecological considerations might affect the profits of the
world's number one oil colossus, Shell.

What makes books—and with them writers—so dan-
gerous that church and state, politburos and the mass
media feel the need to oppose them? Silencing and worse
are seldom the result of direct attacks on the reigning ide-
ology. Often all it takes is a literary allusion to the idea that
truth exists only in the plural—that there is no such thing
as a single truth but only a multitude of truths—to make
the defenders of one or another truth sense danger, mortal
danger. Then there is the problem that writers are by defi-
nition unable to leave the past in peace: they are quick to
open closed wounds, peer behind closed doors, find skele-
tons in the cupboard, consume sacred cows or, as in the
case of Jonathan Swift, offer up Irish children, "stewed,
roasted, baked, or boiled," to the kitchens of the English
nobility. In other words, nothing is sacred to them, not
even capitalism, and that makes them offensive, even crim-
inal. But worst of all they refuse to make common cause
with the victors of history: they take pleasure milling about
the fringes of the historical process with the losers, who
have plenty to say but no platform to say it on. By giving

them a voice, they call the victory into question, by associating with them, they join ranks with them.

Of course the powers-that-be, no matter what period costume they may be wearing, have nothing against literature as such. They enjoy it as an ornament and even promote it. At present its role is to entertain, to serve the fun culture, to de-emphasize the negative side of things and give people hope, a light in the darkness. What is basically called for, though not quite so explicitly as during the Communist years, is a "positive hero." In the jungle of the free market economy he is likely to pave his way to success Rambo-like with corpses and a smile; he is an adventurer who is always up for a quick fuck between battles, a winner who leaves a trail of losers behind him, in short, the perfect role model for our globalized world. And the demand for the hard-boiled he-man who always lands on his feet is unfailingly met by the media: James Bond has spawned any number of Dolly-like children. Good will continue to prevail over evil as long as it assumes his cool-guy pose.

Does that make his opposite or enemy a negative hero? Not necessarily. I have my roots, as you will have noticed from your reading, in the Spanish or Moorish school of the picaresque novel. Tilting at windmills has remained a model for that school down through the ages, and the picaro's very existence derives from the comic nature of defeat. He pees on the pillars of power and saws away at the throne knowing full well he will make no dent in either: once he moves on, the exalted temple may look a bit shabby, the throne may wobble slightly, but that is all. His humor is part and parcel of his despair. While *Die Götterdämmerung* drones on before an elegant Bayreuth audience, he sits sniggering in the back row, because in his theater comedy and tragedy go hand in hand. He scorns the fateful march of the victors and sticks his foot out to trip them, yet much as his failure makes us laugh the laughter sticks in our throat: even his wittiest cynicisms have a tragic cast to them. Besides, from the point of view of the philistine, rightist or leftist, he is a formalist—even a mannerist—of the first order: he holds the spyglass the wrong way; he sees time as a train on a siding; he puts mirrors everywhere; you can never tell whose ventriloquist he is; given his perspective, he can even accept dwarfs and giants into his entourage. The reason Rabelais was constantly on the run from the secular police and the Holy Inquisition is that his larger-than-life Gargantua and Pantagruel had turned the world according to scholasticism on its head. The laughter they unleashed was positively infernal. When Gargantua stooped bare-arsed on the towers of Notre-Dame and pissed the length and breadth of Paris under water, everyone who did not drown guffawed. Or to go back to Swift: his modest culinary proposal for relieving the hunger in Ireland could be brought up-to-date if at the next economic summit the buffet set for the heads of state were groaning with lusciously prepared street children from Brazil or southern Sudan. Satire is the name of the art form I have in mind, and in satire everything is permitted, even tickling the funny bone with the grotesque.

When Heinrich Böll gave his Nobel lecture here on 2 May 1973, he brought the seemingly opposing positions of reason and poetry into closer and closer proximity and bemoaned the lack of time to go into another aspect of the issue: "I have had to pass over humor, which, though no class privilege, is ignored in his poetry as a hiding place for resistance." Now Böll knew that Jean Paul, the poet in question, had a place in the German Culture Hall of Fame, little read though he is nowadays; he knew to what extent Thomas Mann's literary oeuvre was suspected—by both the right and the left—of irony at the time (and still is, I might add). Clearly, what Böll had in mind was not belly-laugh humor but rather inaudible, between-the-lines humor, the chronic susceptibility to melancholy of his clown, the desperate wit of the man who collected silence, an activity, by the way, that has become quite the thing in the media and—under the guise of "voluntary self-control" on the part of the free West—a benign disguise for censorship.

By the early fifties, when I had started writing consciously, Heinrich Böll was a well-known if not always well-received author. With Wolfgang Koeppen, Günter Eich, and Arno Schmidt, he stood apart from the culture industry. Postwar German literature, still young, was having a hard time with German, which had been corrupted by the Nazi regime. In addition, Böll's generation—but also the younger writers like myself—were stymied to a certain extent by a prohibition that came from Theodor Adorno: "It is barbaric to write a poem after Auschwitz, and that is why it has become impossible to write poetry today. . . ."

In other words, no more "To Be Continued . . ." Though write we did. We wrote by bearing in mind, like Adorno in his *Minima Moralia: Reflections from Damaged Life* (1951), that Auschwitz marks a rift, an unbridgeable gap in the history of civilization. It was the only way we could get around the prohibition. Even so, Adorno's writing on the wall has retained its power to this day. All the writers of my generation did public battle with it. No one had the desire or ability to keep silent. It was our duty to take the goosestep out of German, to lure it out of its idylls and fogged inwardness. We, the children who had had our fingers burned, we were the ones to repudiate the absolutes, the ideological black or white. Doubt and scepticism were our godparents and the multitude of gray values their present to us. In any case, such was the asceticism I imposed on myself before discovering the richness of a language I had all too sweepingly pronounced guilty: its seducible softness, its tendency to plumb the depths, its utterly supple hardness, not to mention the sheen of its dialects, its artlessness and artfulness, its eccentricities, and beauty blossoming from its subjunctives. Having won back this capital, we invested it to make more. Despite Adorno's verdict or spurred on by it. The only way writing after Auschwitz, poetry or prose, could proceed was by becoming memory and preventing the past from coming to an end. Only then could postwar literature in German justify applying the generally valid "To Be Continued . . ." to itself and its descendants; only then could the wound be kept open and the much desired and prescribed forgetting be reversed with a steadfast "Once upon a time."

How many times when one or another interest group calls for considering what happened a closed chapter—we need to return to normalcy and put our shameful past behind us—how many times has literature resisted? And rightly so! Because it is a position as foolish as it is understandable; because every time the end of the postwar period is proclaimed in Germany—as it was ten years ago, with the Wall down and unity in the offing—the past catches up with us.

At that time, in February 1990, I gave a talk to students in Frankfurt entitled "Writing After Auschwitz." I wanted to take stock of my works book by book. In *The Diary of a Snail*, which came out in 1972 and in which past and present crisscross but also run parallel or occasionally collide, I am asked by my sons how I define my profession, and I answer, "A writer, children, is someone who writes against the current of time." What I said to the students was: "Such a view presumes that writers are not encapsulated in isolation or the sempiternal, that they see themselves as living in the here and now, and, even more, that they expose themselves to the vicissitudes of time, that they jump in and take sides. The dangers of jumping in and taking sides are well known: The distance a writer is supposed to keep is threatened; his language must live from hand to mouth; the narrowness of current events can make him narrow and curb the imagination he has trained to run free; he runs the danger of running out of breath."

The risk I referred to then has remained with me throughout the years. But what would the profession of writer be like without risk? Granted, the writer would have the security of, say, a cultural bureaucrat, but he would be the prisoner of his fears of dirtying his hands with the present. Out of fear of losing his distance he would lose himself in realms where myths reside and lofty thoughts are all. But the present, which the past is constantly turning into, would catch up to him in the end and put him through the third degree. Because every writer is of his time, no matter how he protests being born too early or late. He does not autonomously choose what he will write about, that choice is made for him. At least I was not free to choose. Left to my own devices, I would have followed the laws of aesthetics and been perfectly happy to seek my place in texts droll and harmless.

But that was not to be. There were extenuating circumstances: mountains of rubble and cadavers, fruit of the womb of German history. The more I shoveled, the more it grew. It simply could not be ignored. Besides, I come from a family of refugees, which means that in addition to everything that drives a writer from book to book — common ambition, the fear of boredom, the mechanisms of egocentricity — I had the irreparable loss of my birthplace. If by telling tales I could not recapture a city both lost and destroyed, I could at least re-conjure it. And this obsession kept me going. I wanted to make it clear to myself and my readers, not without a bit of a chip on my shoulder, that what was lost did not need to sink into oblivion, that it could be resuscitated by the art of literature in all its grandeur and pettiness: the churches and cemeteries, the sounds of the shipyards and smells of the faintly lapping Baltic, a language on its way out yet still stable-warm and grumble-rich, sins in need of confession, and crimes tolerated if never exonerated.

A similar loss has provided other writers with a hotbed of obsessive topics. In a conversation dating back many years, Salman Rushdie and I concurred that my lost Danzig was for me — like his lost Bombay for him — both resource and refuse pit, point of departure and navel of the world. This arrogance, this overkill lies at the very heart of literature. It is the condition for a story that can pull out all the stops. Painstaking detail, sensitive psychologizing, slice-of-life realism — no such techniques can handle our monstrous raw materials. As indebted as we are to the Enlightenment tradition of reason, the absurd course of history spurns all exclusively reasonable explanations.

Just as the Nobel Prize—once we divest it of its ceremonial garb—has its roots in the invention of dynamite, which like such other human headbirths as the splitting of the atom and the likewise Nobelified classification of the gene has wrought both weal and woe in the world, so literature has an explosive quality at its root, though the explosions literature releases have a delayed-action effect and change the world only in the magnifying glass of time, so to speak, it too wreaking cause for both joy and lamentation here below. How long did it take the European Enlightenment from Montaigne to Voltaire, Diderot, Kant, Lessing, and Lichtenberg to introduce a flicker of reason into the dark corners of scholasticism? And even that flicker often died in the process, a process censorship went a long way towards inhibiting. But when the light finally did brighten things up, it turned out to be the light of cold reason, limited to the technically doable, to economic and social progress, a reason that claimed to be enlightened but that merely drummed a reason-based jargon (which amounted to instructions for making progress at all costs) into its offspring, capitalism and socialism (which were at each other's throats from the word go).

Today we can see what those brilliant failures who were the Enlightenment's offspring have wrought. We can see what a dangerous position its delayed-action, word-detonated explosion has hurled us into. And if we are trying to repair the damage with Enlightenment tools, it is only because we have no others. We look on in horror as capitalism—now that his brother, socialism, has been declared dead—rages unimpeded, megalomaniacally replaying the errors of the supposedly extinct brother. It has turned the free market into dogma, the only truth, and intoxicated by its all but limitless power, plays the wildest of games, making merger after merger with no goal other than to maximize profits. No wonder capitalism is proving as impervious to reform as the communism that managed to strangle itself. Globalization is its motto, a motto it proclaims with the arrogance of infallibility: there is no alternative.

Accordingly, history has come to an end. No more "To Be Continued..." No more suspense. Though perhaps there is hope that if not politics, which has abdicated its decision-making power to economics, then at least literature may come up with something to cause the "new dogmatism" to falter.

How can subversive writing be both dynamite and of literary quality? Is there time enough to wait for the delayed action? Is any book capable of supplying a commodity in so short supply as the future? Is it not rather the case that literature is currently retreating from public life and that young writers are using the Internet as a playground? A standstill, to which the suspicious word "communication" lends a certain aura, is making headway. Every scrap of time is planned down to the last nervous breakdown. A cultural industry vale of tears is taking over the world. What is to be done?

My godlessness notwithstanding, all I can do is bend my knee to a saint who has never failed me and cracked some of the hardest nuts. "O Holy and (through the grace of Camus) Nobelified Sisyphus! May thy stone not remain at the top of the hill, may we roll it down again and like thee continue to rejoice in it, and may the story told of the drudgery of our existence have no end. Amen."

But will my prayer be heard? Or are the rumors true? Is the new breed of cloned creature destined to assure the continuation of human history?

Which brings me back to the beginning of my talk. Once more I open *The Rat* to the fifth chapter, in which the laboratory rat, representing millions of other laboratory animals in the cause of research, wins the Nobel Prize, and I am reminded how few prizes have been awarded to projects that would rid the world of the scourge of mankind: hunger. Anyone who can pay the price can get a new pair of kidneys. Hearts can be transplanted. We can phone anywhere in the world wire-free. Satellites and space stations orbit us solicitously. The latest weapon systems, conceived and developed, they too, on the basis of award-winning research, can help their masters to keep death at bay. Anything the human mind comes up with finds astonishing applications. Only hunger seems to resist. It is even increasing. Poverty deeply rooted shades into misery. Refugees are flocking all over the world accompanied by hunger. It takes political will paired with scientific know-how to root out misery of such magnitude, and no one seems resolved to undertake it.

In 1973, just when terror—with the active support of the United States—was beginning to strike in Chile, Willy Brandt spoke before the United Nations General Assembly, the first German chancellor to do so. He brought up the issue of worldwide poverty. The applause following his exclamation "Hunger is war, too!" was stunning.

I was present when he gave the speech. I was working on my novel *The Flounder* at the time. It deals with the very foundations of human existence including food, the lack and superabundance thereof, great gluttons and untold starvelings, the joys of the palate and crusts from the rich man's table.

The issue is still with us. The poor counter growing riches with growing birth rates. The affluent North and West can try to screen themselves off in security-mad fortresses, but the flocks of refugees will catch up with them: no gate can withstand the crush of the hungry.

The future will have something to say about all this. Our common novel must be continued. And even if one day people stop or are forced to stop writing and publishing, if books are no longer available, there will still be storytellers giving us mouth-to-ear artificial respiration, spinning old stories in new ways: loud and soft, heckling and halting, now close to laughter, now on the brink of tears.

Translated by Michael Henry Heim

Mitten im Leben   (1996)

denke ich an die Toten,
die ungezählten und die mit Namen.
Dann klopft der Alltag an,
und übern Zaun
ruft der Garten: Die Kirschen sind reif!

———•••———

In the Midst of Life

I think of the dead,
those uncounted and those with names.
Then Every-Day knocks on the door
and over the fence
the garden calls out: The cherries are ripe!

Translated by Michael Hamburger

I REMEMBER . . .

In October 2000, the Goethe Institute in Vilnius, Lithuania, invited Grass to join Czesław Miłosz, Wisława Symborska, and Tomas Venclova for a conversation on "The Future of Memory." Grass delivered this address on October 2.

. . . OR I AM REMINDED BY SOMETHING THAT STANDS in my way, something that left its smell behind or hid in age-old letters marked with certain treacherous words, waiting to be remembered. Snared by these and other traps, we stumble. From somewhere off to the side, something not immediately nameable surfaces. Speechless objects bump up against us; things that for years surrounded us indifferently, or so we thought, begin blurting out secrets: How embarrassing! And then there are the dreams in which we meet ourselves as strangers, unfathomable, in need of endless interpretation.

And when we travel to the places of our past, which were destroyed and are lost and now bear strange-sounding foreign names, memory suddenly catches up with us. Which is what happened to me in the spring of 1958, when, for the first time after the war, I visited Gdansk, a city slowly reemerging from rubble still being cleared, where I hoped in the back of my mind to run into traces of Danzig. To be sure, the school buildings were still there, their corridors alive with the well-preserved fug of school. The paths I used to take to school, on the other hand, seemed shorter than I remembered. But then, as I was looking for the former fishing village Brösen and discovering that the listless slapping of the Baltic tide had not changed, I suddenly found myself standing in front of the bathhouse, as derelict as the boarded-up kiosk next to its entrance. And all at once I saw that cheapest of my childhood pleasures bubbling up: raspberry- and lemon- and woodruff-flavored fizz powder in little bags, which I would buy at that kiosk for a few pfennigs each. Hardly had the remembered refreshment begun to register in my mind than it began to hatch stories, true stories of lies waiting only for the right code word. The simple, harmless, and water-soluble fizz powder released a chain reaction in my head: The effervescence of first love, that tingling sensation experienced once and never again.

As hazy and fragmentary as it may seem, there is more to memory than total recall. Memories may cheat, gloss over, and simulate, though our ability to recall the past likes to present itself to us as an incorruptible bookkeeper. But we all know that our immediate recollection grows dim with age, while that which was long buried—our childhood—rejoins us in our memory, clearer than ever and often solidified into moments of happiness. Being someone who still enjoys mushroom hunting, I am occasionally overcome with a memory of being a child in the Kashubian woods and encountering there a lone boletus. It was larger and more attractively formed than anything I've seen since. And so I continue looking. My memory is what set the standard.

A writer is a professional rememberer. As a teller of stories he is trained in the field. He knows that memory is the proverbial cat that likes to be stroked, sometimes even the wrong way, until it crackles; then it purrs. In this way he exploits his memories and, if necessary, those of entirely imaginary people. Memory is his gold mine, his garbage dump, his archive. He tends it like a pot of replanted chives. Although he knows what a glutton literature is—how it wolfs down even newspaper copy and similarly unripe or uncooked current news—regurgitated memories are his staple, and in times of drought his memory turns to memories previously grazed. Perhaps it is an occupational perversion that allows him to enjoy putting to use remembered pain, embarrassment, even failures.

That, at any rate, is how my lost home became a permanent occasion for compulsive remembering, for my obsession with writing. On blank paper, page after page, and even if it came out deformed, as if captured in the shards of a mirror, I had to remember, to exorcise, to banish this thing that had been lost forever, leaving a vacuum in its wake, and that was irreplaceable by any surrogate or substitute home. Memory was milked strategically, in order to be ingested in full portions by a first-person-obsessed narrator who from his odd perspective saw small things as big and big things as small. The sluices were all open. Everything was right there again, within reach. The Danzig streetcar lines; movie houses in the old town and the outer precincts. And that Kashubian uncle of mine, who had defended the Polish post office at the start of the war and become an accidental hero, entered the image in my memory, though in an altered form. Afterward my family never talked about his death. By then our talk was only about ambushes, news flashes, victories on an endless feed loop, and there was also the continuous chatter about everyday things, of which only shreds of language have stuck in my mind.

Remembered language: The grousing patter of the oldest refugees, which went to its grave like them decades after the war's end, the Low German dialect that furled further and further out toward western and eastern Prussia, and its Kashubian variant—at least when my relatives spoke German, which I remember in detail. Like the sentence my great-aunt whispered to me in 1958, which will only get lost being translated into High German (or English): "Ech waiß, Ginterchen, ein Wästen is bässer, aber em Osten is scheener" [Oh, little Günter, I know, the West is better, but the East is more beautiful]. Her appraisal grew in the chrysalis of my memory, but what's more, it flitted forth through my books, dispensing assessments of East and West, and still gives me direction today.

So much for these cursory glances at the mania of writers, at remembering as a profession. There is also a collective memory, whether it is only a matter of claim or supposition, or of ritual on ceremonial occasions. Everywhere in Europe this collective memory is invoked, deployed, or refused. Wars and war crimes now burden it. Ideologies continue to leave their mark on it. And it is especially troubling to the older generation. Perhaps this is why we Germans came up with that stereotypical and clichéd expression "memory work," which is demanded as an admission of guilt, dismissed as an imposition, and practiced assiduously. We've performed our memory work as a compulsory exercise for decades, for as long as the past has kept catching up with us; and since the sixties, each succeeding and, one would imagine, unburdened younger generation has done so as well. It is as if the children and grandchildren were remembering on behalf of their close-lipped fathers and grandfathers.

At present, not a week goes by in which we are not warned against forgetting. Now that we have sufficiently often remembered the Jews who emigrated, who were persecuted, and who were murdered in inconceivable numbers, we're belatedly remembering the transport and murder of tens of thousands of Roma and Sinti. For many, even our most recent commitment comes too late: that of remembering the fate of hundreds of thousands of forced laborers who came from Poland, Lithuania, the Soviet Union, and many other countries and were put to work on the assembly lines of the German war industry. It is as if the evils that took only twelve years to commit, the crimes that now get lumped together into a single iniquity, have gained in gravity in proportion to their distance from us in time. Ineffectual attempts are made to give form to memory through monuments. In Berlin, for example, a controversy broke out, and aesthetic issues weren't the only ones on the table. "Never forget!" cried some. "We've had enough!" declared others. At times, strangers who observe our way of dealing with the past, of remembering it, call it masochistic, implying that for Germans, remembering is torturous. But there is no foreseeable end to this. No matter what plan we make for the future, the past has already marked the supposedly virgin territory with its scent and everywhere staked signposts pointing back to our history.

Yet it is strange and troubling to think how lately and with what hesitation we remember the suffering inflicted on Germans during the war. The consequences for us of that unscrupulously initiated and criminally executed war, that is, the destruction of German cities, the death of hundreds of thousands of civilians through Allied carpet bombing, and the forced expulsion and privation of twelve million emigrant Germans from the East, have been relegated to the background. Even in postwar literature there has been little room for remembering the bombings and mass migrations, and their casualties. One injustice concealed the other. It was forbidden to compare them or even to estimate damages. But experience tells us that victims of violence, regardless of who its perpetrators are, tend not to want to remember what they have suffered, and for their part, they have the right to forget, even to repress, those horrors.

So even if these painful memories force their way back to our consciousness, much will remain unsaid. But the silence of the victims is irresistible: we cannot pretend not to hear it. And since there has never been peace—and in the Balkans and the Caucasus and many other places of horror on this planet, murder, flight, and expulsion are part of everyday life even now—memory will continue to be the echo of past suffering. Recently the Hungarian author György Konrád wrote, with regard to European history, "To remember is human, we could even say it is the essence of humanity." What he says about nature being indifferent to history construes the distinctly human capacity to remember as something ambivalent, as if this gift were both blessing and curse: a curse in that we are captive to it, a blessing in that it vitiates death. In memory we converse with both the living and the dead. In being remembered, we survive. Forgetting, however, is the seal of death.

Translated by W. Martin

KLECKERBURG (1967)

Gestrichnes Korn, gezielte Fragen
verlangt die Kimme lebenslang:
Als ich verliess den Zeugenstand,
an Wände, vor Gericht gestellt,
wo Grenzen Flüsse widerlegen,
sechstausend Meter überm Mief,
zuhause, der Friseur behauchte
den Spiegel und sein Finger schreib:
Geboren wann? Nun sag schon, wo?
      Das liegt nordöstlich, westlich von
      und nährt noch immer Fotografen.
      Das hiess mal so, heut heisst es so.
      Dort wohnten bis, von dann an wohnten.
      Ich buchstabiere: Wrzeszcz heiss früher.
      Das Haus blieb stehen, nur der Putz.
      Den Friedhof, den ich, gibts nicht mehr.
      Wo damals Zäune, kann heut jeder.
      So gotisch denkt sich Gott was aus.
      Denn man hat wieder für viel Geld.
      Ich zählte Giebel, keiner fehlte:
      das Mittelalter holt sich ein.
      Nur jenes Denkmal mit dem Schwanz
      ist westwärts und davon geritten.
Und jedes Pausenzeichen fragt;
denn als ich, zwischen Muscheln, kleckerte mit Sand,
als ich bei Brenntau einen Grabstein fand,
als ich Papier bewegte im Archiv
und im Hotel die Frage in fünf Sprachen:

(continued on p. 290)

KLECKERBURG

Aimed questions, foresight well aligned
lifelong the backsight will demand:
When I had left the witness box,
stood up in court, before a wall,
where frontiers contravert the rivers,
twelve thousand feet above the smog,
at home, the barber breathed upon
his mirror, and his finger wrote:
Born when? And — out with it — born where?
　　　It lies to the northeast, west of,
　　　and still can feed photographers.
　　　Its name was this and now is that.
　　　There lived until, from then on lived.
　　　I spell: Its name was Wrzeszcz before.
　　　The house still stands, but the façade.
　　　The graveyard, which, has ceased to be.
　　　Where fences were now anyone.
　　　Such gothic things does God think up.
　　　For once again at great expense.
　　　I counted gables, none was missing:
　　　The Middle Ages catch us up.
　　　Only that statue with the tail
　　　has ridden off now, has gone west.
And every station signal also asks;
for when, between small shells, I built sand castles,
when I unearthed a tombstone outside Brenntau,
when I turned over papers in the archives
and in five languages the form in the hotel:

(continued on p. 291)

Geboren wann und wo, warum?
nach Antwort schnappte, beichtete mein Stift:
    Das war zur Zeit der Rentenmark.
    Hier, nah der Mottlau, die ein Nebenfluss,
    wo Forster brüllte und Hirsch Fajngold schwieg,
    hier, wo ich meine ersten Schuhe
    zerlief, und als ich sprechen konnte,
    das Stottern lernte: Sand, klatschnass,
    zum Kleckern, bis mein Kinder-Gral
    sich gotisch türmte und zerfiel.
    Das war knapp zwanzig Jahre nach Verdun;
    und dreissig Jahre Frist, bis mich die Söhne
    zum Vater machten; Stallgeruch
    hat diese Sprache, Sammeltrieb,
    als ich Geschichten, Schmetterlinge spiesste
    und Worte fischte, die gleich Katzen
    auf Treibholz zitterten, an Land gesetzt,
    zwölf Junge warfen: grau und blind.
Geboren wann? Und wo? Warum?
Das hab ich hin und her geschleppt,
im Rhein versenkt, bei Hildesheim begraben;
doch Taucher fanden und mit Förderkörben
kam Strandgut Rollgut hoch, ans Licht.
    Bucheckern, Bernstein, Brausepulver,
    dies Taschenmesser und dies Abziehbild,
    ein Stück vom Stück, Tonnagezahlen,
    Minutenzeiger, Knöpfe, Münzen,
    für jeden Platz ein Tütchen Wind.
    Hochstapeln lehrt mein Fundbüro:
    Gerüche, abgetretne Schwellen,
    verjährte Schulden, Batterien,

(continued on p. 292)

Born when and where, born why?
Yapped for the answers, my ball pen confessed:
    It was when *Rentenmarks* were current.
    Here, by the Mottlau, a small tributary,
    where Forster roared, Hirsch Fajngold held his tongue,
    where I wore out the soles of my first pair
    of shoes, and being old enough to speak
    learned how to stammer: sand, all clammy
    for making castles, until my childhood grail
    gothically towered and collapsed.
    That was some twenty years after Verdun;
    came thirty years of respite, till my sons
    made me a father; stable smells
    talk in this lilt, collector's mania
    when stories, butterflies I impaled
    and fished for words that cat-like trembled
    on rafts of driftwood washed ashore,
    gave birth to twelve, all gray and blind.
Born when? And where? And why?
Those questions I have dragged around,
sunk in the Rhine, buried near Hildesheim;
but divers found them and in dragging nets
flotsam and jetsam rose, were brought to light.
    Beechnuts and amber, sherbet fizz,
    this penknife and this transfer picture,
    piece of a piece, ship tonnage figures,
    buttons and coins and minute hands,
    for every square a bag of wind.
    To confidence tricks I'm driven by
    my treasure trove, lost property office:
    The smells, the thresholds trodden down,

(continued on p. 293)

die nur in Taschenlampen glücklich,
und Namen, die nur Namen sind:
Elfriede Broschke, Siemoneit,
Guschnerus, Lusch und Heinz Stanowski;
auch Chodowiecki, Schopenhauer
sind dort geboren. Wann? Warum?
Ja, in Geschichte war ich immer gut.
Fragt mich nach Pest und Teuerung.
Ich bete läufig Friedensschlüsse,
die Ordensmeister, Schwedennot,
und kennen alle Jagellonen
und alle Kirchen, von Johann
bis Trinitatis, backsteinrot.
Wer fragt noch wo? Mein Zungenschlag
ist baltisch tückisch stubenwarm.
Wie macht die Ostsee? —Blubb, pifff, pschsch . . .
Auf deutsch, auf polnisch: Blubb, pifff, pschsch . . .
Doch als ich auf dem volksfestmüden,
von Sonderbussen, Bundesbahn
gespeisten Flüchtlingstreffen in Hannover
die Funktionäre fragte, hatten sie
vergessen, wie die Ostsee macht,
und liessen den Atlantik röhren;
ich blieb beharrlich: Blubb, pifff, pschsch . . .
Da schrien alle: Schlagt ihn tot!
Er hat auf Menschenrecht und Renten,
auf Lastenausgleich, Vaterstadt
verzichtet, hört den Zungenschlag:
Das ist die Ostsee nicht, das ist Verrat.

(continued on p. 294)

debts never paid, small batteries
happy in torches, only torches,
and names that are no more than names:
Elfriede Broschke, Siemoneit,
Guschnerus, Lusch and Heinz Stanowski;
and Chodowiecki, Schopenhauer
were born there too. Born when? Born why?
Yes, I was always good at history.
Ask me about the plagues and price increases.
Peace treaties fluently I can pray,
masters of orders, Swedish war,
and all the Jagellons I know,
and all the churches, from St. John's
to Holy Trinity, red brick.
      Who still asks where? My intonation
is Baltic, wily, warm as rooms.
What says the Baltic? Blubb, pfff, pshsh . . .
In German, Polish: Blubb, pfff, pshsh . . .
But when I asked the functionaries
at the assembly-weary, coach-
and-special-train-fed gathering
of eastern refugees at Hanover,
they had forgotten what the Baltic says
and made the Atlantic Ocean roar;
I kept insisting: Blubb, pfff, pshsh . . .
So: Hit him! Kill him! all yelled out,
he's turned his back on human rights,
on pensions, on his native city,
on compensations, restitutions,
just listen to his intonation:
That's not the Baltic, that's high treason.

(continued on p. 295)

Befragt ihn peinlich, holt den Stockturm her,
streckt, rädert, blendet, brecht und glüht,
passt dem Gedächtnis Schrauben an.
Wir wollen wissen, wo und wann.
Nicht auf Strohdeich und Bürgerwiesen,
nicht in der Pfefferstadt, —ach, wär ich doch
geboren zwischen Speichern auf dem Holm! —
in Striessbachnähe, nah dem Heeresanger
ist es passiert, heut heisst die Strasse
auf polnisch Lelewela, —nur die Nummer
links von der Haustür blieb und blieb.
Und Sand, klatschnass, zum Kleckern: Gral . . .
In Kleckerburg gebürtig, westlich von.
Das liegt nordwestlich, südlich von.
Dort wechselt Licht viel schneller als.
Die Möwen sind nicht Möwen, sondern.
Und auch die Milch, ein Nebenarm der Weichsel,
floss mit dem Honig brückenreich vorbei.

Getauft geimpft gefirmt geschult.
Gespielt hab ich mit Bombensplittern.
Und aufgewachsen bin ich zwischen
dem Heilgen Geist und Hitlers Bild.
Im Ohr verblieben Schiffssirenen,
gekappte Sätze, Schreie gegen Wind,
paar heile Glocken, Mündungsfeuer
und etwas Ostsee: Blubb, pifff, pschsch . . .

Put screws on him and make him talk,
get wheels and tongs and pokers, blind him,
and stretch his memory on the rack.
We want his answer: when and where.
Not on the Straw Dyke, nor in Merchants' Meadows,
nor yet in Peppertown—would that I had
been born between great store lofts on the Holm! —
Near the small Striessbach, by the Rifle Range
it happened, and today the street
in Polish is called Lelewela—only
the number left of the door remains, remains.
And sand, for castles, clammy, muddy: grail . . .
At Kleckerburg was born, west of.
It lies to the northwest, south of.
The light there changes much more than.
The seagulls are not seagulls, but.
And there the Milch, a Vistula tributary,
honeyed and many-bridged flowed by.

    Baptized and vaccinated, schooled, confirmed.
    Bomb splinters, meanwhile, were my toys.
    And I grew up, was reared between
    the Holy Ghost and Hitler's photograph.
    Ships' sirens echo in my ears,
    lopped sentences and windblown cries,
    a few sound churchbells, rifle fire
    and Baltic snatches: Blubb, pfff, pshsh . . .

Translated by Michael Hamburger

When Time Had Run Out

from Crabwalk (2001)

After almost two hours on the surface, the U-boat had accomplished its circumnavigation maneuver. *S-13* was now sailing parallel to the enemy vessel, which to the astonishment of the tower crew had running lights lit and was not tacking. Since it had completely stopped snowing, there was a risk that the clouds might part, leaving not only the huge transport and its escort ship exposed in the moonlight but also the U-boat.

Marinesko nonetheless adhered to his decision to launch an above-water attack. An advantage for *S-13*, which no one on the submarine could have guessed, was that the U-boat locater on the torpedo boat *Löwe* was frozen and unable to pick up any echoes. In their account, the English authors Dobson, Miller, and Payne assume that the Soviet commander had been practicing surface attacks for a long time because German submarines had had great success with this method in the Atlantic, and now he wanted a chance to try it out. An above-water attack provides better visibility, as well as greater speed and precision.

Marinesko now gave an order to reduce buoyancy until the body of the boat was underwater, leaving only the tower poking out of the choppy sea. Allegedly a signal flare was seen coming from the bridge of the target vessel shortly before the attack, and light signals were spotted; but none of the German sources—the accounts of the surviving captains—confirm this report.

Thus *S-13* approached the port side of the target vessel unimpeded. On instructions from the commander, the four torpedoes in the bow were set to strike at three meters below the surface. The estimated distance to the target was six hundred meters. The periscope had the ship's bow in its crosshairs. It was 2304 hours Moscow Time, precisely two hours earlier German Time.

But before Marinesko's order to fire is issued and can no longer be retracted, I must insert into this report a legend that has been passed down. Before *S-13* left Hangö Harbor, a crew member by the name of Pichur allegedly took a brush and painted dedications on all the torpedoes, including the four that were now ready to be fired. The first read FOR THE MOTHERLAND, the torpedo in tube 2 was marked FOR STALIN, and in tubes 3 and 4 the dedications painted onto the eel-smooth surfaces read FOR THE SOVIET PEOPLE and FOR LENINGRAD.

Their significance thus predetermined, when the order was finally issued, three of the four torpedoes—the one dedicated to Stalin stuck in its tube and had to be hastily

disarmed—zoomed toward the ship, nameless from Mari-
nesko's point of view, in whose maternity ward Mother was
still asleep, lulled by soft music on the radio.

WHILE THE THREE inscribed torpedoes are speeding to-
ward their target, I am tempted to think my way aboard the
Gustloff. I have no trouble finding the last group of naval
auxiliary girls to embark, who were billeted in the drained
swimming pool, also in the adjacent youth hostel area, used
originally for members of the Hitler Youth and League of
German Girls when they were sent on holiday cruises. The
girls sit and lie there, packed in tightly. Their hairdos are
still in place. But no more laughter, no more easygoing or
sharp-tongued gossip. Some of the girls are seasick. There
and throughout the corridors of the other decks, in the for-
mer reception rooms and dining rooms, is the smell of
vomit. The toilets, in any case far too few for the mass of
refugees and navy personnel, are stopped up. The ventila-
tion system is not powerful enough to draw off the stench
along with the stale air. Since the ship got under way, all the
passengers have had orders to wear the life jackets that
were handed out earlier, but because of the increasing heat
many people are stripping off their warm underwear and
also their life jackets. Old folks and children are whining
plaintively. No more announcements over the public ad-
dress system. All sounds subdued. Resigned sighing and
whimpering. What I picture is not a sense of impending
doom but its precursor: fear creeping in.

Only on the bridge, with the worst of the conflict re-
solved, was the mood reportedly somewhat optimistic. The
four captains thought that having reached the Stolpe Bank,

they had put the greatest danger behind them. In the first officer's cabin a meal was being consumed: pea soup with ham. Afterward, Lieutenant Commander Zahn had the steward pour a round of cognac. It seemed appropriate to drink to a voyage on which Fortune was smiling. At his master's feet slept the German shepherd Hassan. Only Captain Weller was on watch on the bridge. Meanwhile time had run out.

From childhood on, I have heard Mother's often repeated formulation: "The first time it went boom I was wide awake, and then it came again, and again. . . ."

The first torpedo hit the bow of the ship far below the waterline, in the area where the crew quarters lay. Any crew member who was off watch, munching a hunk of bread or sleeping in his bunk, and survived the explosion, nonetheless did not escape, because after the first report of damage Captain Weller ordered the automatic closing of the watertight doors, sealing off the forward part of the ship, to prevent the vessel from sinking rapidly at the bow; an emergency drill in closing the watertight doors had been conducted just before the ship put out to sea. Among the sailors and Croatian volunteers thus sacrificed were many who had been drilled in loading and lowering the lifeboats in an orderly fashion.

What took place—suddenly, gradually, finally—in the closed-off forward portion of the ship no one knows.

Mother's next utterance also made an indelible impression: "At the second boom I fell out of bed, that's how bad it was. . . ." This torpedo from tube 3, whose smooth surface carried the inscription FOR THE SOVIET PEOPLE, exploded beneath the swimming pool on E deck. Only two or three girls from the naval auxiliary survived. Later they spoke of smelling gas, and of seeing girls cut to pieces by glass shards from the mosaic that had adorned the front wall of the pool area and by splintered tiles from the pool itself. As the water rushed in, one could see corpses and body parts floating in it, along with sandwiches and other remains of supper, also empty life jackets. Hardly any screaming. Then the light went out. These two or three naval auxiliaries, of whom I have no passport-sized photos, managed to escape through an emergency exit, behind which a companionway led steeply up to the higher decks.

And then Mother said, "Not till the third boom" had Dr. Richter turned up to check on the women in the maternity ward. "By that time all hell'd broke loose!" she exclaimed every time her neverending story reached "number 3."

The last torpedo hit the engine room amidships, knocking out not only the engines but also the interior lighting on all decks, as well as the ship's other systems. After that everything took place in darkness. Only the emergency lighting that came on a few minutes later provided some sense of orientation amid the chaos, as panic broke out everywhere on the two-hundred-meter-long and ten-story-high ship, which could no longer send out an SOS; the equipment in the radio room had also gone dead. Only from the torpedo boat *Löwe* did the repeated call go out into the ether: "*Gustloff* sinking after three torpedo strikes!" In between, the location of the sinking ship was transmitted over and over, for hours: "Position Stolpmünde, 55.07 degrees north, 17.42 degrees east. Request assistance . . ."

On *S-13,* the successful hits and the soon unmistakable sinking of the target gave rise to quiet rejoicing. Captain

Marinesko issued an order for the partially preflooded submarine to submerge, because he knew that this close to the coast, and especially over the Stolpe Bank, there was little protection from depth charges. First the torpedo stuck in tube 2 had to be disarmed; if it remained sitting there, ready for ignition, with the firing motor running, the slightest vibration could cause it to explode. Fortunately no depth charges were dropped. The torpedo boat *Löwe*, its engines cut, was sweeping the mortally wounded ship with its searchlights.

Translated by Krishna Winston

NACH MITTERNACHT   (2002)

Nein, kein knöcherner Sensenmann,
der tänzelnd Bauer und Bürger,
das adlige Fräulein, den feisten Pfaff,
Bettler und Kaiser mitnimmt,
auch nicht der tanzende Gott
überm bergspiegelnden Wasser von Sils Maria,
wie er mit Sprüngen über sich weist
und als Superman Sprechblasen füllt;
einzig wir beide gepaart,
wenn uns um Mitternacht,
gleich nach den Spätnachrichten—
schon wieder droht Krieg—
das Küchenradio führt:
ein Slowfox, altmodisch, fügt zusammen,
was tagsüber zerstreut seinen Lauf nahm.

Liebste, nur wenige Takte,
bevor du mich und dich—
wie immer um diese Zeit—
mit Tabletten versorgst: einzelne
und gezählte.

AFTER MIDNIGHT

No, this is no grim reaper,
skipping along, taking farmer and townsman,
the upright girl, the plump priest,
beggar and emperor alike,
nor is it the dancing god,
hovering over the alpine waters of Sils Maria,
pointing beyond himself as he leaps
filling speech balloons like Superman.
It's just the two of us, paired,
when around midnight,
war threatens yet again,
after the late news
led by the kitchen radio:
in an old-fashioned fox-trot
we draw together
all that's about to pull us apart.

Just a few measures, love,
before you see to it—
as you always do around this time—
that we get our pills:
single ones and numbered.

Translated by Charles Simic

TANGO NOCTURNO   (2002)

Der Herr knickt die Dame,
nein, biegt sie, so beugsam die Dame,
der Herr gibt sich steif.

Zwei Körper, die eins sind, doch nichts
von sich wissen, geschieden in Treue,
in Treue vereint.

Die Hand in der Beuge, gedehnt tropft die Zeit,
bis plötzlich die Uhr schlägt:
fünf eilige Schritte.

Wir stürzen nach vorne und retten uns rücklings,
wo nichts ist als Fläche,
nach vorne zurück.

In Angst, doch ich fange — der Sturz
ist gespielt nur — mit rettendem Händchen
dich oftgeübt auf.

Sind leer jetzt mit Haltung und schauen
im Schleppschritt, beim Leerlauf mit Haltung
uns unbewegt zu.

Das ist der Tango, die Diagonale.
Aus Fallsucht zum Stillstand.
Ich höre dein Herz.

Tango Nocturno

The man cracks the woman in half,
no, bends her, the woman so pliant,
the man remains stiff.

Two bodies unaware of one another,
separated in good faith,
in good faith united.

The hand in the curve of the back, time in slow motion,
until suddenly the clock strikes:
in five quick steps.

We lurch forward and catch ourselves backward,
where there is nothing but space,
then back-forward we go again.

Afraid, I catch you
with the well-trained hands of a savior—
but your slip is feigned.

Empty now with composure, watching ourselves
running on empty, still composed,
drag our feet back to us.

This is the tango, the diagonal.
From lust for falling
to a standstill where I hear your heart.

Translated by Charles Simic

306   THE GÜNTER GRASS READER

TANGO MORTALE   (2002)

Befehl wie von oben: der Leib, der den Leib flieht,
gestreckt auf der Flucht ist,
so reißt es uns hin.

Kein Abgrund, doch Weite, in die wir,
als stünden rings Spiegel,
Blicke verwerfen.

Und nochmals befohlen: die Einkehr nach innen.
Wir treten die Stelle, zuinnerst die Stelle
und bleiben im Takt.

Gezählt sind die Stürze, die Beinahestürze,
der Fortgang der Schritte, die zögernd, verzögernd
das Ende verschleppen.

Unsterblich, unsterblich! Das doppelte Ich,
solange beim Tango, beim Tango Mortale
ein Schrittmuster führt.

Mit restlichem Atem beim Fest ohne Gäste.
Das Paar, das sich feiert, ist dennoch und endlich
auf Beifall bedacht.

Der Schmerz ist nur Maske. Wir gleiten verkleidet
auf grenzloser Fläche, dem Tod auf den Fersen,
uns selbst hinterdrein.

TANGO MORTALE

A command from above:
the body that flees the body,
trails in flight drawing us in.

No abyss, but a breadth of space
in which we exchange glances,
as if mirrors surrounded us.

Another command: to turn within.
We tread on the spot,
the innermost spot, always in rhythm.

Our falls are numbered, the near-falls,
the movement of feet, hesitant, deferred,
postponing the end.

Immortal, immortal! My double,
so long as the tango, the mortal tango,
executes its pattern of steps.

At a party without guests, with their last breaths,
the pair celebrating themselves
is still waiting for applause.

The pain is just a mask. Smartly dressed,
we glide with death on our heels
across space with no boundaries.

Translated by Charles Simic

PERMISSION ACKNOWLEDGMENTS

Translated by William Martin:
"A Look Back at *The Tin Drum* . . . ," "Literature and Politics," "A Father's Difficulties in Explaining Auschwitz to His Children," "Israel and Me," "By a Rough Estimate," "Literature and Myth," "Berlin—A Projected Fiction," "Willy Brandt at the Warsaw Ghetto," "Obituary for Helen Wolff," "Literature and History," "I remember . . ."

Translated by Philip Boehm:
"In the Tunnel," "Roll Your Own," "Two Left-handers," "I Like Riding the Escalator," "When Father Wanted to Remarry," "Police Radio," "Immured," "The Hare and the Hedgehog," "Bikini Atoll"

Translated by Charles Simic:
"The Stone," "My Old Olivetti," "After Midnight," "Tango Nocturno," "Tango Mortale"

Translated by Michael Hamburger:
"Nursery Rhyme," "In the Midst of Life"

Translated by Michael Henry Heim:
"When the *LZ-126* Drew Close to New York," "Execution on the Playground," "Dixieland!," "Operation Travel Bureau," "A Call to the Special Unit," "Madness! Sheer Madness!," "To Be Continued . . ."

"The Stockturm. Long-Distance Song Effects" from *The Tin Drum* by Günter Grass, translated by Ralph Manheim, copyright © 1961, 1962 by Pantheon Books, a division of Random House, Inc. Renewed 1989, 1990 by Random House, Inc. Used by permission of Pantheon Books, a division of Random House, Inc.

"By the Time the War Broke Out" from *Cat and Mouse* by Günter Grass, English translation by Ralph Manheim copyright © 1963 by Harcourt, Inc. and Martin Secker & Warburg Limited and renewed 1991 by Ralph Manheim, reprinted by permission of Harcourt, Inc.

"Isn't It Nice to Be Rich and Famous?" from *From the Diary of a Snail*, copyright © 1972 by Hermann Luchterhand Verlag, Darmstadt und Neuwied, English translation by Ralph Manheim copyright © 1973 by Harcourt, Inc., reprinted by permission of Harcourt, Inc.

"The Artist's Freedom of Opinion" and "The Destruction of Mankind Has Begun" from *On Writing and Politics 1967–1983* by Günter Grass, English translation by Ralph Manheim copyright © 1985 by Harcourt, Inc., reprinted by permission of the publisher.